WILLIAM GOLDING
Nobel Laureate for Literature

"His novels . . . with the perspicuity of realistic narrative art and universality of myth, illuminate the human condition in the world today."

—from the Swedish Academy Nobel Prize Citation, 1983

"Golding's novels seem easy. His prose is forceful and compact. He tells a rousing good story. Yet his technical virtuosity, his use of image and symbol, among other literary devices . . . are what account for his reputation."

—George Plimpton, *The New York Times Book Review*

WILLIAM GERALD GOLDING was born in Cornwall, England, in 1911, and educated at Oxford University. He joined the Royal Navy in 1940. His first book, *Poems*, was published in 1935. His first novel, *Lord of the Flies* (1954), was written while he was teaching school after the war. His other novels include *Pincher Martin* (1957), *Free Fall* (1960), *The Inheritors* (1962), *The Spire* (1964), and *The Pyramid* (1967). He also had a play produced on the London stage, *The Brass Butterfly* (1958), and published a collection of shorter works entitled *Hot Gates and Other Occasional Pieces* (1965). In 1983, William Golding was awarded the Nobel Prize for Literature.

LORD
of the
FLIES

A NOVEL BY
William Golding

Introduction by
E. M. Forster

With a biographical and critical note by
E. L. Epstein

RIVERHEAD BOOKS, NEW YORK

Riverhead Books
Published by The Berkley Publishing Group
A division of Penguin Putnam Inc.
375 Hudson Street
New York, New York 10014

Mr. Forster's Introduction appeared in *Lord of the Flies*, New York:
Coward-McCann, Inc., 1962.

Copyright © 1954 by William Golding
Book design by Casey Hampton
Cover design by Marc J. Cohen
Cover photographs by Masatomo Kuriya / Photonica, Koichiro Shimanchi /
Photonica, and Masakatsu Yamazaki / Photonica

Originally published in Great Britain by Faber and Faber, Ltd.
Capricorn edition: July 1959, with ninety-four subsequent Capricorn printings
Forty-eight subsequent Perigee printings
Coward-McCann, Inc., edition published in 1962
First Riverhead trade paperback edition: August 1997

The Penguin Putnam Inc. World Wide Web site address is
http://www.penguinputnam.com

The Library of Congress Cataloging-in-Publication Data

Golding, William, 1911–
    Lord of the flies: a novel / by William Golding; introduction by
  E.M. Forster; with a biographical and critical note by E. L.
  Epstein.—1st Riverhead trade pbk. ed.
      p. cm.
    ISBN 1-57322-612-2
    1. Survival after airplane accidents, shipwrecks, etc.—Fiction.
  2. Islands—Fiction. 3. Boys—Fiction. I. Title.
PR6013.O35L6 1997
823'.914—dc21   97-2124
                                                                   CIP

Printed in the United States of America

20

introduction

E. M. FORSTER

I T IS A PLEASURE AND AN HONOUR TO WRITE AN IN-
troduction to this remarkable book, but there is also a difficulty, for the reason that the book contains surprises, and its
reader ought to encounter them for himself. If he knows too
much he will lean back complacently. And complacency is not a
quality that Mr. Golding values. The universe, in his view, secretes
something that we do not expect and shall probably dislike, and
he here presents the universe, under the guise of a school adventure story on a coral island.

How romantically it starts! Several bunches of boys are being
evacuated during a war. Their plane is shot down, but the "tube"
in which they are packed is released, falls on an island, and having
peppered them over the jungle slides into the sea. None of them
are hurt, and presently they collect and prepare to have a high
old time. A most improbable start. But Mr. Golding's magic is
already at work and he persuades us to accept it. And though the
situation is improbable the boys are not. He understands them
thoroughly, partly through innate sympathy, partly because he has
spent much of his life teaching. He makes us feel at once that
we are with real human beings, even if they are small ones, and
thus lays a solid foundation for the horrors to come.

Meet three boys.

Ralph is aged a little over twelve. He is fair and well built, might grow into a boxer but never into a devil, for he is sunny and decent, sensible, considerate. He doesn't understand a lot, but has two things clear: firstly, they will soon be rescued—why, his daddy is in the Navy!—and secondly, until they are rescued they must hang together. It is he who finds the conch and arranges that when there is a meeting he who holds the conch shall speak. He is chosen as leader. He is democracy. And as long as the conch remains, there is some semblance of cooperation. But it gets smashed.

Meet Piggy.

Piggy is stout, asthmatic, shortsighted, underprivileged and wise. He is the brains of the party. It is the lenses of his spectacles that kindle fire. He also possesses the wisdom of the heart. He is loyal to Ralph, and tries to stop him from making mistakes, for he knows where mistakes may lead to in an unknown island. He knows that nothing is safe, nothing is neatly ticketed. He is the human spirit, aware that the universe has not been created for his convenience, and doing the best he can. And as long as he survives there is some semblance of intelligence. But he too gets smashed. He hurtles through the air under a rock dislodged by savages. His skull cracks and his brains spill out.

Meet Jack.

Jack is head of a choir—a bizarre assignment considering his destiny. He marches them two and two up the sun-drenched beach. He loves adventure, excitement, foraging in groups, orders when issued by himself, and though he does not yet know it and shrinks from it the first time, he loves shedding blood. Ralph he rather likes, and the liking is mutual. Piggy he despises and insults. He is dictatorship versus democracy. It is possible to read the book at a political level, and to see in its tragic trend the tragedy of our inter-war world. There is no doubt as to whose side the author is on here. He is on Ralph's. But if one shifts the vision to a still deeper level—the psychological—he is on the side of Piggy. Piggy knows that things mayn't go well because he knows what boys are, and he knows that the island, for all its apparent friendliness, is equivocal.

The hideous accidents that promote the reversion to savagery fill most of the book, and the reader must be left to endure them—and also to embrace them, for somehow or other they are entangled with beauty. The greatness of the vision transcends what is visible. At the close, when the boys are duly rescued by the trim British cruiser, we find ourselves on their side. We have shared their experience and resent the smug cheeriness of their rescuers. The naval officer is a bit disappointed with what he finds—everyone filthy dirty, swollen bellies, faces daubed with clay, two missing at least and the island afire. It ought to have been more like Coral Island, he suggests.

Ralph looked at him dumbly. For a moment he had a fleeting picture of the strange glamour that had once invested the beaches. But the island was scorched up like dead wood—Simon was dead—and Jack had . . . The tears began to flow and sobs shook him. He gave himself up to them now for the first time on the island; great, shuddering spasms of grief that seemed to wrench his whole body. His voice rose under the black smoke before the burning wreckage of the island; and infected by that emotion, the other little boys began to shake and sob too. And in the middle of them, with filthy body, matted hair, and unwiped nose, Ralph wept for the end of innocence, the darkness of man's heart, and the fall through the air of the true, wise friend called Piggy.

This passage—so pathetic—is also revealing. Phrases like "the end of innocence" and "the darkness of man's heart" show us the author's attitude more clearly than has appeared hitherto. He believes in the Fall of Man and perhaps in Original Sin. Or if he does not exactly believe, he fears; the same fear infects his second novel, a difficult and profound work called *The Inheritors*. Here the innocent (the boys as it were) are Neanderthal Man, and the corrupters are Homo Sapiens, our own ancestors, who eat other animals, discover intoxicants, and destroy. Similar notions occur in his other novels.

Thus his attitude approaches the Christian: we are all born in sin, or will all lapse into it. But he does not complete the Christian attitude, for the reason that he never introduces the idea of a Redeemer. When a deity does appear, he is the Lord of the Flies, Beelzebub, and he sends a messenger to prepare his way before him.

The approach of doom is gradual. When the little boys land they are delighted to find that there are no grownups about. Ralph stands on his head with joy, and led by him they have a short period of happiness. Soon problems arise, work has to be assigned and executed, and Ralph now feels "we must make a good job of this, as grownups would, we mustn't let them down." Problems increase and become terrifying. In his desperation the child cries, "If only they could get a message to us, if only they could send us something grown-up . . . a sign or something." And they do. They send something grown-up. A dead parachutist floats down from the upper air, where they have been killing each other, is carried this way and that by the gentle winds, and hooks onto the top of the island.

This is not the end of the horrors. But it is the supreme irony.

And it remains with us when the breezy rescuers arrive at the close and wonder why a better show wasn't put up.

Lord of the Flies is a very serious book which has to be introduced seriously. The danger of such an introduction is that it may suggest that the book is stodgy. It is not. It is written with taste and liveliness, the talk is natural, the descriptions of scenery enchanting. It is certainly not a comforting book. But it may help a few grownups to be less complacent and more compassionate, to support Ralph, respect Piggy, control Jack, and lighten a little the darkness of man's heart. At the present moment (if I may speak personally) it is respect for Piggy that seems needed most. I do not find it in our leaders.

—E. M. FORSTER

King's College
Cambridge
May 14, 1962

CONTENTS

CONTENTS

LORD
of the
FLIES

For my mother and father

one

THE SOUND OF
THE SHELL

THE BOY WITH FAIR HAIR LOWERED HIMSELF
down the last few feet of rock and began to pick his way
toward the lagoon. Though he had taken off his school sweater
and trailed it now from one hand, his grey shirt stuck to him
and his hair was plastered to his forehead. All round him the
long scar smashed into the jungle was a bath of heat. He was
clambering heavily among the creepers and broken trunks when
a bird, a vision of red and yellow, flashed upwards with a witch-
like cry; and this cry was echoed by another.

"Hi!" it said. "Wait a minute!"

The undergrowth at the side of the scar was shaken and a
multitude of raindrops fell pattering.

"Wait a minute," the voice said. "I got caught up."

The fair boy stopped and jerked his stockings with an auto-
matic gesture that made the jungle seem for a moment like the
Home Counties.

The voice spoke again.

"I can't hardly move with all these creeper things."

The owner of the voice came backing out of the undergrowth
so that twigs scratched on a greasy wind-breaker. The naked
crooks of his knees were plump, caught and scratched by thorns.

1

He bent down, removed the thorns carefully, and turned around. He was shorter than the fair boy and very fat. He came forward, searching out safe lodgments for his feet, and then looked up through thick spectacles.

"Where's the man with the megaphone?"

The fair boy shook his head.

"This is an island. At least I think it's an island. That's a reef out in the sea. Perhaps there aren't any grownups anywhere."

The fat boy looked startled.

"There was that pilot. But he wasn't in the passenger cabin, he was up in front."

The fair boy was peering at the reef through screwed-up eyes.

"All them other kids," the fat boy went on. "Some of them must have got out. They must have, mustn't they?"

The fair boy began to pick his way as casually as possible toward the water. He tried to be offhand and not too obviously uninterested, but the fat boy hurried after him.

"Aren't there any grownups at all?"

"I don't think so."

The fair boy said this solemnly; but then the delight of a realized ambition overcame him. In the middle of the scar he stood on his head and grinned at the reversed fat boy.

"No grownups!"

The fat boy thought for a moment.

"That pilot."

The fair boy allowed his feet to come down and sat on the steamy earth.

"He must have flown off after he dropped us. He couldn't land here. Not in a place with wheels."

"We was attacked!"

"He'll be back all right."

The fat boy shook his head.

"When we was coming down I looked through one of them windows. I saw the other part of the plane. There were flames coming out of it."

He looked up and down the scar.

"And this is what the cabin done."

The fair boy reached out and touched the jagged end of a trunk. For a moment he looked interested.

"What happened to it?" he asked. "Where's it got to now?"

"That storm dragged it out to sea. It wasn't half dangerous with all them tree trunks falling. There must have been some kids still in it."

He hesitated for a moment, then spoke again.

"What's your name?"

"Ralph."

The fat boy waited to be asked his name in turn but this proffer of acquaintance was not made; the fair boy called Ralph smiled vaguely, stood up, and began to make his way once more toward the lagoon. The fat boy hung steadily at his shoulder.

"I expect there's a lot more of us scattered about. You haven't seen any others, have you?"

Ralph shook his head and increased his speed. Then he tripped over a branch and came down with a crash.

The fat boy stood by him, breathing hard.

"My auntie told me not to run," he explained, "on account of my asthma."

"Ass-mar?"

"That's right. Can't catch my breath. I was the only boy in our school what had asthma," said the fat boy with a touch of pride. "And I've been wearing specs since I was three."

He took off his glasses and held them out to Ralph, blinking and smiling, and then started to wipe them against his grubby wind-breaker. An expression of pain and inward concentration altered the pale contours of his face. He smeared the sweat from his cheeks and quickly adjusted the spectacles on his nose.

"Them fruit."

He glanced round the scar.

"Them fruit," he said, "I expect—"

He put on his glasses, waded away from Ralph, and crouched down among the tangled foliage.

"I'll be out again in just a minute—"

Ralph disentangled himself cautiously and stole away through the branches. In a few seconds the fat boy's grunts were behind him and he was hurrying toward the screen that still lay between him and the lagoon. He climbed over a broken trunk and was out of the jungle.

The shore was fledged with palm trees. These stood or leaned or reclined against the light and their green feathers were a hundred feet up in the air. The ground beneath them was a bank covered with coarse grass, torn everywhere by the upheavals of fallen trees, scattered with decaying coconuts and palm saplings. Behind this was the darkness of the forest proper and the open space of the scar. Ralph stood, one hand against a grey trunk, and screwed up his eyes against the shimmering water. Out there, perhaps a mile away, the white surf flinked on a coral reef, and beyond that the open sea was dark blue. Within the irregular arc of coral the lagoon was still as a mountain lake—blue of all shades and shadowy green and purple. The beach between the palm terrace and the water was a thin stick, endless apparently, for to Ralph's left the perspectives of palm and beach and water drew to a point at infinity; and always, almost visible, was the heat.

He jumped down from the terrace. The sand was thick over his black shoes and the heat hit him. He became conscious of the weight of clothes, kicked his shoes off fiercely and ripped off each stocking with its elastic garter in a single movement. Then he leapt back on the terrace, pulled off his shirt, and stood there among the skull-like coconuts with green shadows from the palms and the forest sliding over his skin. He undid the snake-clasp of his belt, lugged off his shorts and pants, and stood there naked, looking at the dazzling beach and the water.

He was old enough, twelve years and a few months, to have lost the prominent tummy of childhood and not yet old enough for adolescence to have made him awkward. You could see now that he might make a boxer, as far as width and heaviness of shoulders went, but there was a mildness about his mouth and eyes that proclaimed no devil. He patted the palm trunk softly, and, forced at last to believe in the reality of the island laughed delightedly again and stood on his head. He turned neatly on to his feet, jumped down to the beach, knelt and swept a double armful of sand into a pile against his chest. Then he sat back and looked at the water with bright, excited eyes.

"Ralph—"

The fat boy lowered himself over the terrace and sat down carefully, using the edge as a seat.

"I'm sorry I been such a time. Them fruit—"

He wiped his glasses and adjusted them on his button nose. The frame had made a deep, pink "V" on the bridge. He looked critically at Ralph's golden body and then down at his own clothes. He laid a hand on the end of a zipper that extended down his chest.

"My auntie——"

Then he opened the zipper with decision and pulled the whole wind-breaker over his head.

"There!"

Ralph looked at him sidelong and said nothing.

"I expect we'll want to know all their names," said the fat boy, "and make a list. We ought to have a meeting."

Ralph did not take the hint so the fat boy was forced to continue.

"I don't care what they call me," he said confidentially, "so long as they don't call me what they used to call me at school."

Ralph was faintly interested.

"What was that?"

The fat boy glanced over his shoulder, then leaned toward Ralph.

He whispered.

"They used to call me 'Piggy.'"

Ralph shrieked with laughter. He jumped up.

"Piggy! Piggy!"

"Ralph—please!"

Piggy clasped his hands in apprehension.

"I said I didn't want——"

"Piggy! Piggy!"

Ralph danced out into the hot air of the beach and then returned as a fighter-plane, with wings swept back, and machine-gunned Piggy.

"Sche-aa-ow!"

He dived in the sand at Piggy's feet and lay there laughing.

"Piggy!"

Piggy grinned reluctantly, pleased despite himself at even this much recognition.

"So long as you don't tell the others—"

Ralph giggled into the sand. The expression of pain and concentration returned to Piggy's face.

"Half a sec'."

He hastened back into the forest. Ralph stood up and trotted along to the right.

Here the beach was interrupted abruptly by the square motif of the landscape; a great platform of pink granite thrust up uncompromisingly through forest and terrace and sand and lagoon to make a raised jetty four feet high. The top of this was covered with a thin layer of soil and coarse grass and shaded with young palm trees. There was not enough soil for them to grow to any height and when they reached perhaps twenty feet they fell and dried, forming a criss-cross pattern of trunks, very convenient to sit on. The palms that still stood made a green roof, covered on the underside with a quivering tangle of reflections from the lagoon. Ralph hauled himself onto this platform, noted the coolness and shade, shut one eye, and decided that the shadows on his body were really green. He picked his way to the seaward edge of the platform and stood looking down into the water. It was clear to the bottom and bright with the efflorescence of tropical weed and coral. A school of tiny, glittering fish flicked hither and thither. Ralph spoke to himself, sounding the bass strings of delight.

"Whizzoh!"

Beyond the platform there was more enchantment. Some act of God—a typhoon perhaps, or the storm that had accompanied his own arrival—had banked sand inside the lagoon so that there was a long, deep pool in the beach with a high ledge of pink granite at the further end. Ralph had been deceived before now by the specious appearance of depth in a beach pool and he approached this one preparing to be disappointed. But the island ran true to form and the incredible pool, which clearly was only invaded by the sea at high tide, was so deep at one end as to be dark green. Ralph inspected the whole thirty yards carefully and then plunged in. The water was warmer than his blood and he might have been swimming in a huge bath.

Piggy appeared again, sat on the rocky ledge, and watched Ralph's green and white body enviously.

"You can't half swim."

"Piggy."

Piggy took off his shoes and socks, ranged them carefully on the ledge, and tested the water with one toe.

"It's hot!"

"What did you expect?"

"I didn't expect nothing. My auntie—"

"Sucks to your auntie!"

Ralph did a surface dive and swam under water with his eyes open; the sandy edge of the pool loomed up like a hillside. He turned over, holding his nose, and a golden light danced and shattered just over his face. Piggy was looking determined and began to take off his shorts. Presently he was palely and fatly naked. He tiptoed down the sandy side of the pool, and sat there up to his neck in water smiling proudly at Ralph.

"Aren't you going to swim?"

Piggy shook his head.

"I can't swim. I wasn't allowed. My asthma—"

"Sucks to your ass-mar!"

Piggy bore this with a sort of humble patience.

"You can't half swim well."

Ralph paddled backwards down the slope, immersed his mouth and blew a jet of water into the air. Then he lifted his chin and spoke.

"I could swim when I was five. Daddy taught me. He's a commander in the Navy. When he gets leave he'll come and rescue us. What's your father?"

Piggy flushed suddenly.

"My dad's dead," he said quickly, "and my mum—"

He took off his glasses and looked vainly for something with which to clean them.

"I used to live with my auntie. She kept a candy store. I used to get ever so many candies. As many as I liked. When'll your dad rescue us?"

"Soon as he can."

Piggy rose dripping from the water and stood naked, cleaning his glasses with a sock. The only sound that reached them now through the heat of the morning was the long, grinding roar of the breakers on the reef.

"How does he know we're here?"

Ralph lolled in the water. Sleep enveloped him like the swathing mirages that were wrestling with the brilliance of the lagoon.

"How does he know we're here?"

Because, thought Ralph, because, because. The roar from the reef became very distant.

"They'd tell him at the airport."

Piggy shook his head, put on his flashing glasses and looked down at Ralph.

"Not them. Didn't you hear what the pilot said? About the atom bomb? They're all dead."

Ralph pulled himself out of the water, stood facing Piggy, and considered this unusual problem.

Piggy persisted.

"This an island, isn't it?"

"I climbed a rock," said Ralph slowly, "and I think this is an island."

"They're all dead," said Piggy, "an' this is an island. Nobody don't know we're here. Your dad don't know, nobody don't know—"

His lips quivered and the spectacles were dimmed with mist.

"We may stay here till we die."

With that word the heat seemed to increase till it became a threatening weight and the lagoon attacked them with a blinding effulgence.

"Get my clothes," muttered Ralph. "Along there."

He trotted through the sand, enduring the sun's enmity, crossed the platform and found his scattered clothes. To put on a grey shirt once more was strangely pleasing. Then he climbed the edge of the platform and sat in the green shade on a convenient trunk. Piggy hauled himself up, carrying most of his clothes under his arms. Then he sat carefully on a fallen trunk near the little cliff that fronted the lagoon; and the tangled reflections quivered over him.

Presently he spoke.

"We got to find the others. We got to do something."

Ralph said nothing. Here was a coral island. Protected from the sun, ignoring Piggy's ill-omened talk, he dreamed pleasantly.

Piggy insisted.

"How many of us are there?"

Ralph came forward and stood by Piggy.

"I don't know."

Here and there, little breezes crept over the polished waters beneath the haze of heat. When these breezes reached the platform the palm fronds would whisper, so that spots of blurred sunlight slid over their bodies or moved like bright, winged things in the shade.

Piggy looked up at Ralph. All the shadows on Ralph's face were reversed; green above, bright below from the lagoon. A blur of sunlight was crawling across his hair.

"We got to do something."

Ralph looked through him. Here at last was the imagined but never fully realized place leaping into real life. Ralph's lips parted in a delighted smile and Piggy, taking this smile to himself as a mark of recognition, laughed with pleasure.

"If it really is an island—"

"What's that?"

Ralph had stopped smiling and was pointing into the lagoon. Something creamy lay among the ferny weeds.

"A stone."

"No. A shell."

Suddenly Piggy was a-bubble with decorous excitement.

"S'right. It's a shell! I seen one like that before. On someone's back wall. A conch he called it. He used to blow it and then his mum would come. It's ever so valuable—"

Near to Ralph's elbow a palm sapling leaned out over the lagoon. Indeed, the weight was already pulling a lump from the poor soil and soon it would fall. He tore out the stem and began to poke about in the water, while the brilliant fish flicked away on this side and that. Piggy leaned dangerously.

"Careful! You'll break it—"

"Shut up."

Ralph spoke absently. The shell was interesting and pretty and a worthy plaything; but the vivid phantoms of his day-dream still interposed between him and Piggy, who in this context was an irrelevance. The palm sapling, bending, pushed the shell across the weeds. Ralph used one hand as a fulcrum and pressed down with the other till the shell rose, dripping, and Piggy could make a grab.

Now the shell was no longer a thing seen but not to be touched, Ralph too became excited. Piggy babbled:

"—a conch; ever so expensive. I bet if you wanted to buy one, you'd have to pay pounds and pounds and pounds—he had it on his garden wall, and my auntie—"

Ralph took the shell from Piggy and a little water ran down his arm. In color the shell was deep cream, touched here and there with fading pink. Between the point, worn away into a little hole, and the pink lips of the mouth, lay eighteen inches of shell with a slight spiral twist and covered with a delicate, embossed pattern. Ralph shook sand out of the deep tube.

"—mooed like a cow," he said. "He had some white stones too, an' a bird cage with a green parrot. He didn't blow the white stones, of course, an' he said—"

Piggy paused for breath and stroked the glistening thing that lay in Ralph's hands.

"Ralph!"

Ralph looked up.

"We can use this to call the others. Have a meeting. They'll come when they hear us—"

He beamed at Ralph.

"That was what you meant, didn't you? That's why you got the conch out of the water?"

Ralph pushed back his fair hair.

"How did your friend blow the conch?"

"He kind of spat," said Piggy. "My auntie wouldn't let me blow on account of my asthma. He said you blew from down

here." Piggy laid a hand on his jutting abdomen. "You try, Ralph.
You'll call the others."

Doubtfully, Ralph laid the small end of the shell against his
mouth and blew. There came a rushing sound from its mouth
but nothing more. Ralph wiped the salt water off his lips and
tried again, but the shell remained silent.

"He kind of spat."

Ralph pursed his lips and squirted air into the shell, which
emitted a low, farting noise. This amused both boys so much
that Ralph went on squirting for some minutes, between bouts
of laughter.

"He blew from down here."

Ralph grasped the idea and hit the shell with air from his
diaphragm. Immediately the thing sounded. A deep, harsh note
boomed under the palms, spread through the intricacies of the
forest and echoed back from the pink granite of the mountain.
Clouds of birds rose from the treetops, and something squealed
and ran in the undergrowth.

Ralph took the shell away from his lips.

"Gosh!"

His ordinary voice sounded like a whisper after the harsh note
of the conch. He laid the conch against his lips, took a deep
breath and blew once more. The note boomed again: and then
at his firmer pressure, the note, fluking up an octave, became a
strident blare more penetrating than before. Piggy was shouting
something, his face pleased, his glasses flashing. The birds cried,
small animals scuttered. Ralph's breath failed; the note dropped
the octave, became a low wubber, was a rush of air.

The conch was silent, a gleaming tusk; Ralph's face was dark
with breathlessness and the air over the island was full of bird-
clamor and echoes ringing.

"I bet you can hear that for miles."

Ralph found his breath and blew a series of short blasts.

Piggy exclaimed: "There's one!"

A child had appeared among the palms, about a hundred yards along the beach. He was a boy of perhaps six years, sturdy and fair, his clothes torn, his face covered with a sticky mess of fruit. His trousers had been lowered for an obvious purpose and had only been pulled back half-way. He jumped off the palm terrace into the sand and his trousers fell about his ankles; he stepped out of them and trotted to the platform. Piggy helped him up. Meanwhile Ralph continued to blow till voices shouted in the forest. The small boy squatted in front of Ralph, looking up brightly and vertically. As he received the reassurance of something purposeful being done he began to look satisfied, and his only clean digit, a pink thumb, slid into his mouth.

Piggy leaned down to him.

"What's yer name?"

"Johnny."

Piggy muttered the name to himself and then shouted it to Ralph, who was not interested because he was still blowing. His face was dark with the violent pleasure of making this stupendous noise, and his heart was making the stretched shirt shake. The shouting in the forest was nearer.

Signs of life were visible now on the beach. The sand, trembling beneath the heat haze, concealed many figures in its miles of length; boys were making their way toward the platform through the hot, dumb sand. Three small children, no older than Johnny, appeared from startlingly close at hand, where they had been gorging fruit in the forest. A dark little boy, not much younger than Piggy, parted a tangle of undergrowth, walked on to the platform, and smiled cheerfully at everybody. More and more of them came. Taking their cue from the innocent Johnny, they sat down on the fallen palm trunks and waited. Ralph continued to blow short, penetrating blasts. Piggy moved among the crowd, asking names and frowning to remember them. The children gave him the same simple obedience that they had given to the men with megaphones. Some were naked and carrying their clothes; others half-naked, or more or less dressed, in school uniforms, grey, blue, fawn, jacketed, or jerseyed. There were badges, mottoes even, stripes of color in stockings and pullovers. Their heads clustered above the trunks in the green shade; heads brown, fair, black, chestnut, sandy, mouse-colored; heads muttering, whispering, heads full of eyes that watched Ralph and speculated. Something was being done.

The children who came along the beach, singly or in twos, leapt into visibility when they crossed the line from heat haze to nearer sand. Here, the eye was first attracted to a black, bat-like creature that danced on the sand, and only later perceived the body above it. The bat was the child's shadow, shrunk by the vertical sun to a patch between the hurrying feet. Even while he blew, Ralph noticed the last pair of bodies that reached the platform above a fluttering patch of black. The two boys, bullet-headed and with hair like tow, flung themselves down and lay grinning and panting at Ralph like dogs. They were twins, and the eye was shocked and incredulous at such cheery duplication. They breathed together, they grinned together, they were chunky and vital. They raised wet lips at Ralph, for they seemed provided with not quite enough skin, so that their profiles were blurred and their mouths pulled open. Piggy bent his flashing glasses to them and could be heard between the blasts, repeating their names.

"Sam, Eric, Sam, Eric."

Then he got muddled; the twins shook their heads and pointed at each other and the crowd laughed.

At last Ralph ceased to blow and sat there, the conch trailing from one hand, his head bowed on his knees. As the echoes died away so did the laughter, and there was silence.

Within the diamond haze of the beach something dark was fumbling along. Ralph saw it first, and watched till the intentness of his gaze drew all eyes that way. Then the creature stepped from mirage on to clear sand, and they saw that the darkness was not all shadow but mostly clothing. The creature was a party of boys, marching approximately in step in two parallel lines and dressed in strangely eccentric clothing. Shorts, shirts, and different garments they carried in their hands; but each boy wore a square black cap with a silver badge on it. Their bodies, from throat to ankle, were hidden by black cloaks which bore a long silver cross on the left breast and each neck was finished off with a hambone frill. The heat of the tropics, the descent, the search for food, and now this sweaty march along the blazing beach had given them the complexions of newly washed plums. The boy who controlled them was dressed in the same way though his cap badge was golden. When his party was about ten yards from the platform he shouted an order and they halted, gasping, sweating, swaying in the fierce light. The boy himself came forward, vaulted on to the platform with his cloak flying, and peered into what to him was almost complete darkness.

"Where's the man with the trumpet?"

Ralph, sensing his sun-blindness, answered him.

"There's no man with a trumpet. Only me."

The boy came close and peered down at Ralph, screwing up his face as he did so. What he saw of the fair-haired boy with the creamy shell on his knees did not seem to satisfy him. He turned quickly, his black cloak circling.

"Isn't there a ship, then?"

Inside the floating cloak he was tall, thin, and bony; and his hair was red beneath the black cap. His face was crumpled and freckled, and ugly without silliness. Out of this face stared two light blue eyes, frustrated now, and turning, or ready to turn, to anger.

"Isn't there a man here?"

Ralph spoke to his back.

"No. We're having a meeting. Come and join in."

The group of cloaked boys began to scatter from close line. The tall boy shouted at them.

"Choir! Stand still!"

Wearily obedient, the choir huddled into line and stood there swaying in the sun. None the less, some began to protest faintly.

"But, Merridew. Please, Merridew . . . can't we?"

Then one of the boys flopped on his face in the sand and the line broke up. They heaved the fallen boy to the platform and let him lie. Merridew, his eyes staring, made the best of a bad job.

"All right then. Sit down. Let him alone."

"But Merridew."

"He's always throwing a faint," said Merridew. "He did in Gib.; and Addis; and at matins over the precentor."

This last piece of shop brought sniggers from the choir, who perched like black birds on the criss-cross trunks and examined Ralph with interest. Piggy asked no names. He was intimidated by this uniformed superiority and the offhand authority in Merridew's voice. He shrank to the other side of Ralph and busied himself with his glasses.

Merridew turned to Ralph.

"Aren't there any grownups?"

"No."

Merridew sat down on a trunk and looked round the circle.

"Then we'll have to look after ourselves."

Secure on the other side of Ralph, Piggy spoke timidly.

"That's why Ralph made a meeting. So as we can decide what to do. We've heard names. That's Johnny. Those two—they're twins, Sam 'n Eric. Which is Eric—? You? No—you're Sam—"

"I'm Sam—"

"'n I'm Eric."

"We'd better all have names," said Ralph, "so I'm Ralph."

"We got most names," said Piggy. "Got 'em just now."

"Kids' names," said Merridew. "Why should I be Jack? I'm Merridew."

Ralph turned to him quickly. This was the voice of one who knew his own mind.

"Then," went on Piggy, "that boy—I forget—"

"You're talking too much," said Jack Merridew. "Shut up, Fatty."

Laughter arose.

"He's not Fatty," cried Ralph, "his real name's Piggy!"

"Piggy!"

"Piggy!"

"Oh, Piggy!"

A storm of laughter arose and even the tiniest child joined in. For the moment the boys were a closed circuit of sympathy with Piggy outside: he went very pink, bowed his head and cleaned his glasses again.

Finally the laughter died away and the naming continued.

There was Maurice, next in size among the choir boys to Jack, but broad and grinning all the time. There was a slight, furtive boy whom no one knew, who kept to himself with an inner intensity of avoidance and secrecy. He muttered that his name was Roger and was silent again. Bill, Robert, Harold, Henry; the choir boy who had fainted sat up against a palm trunk, smiled pallidly at Ralph and said that his name was Simon.

Jack spoke.

"We've got to decide about being rescued."

There was a buzz. One of the small boys, Henry, said that he wanted to go home.

"Shut up," said Ralph absently. He lifted the conch. "Seems to me we ought to have a chief to decide things."

"A chief! A chief!"

"I ought to be chief," said Jack with simple arrogance, "because I'm chapter chorister and head boy. I can sing C sharp."

Another buzz.

"Well then," said Jack, "I—"

He hesitated. The dark boy, Roger, stirred at last and spoke up.

"Let's have a vote."

"Yes!"

"Vote for chief!"

"Let's vote—"

This toy of voting was almost as pleasing as the conch. Jack started to protest but the clamor changed from the general wish for a chief to an election by acclaim of Ralph himself. None of the boys could have found good reason for this; what intelligence had been shown was traceable to Piggy while the most obvious leader was Jack. But there was a stillness about Ralph as he sat that marked him out: there was his size, and attractive appearance; and most obscurely, yet most powerfully, there was the conch. The being that had blown that, had sat waiting for them on the platform with the delicate thing balanced on his knees, was set apart.

"Him with the shell."

"Ralph! Ralph!"

"Let him be chief with the trumpet-thing."

Ralph raised a hand for silence.

"All right. Who wants Jack for chief?"

With dreary obedience the choir raised their hands.

"Who wants me?"

Every hand outside the choir except Piggy's was raised immediately. Then Piggy, too, raised his hand grudgingly into the air.

Ralph counted.

"I'm chief then."

The circle of boys broke into applause. Even the choir applauded; and the freckles on Jack's face disappeared under a blush of mortification. He started up, then changed his mind and sat down again while the air rang. Ralph looked at him, eager to offer something.

"The choir belongs to you, of course."

"They could be the army—"

"Or hunters—"

"They could be—"

The suffusion drained away from Jack's face. Ralph waved again for silence.

"Jack's in charge of the choir. They can be—what do you want them to be?"

"Hunters."

Jack and Ralph smiled at each other with shy liking. The rest began to talk eagerly.

Jack stood up.

"All right, choir. Take off your togs."

As if released from class, the choir boys stood up, chattered, piled their black cloaks on the grass. Jack laid his on the trunk by Ralph. His grey shorts were sticking to him with sweat. Ralph glanced at them admiringly, and when Jack saw his glance he explained.

"I tried to get over that hill to see if there was water all round. But your shell called us."

Ralph smiled and held up the conch for silence.

"Listen, everybody. I've got to have time to think things out. I can't decide what to do straight off. If this isn't an island we might be rescued straight away. So we've got to decide if this is an island. Everybody must stay round here and wait and not go away. Three of us—if we take more we'd get all mixed, and lose each other—three of us will go on an expedition and find out. I'll go, and Jack, and, and...."

He looked round the circle of eager faces. There was no lack of boys to choose from.

"And Simon."

The boys round Simon giggled, and he stood up, laughing a little. Now that the pallor of his faint was over, he was a skinny, vivid little boy, with a glance coming up from under a hut of straight hair that hung down, black and coarse.

He nodded at Ralph.

"I'll come."

"And I—"

Jack snatched from behind him a sizable sheath-knife and clouted it into a trunk. The buzz rose and died away.

Piggy stirred.

"I'll come."

Ralph turned to him.

"You're no good on a job like this."

"All the same—"

"We don't want you," said Jack, flatly. "Three's enough."

Piggy's glasses flashed.

"I was with him when he found the conch. I was with him before anyone else was."

Jack and the others paid no attention. There was a general dispersal. Ralph, Jack and Simon jumped off the platform and walked along the sand past the bathing pool. Piggy hung bumbling behind them.

"If Simon walks in the middle of us," said Ralph, "then we could talk over his head."

The three of them fell into step. This meant that every now and then Simon had to do a double shuffle to catch up with the others. Presently Ralph stopped and turned back to Piggy.

"Look."

Jack and Simon pretended to notice nothing. They walked on.

"You can't come."

Piggy's glasses were misted again—this time with humiliation.

"You told 'em. After what I said."

His face flushed, his mouth trembled.

"After I said I didn't want—"

"What on earth are you talking about?"

"About being called Piggy. I said I didn't care as long as they didn't call me Piggy; an' I said not to tell and then you went an' said straight out—"

Stillness descended on them. Ralph, looking with more understanding at Piggy, saw that he was hurt and crushed. He hovered between the two courses of apology or further insult.

"Better Piggy than Fatty," he said at last, with the directness of genuine leadership, "and anyway, I'm sorry if you feel like that. Now go back, Piggy, and take names. That's your job. So long."

He turned and raced after the other two. Piggy stood and the rose of indignation faded slowly from his cheeks. He went back to the platform.

The three boys walked briskly on the sand. The tide was low and there was a strip of weed-strewn beach that was almost as firm as a road. A kind of glamour was spread over them and the scene and they were conscious of the glamour and made happy by it. They turned to each other, laughing excitedly, talking, not listening. The air was bright. Ralph, faced by the task of translating all this into an explanation, stood on his head and fell over. When they had done laughing, Simon stroked Ralph's arm shyly; and they had to laugh again.

"Come on," said Jack presently, "we're explorers."

"We'll go to the end of the island," said Ralph, "and look round the corner."

"If it is an island—"

Now, toward the end of the afternoon, the mirages were settling a little. They found the end of the island, quite distinct, and not magicked out of shape or sense. There was a jumble of the usual squareness, with one great block sitting out in the lagoon. Sea birds were nesting there.

"Like icing," said Ralph, "on a pink cake."

"We shan't see round this corner," said Jack, "because there isn't one. Only a slow curve—and you can see, the rocks get worse—"

Ralph shaded his eyes and followed the jagged outline of the crags up toward the mountain. This part of the beach was nearer the mountain than any other that they had seen.

"We'll try climbing the mountain from here," he said. "I should think this is the easiest way. There's less of that jungly stuff; and more pink rock. Come on."

The three boys began to scramble up. Some unknown force had wrenched and shattered these cubes so that they lay askew, often piled diminishingly on each other. The most usual feature of the rock was a pink cliff surmounted by a skewed block; and that again surmounted, and that again, till the pinkness became a stack of balanced rock projecting through the looped fantasy of the forest creepers. Where the pink cliffs rose out of the ground there were often narrow tracks winding upwards. They could edge along them, deep in the plant world, their faces to the rock.

"What made this track?"

Jack paused, wiping the sweat from his face. Ralph stood by him, breathless.

"Men?"

Jack shook his head.

"Animals."

Ralph peered into the darkness under the trees. The forest minutely vibrated.

"Come on."

The difficulty was not the steep ascent round the shoulders of rock, but the occasional plunges through the undergrowth to get to the next path. Here the roots and stems of creepers were in such tangles that the boys had to thread through them like pliant needles. Their only guide, apart from the brown ground and occasional flashes of light through the foliage, was the tendency of slope: whether this hole, laced as it was with the cables of creeper, stood higher than that.

Somehow, they moved up.

Immured in these tangles, at perhaps their most difficult moment, Ralph turned with shining eyes to the others.

"Wacco."

"Wizard."

"Smashing."

The cause of their pleasure was not obvious. All three were hot, dirty and exhausted. Ralph was badly scratched. The creepers were as thick as their thighs and left little but tunnels for further penetration. Ralph shouted experimentally and they listened to the muted echoes.

"This is real exploring," said Jack. "I bet nobody's been here before."

"We ought to draw a map," said Ralph, "only we haven't any paper."

"We could make scratches on bark," said Simon, "and rub black stuff in."

Again came the solemn communion of shining eyes in the gloom.

"Wacco."

"Wizard."

There was no place for standing on one's head. This time Ralph expressed the intensity of his emotion by pretending to knock Simon down; and soon they were a happy, heaving pile in the under-dusk.

When they had fallen apart Ralph spoke first.

"Got to get on."

The pink granite of the next cliff was further back from the creepers and trees so that they could trot up the path. This again led into more open forest so that they had a glimpse of the spread sea. With openness came the sun; it dried the sweat that had soaked their clothes in the dark, damp heat. At last the way to the top looked like a scramble over pink rock, with no more plunging through darkness. The boys chose their way through defiles and over heaps of sharp stone.

"Look! Look!"

High over this end of the island, the shattered rocks lifted up their stacks and chimneys. This one, against which Jack leaned, moved with a grating sound when they pushed.

"Come on—"

But not "Come on" to the top. The assault on the summit must wait while the three boys accepted this challenge. The rock was as large as a small motor car.

"Heave!"

Sway back and forth, catch the rhythm.

"Heave!"

Increase the swing of the pendulum, increase, increase, come up and bear against that point of furthest balance—increase—increase—

"Heave!"

The great rock loitered, poised on one toe, decided not to return, moved through the air, fell, struck, turned over, leapt droning through the air and smashed a deep hole in the canopy of the forest. Echoes and birds flew, white and pink dust floated, the forest further down shook as with the passage of an enraged monster: and then the island was still.

"Wacco!"

"Like a bomb!"

"Whee-aa-oo!"

Not for five minutes could they drag themselves away from this triumph. But they left at last.

The way to the top was easy after that. As they reached the last stretch Ralph stopped.

"Golly!"

They were on the lip of a circular hollow in the side of the mountain. This was filled with a blue flower, a rock plant of some sort, and the overflow hung down the vent and spilled lavishly among the canopy of the forest. The air was thick with butterflies, lifting, fluttering, settling.

Beyond the hollow was the square top of the mountain and soon they were standing on it.

They had guessed before that this was an island: clambering among the pink rocks, with the sea on either side, and the crystal heights of air, they had known by some instinct that the sea lay on every side. But there seemed something more fitting in leaving the last word till they stood on the top, and could see a circular horizon of water.

Ralph turned to the others.

"This belongs to us."

It was roughly boat-shaped: humped near this end with behind them the jumbled descent to the shore. On either side rocks, cliffs, treetops and a steep slope: forward there, the length of the boat, a tamer descent, tree-clad, with hints of pink: and then the jungly flat of the island, dense green, but drawn at the end to a pink tail. There, where the island petered out in water, was another island; a rock, almost detached, standing like a fort, facing them across the green with one bold, pink bastion.

The boys surveyed all this, then looked out to sea. They were high up and the afternoon had advanced; the view was not robbed of sharpness by mirage.

"That's a reef. A coral reef. I've seen pictures like that."

The reef enclosed more than one side of the island, lying perhaps a mile out and parallel to what they now thought of as their beach. The coral was scribbled in the sea as though a giant had bent down to reproduce the shape of the island in a flowing chalk line but tired before he had finished. Inside was peacock water, rocks and weeds showing as in an aquarium; outside was the dark blue of the sea. The tide was running so that long streaks of foam tailed away from the reef and for a moment they felt that the boat was moving steadily astern.

Jack pointed down.

"That's where we landed."

Beyond falls and cliffs there was a gash visible in the trees; there were the splintered trunks and then the drag, leaving only a fringe of palm between the scar and the sea. There, too, jutting into the lagoon, was the platform, with insect-like figures moving near it.

Ralph sketched a twining line from the bald spot on which they stood down a slope, a gully, through flowers, round and down to the rock where the scar started.

"That's the quickest way back."

Eyes shining, mouths open, triumphant, they savored the right of domination. They were lifted up: were friends.

"There's no village smoke, and no boats," said Ralph wisely. "We'll make sure later, but I think it's uninhabited."

"We'll get food," cried Jack. "Hunt. Catch things . . . until they fetch us."

Simon looked at them both, saying nothing but nodding till his black hair flopped backwards and forwards: his face was glowing.

Ralph looked down the other way where there was no reef.

"Steeper," said Jack.

Ralph made a cupping gesture.

"That bit of forest down there . . . the mountain holds it up."

Every point of the mountain held up trees—flowers and trees. Now the forest stirred, roared, flailed. The nearer acres of rock flowers fluttered and for half a minute the breeze blew cool on their faces.

Ralph spread his arms.

"All ours."

They laughed and tumbled and shouted on the mountain.

"I'm hungry."

When Simon mentioned his hunger the others became aware of theirs.

"Come on," said Ralph. "We've found out what we wanted to know."

They scrambled down a rock slope, dropped among flowers and made their way under the trees. Here they paused and examined the bushes round them curiously.

Simon spoke first.

"Like candles. Candle bushes. Candle buds."

The bushes were dark evergreen and aromatic and the many buds were waxen green and folded up against the light. Jack slashed at one with his knife and the scent spilled over them.

"Candle buds."

"You couldn't light them," said Ralph. "They just look like candles."

"Green candles," said Jack contemptuously. "We can't eat them. Come on."

They were in the beginnings of the thick forest, plonking with weary feet on a track, when they heard the noises—squeakings—and the hard strike of hoofs on a path. As they pushed forward the squeaking increased till it became a frenzy. They found a piglet caught in a curtain of creepers, throwing itself at the elastic traces in all the madness of extreme terror. Its voice was thin, needle-sharp and insistent. The three boys rushed forward and Jack drew his knife again with a flourish. He raised his arm in the air. There came a pause, a hiatus, the pig continued to scream and the creepers to jerk, and the blade continued to flash at the end of a bony arm. The pause was only long enough for them to understand what an enormity the downward stroke would be. Then the piglet tore loose from the creepers and scurried into the undergrowth. They were left looking at each other and the place of terror. Jack's face was white under the freckles. He noticed that he still held the knife aloft and brought his arm down replacing the blade in the sheath. Then they all three laughed ashamedly and began to climb back to the track.

"I was choosing a place," said Jack. "I was just waiting for a moment to decide where to stab him."

"You should stick a pig," said Ralph fiercely. "They always talk about sticking a pig."

"You cut a pig's throat to let the blood out," said Jack, "otherwise you can't eat the meat."

"Why didn't you—?"

They knew very well why he hadn't: because of the enormity of the knife descending and cutting into living flesh; because of the unbearable blood.

"I was going to," said Jack. He was ahead of them, and they could not see his face. "I was choosing a place. Next time—!"

He snatched his knife out of the sheath and slammed it into a tree trunk. Next time there would be no mercy. He looked round fiercely, daring them to contradict. Then they broke out into the sunlight and for a while they were busy finding and devouring food as they moved down the scar toward the platform and the meeting.

t w o

FIRE ON THE MOUNTAIN

B Y THE TIME RALPH FINISHED BLOWING THE conch the platform was crowded. There were differences between this meeting and the one held in the morning. The afternoon sun slanted in from the other side of the platform and most of the children, feeling too late the smart of sunburn, had put their clothes on. The choir, noticeably less of a group, had discarded their cloaks.

Ralph sat on a fallen trunk, his left side to the sun. On his right were most of the choir; on his left the larger boys who had not known each other before the evacuation; before him small children squatted in the grass.

Silence now. Ralph lifted the cream and pink shell to his knees and a sudden breeze scattered light over the platform. He was uncertain whether to stand up or remain sitting. He looked sideways to his left, toward the bathing pool. Piggy was sitting near but giving no help.

Ralph cleared his throat.

"Well then."

All at once he found he could talk fluently and explain what he had to say. He passed a hand through his fair hair and spoke.

"We're on an island. We've been on the mountain top and seen water all round. We saw no houses, no smoke, no footprints, no boats, no people. We're on an uninhabited island with no other people on it."

Jack broke in.

"All the same you need an army—for hunting. Hunting pigs—"

"Yes. There are pigs on the island."

All three of them tried to convey the sense of the pink live thing struggling in the creepers.

"We saw—"

"Squealing—"

"It broke away—"

"Before I could kill it—but—next time!"

Jack slammed his knife into a trunk and looked round challengingly.

The meeting settled down again.

"So you see," said Ralph, "we need hunters to get us meat. And another thing."

He lifted the shell on his knees and looked round the sunslashed faces.

"There aren't any grownups. We shall have to look after ourselves."

The meeting hummed and was silent.

"And another thing. We can't have everybody talking at once. We'll have to have 'Hands up' like at school."

He held the conch before his face and glanced round the mouth.

"Then I'll give him the conch."

"Conch?"

"That's what this shell's called. I'll give the conch to the next person to speak. He can hold it when he's speaking."

"But—"

"Look—"

"And he won't be interrupted. Except by me."

Jack was on his feet.

"We'll have rules!" he cried excitedly. "Lots of rules! Then when anyone breaks 'em—"

"Whee—oh!"

"Wacco!"

"Bong!"

"Doink!"

Ralph felt the conch lifted from his lap. Then Piggy was standing cradling the great cream shell and the shouting died down. Jack, left on his feet, looked uncertainly at Ralph who smiled and patted the log. Jack sat down. Piggy took off his glasses and blinked at the assembly while he wiped them on his shirt.

"You're hindering Ralph. You're not letting him get to the most important thing."

He paused effectively.

"Who knows we're here? Eh?"

"They knew at the airport."

"The man with a trumpet-thing—"

"My dad."

Piggy put on his glasses.

"Nobody knows where we are," said Piggy. He was paler than before and breathless. "Perhaps they knew where we was going to; and perhaps not. But they don't know where we are 'cos we never got there." He gaped at them for a moment, then swayed and sat down. Ralph took the conch from his hands.

"That's what I was going to say," he went on, "when you all, all...." He gazed at their intent faces. "The plane was shot down in flames. Nobody knows where we are. We may be here a long time."

The silence was so complete that they could hear the unevenness of Piggy's breathing. The sun slanted in and lay golden over half the platform. The breezes that on the lagoon had chased their tails like kittens were finding their way across the platform and into the forest. Ralph pushed back the tangle of fair hair that hung on his forehead.

"So we may be here a long time."

Nobody said anything. He grinned suddenly.

"But this is a good island. We—Jack, Simon and me—we climbed the mountain. It's wizard. There's food and drink, and—"

"Rocks—"

"Blue flowers—"

Piggy, partly recovered, pointed to the conch in Ralph's hands, and Jack and Simon fell silent. Ralph went on.

"While we're waiting we can have a good time on this island."

He gesticulated widely.

"It's like in a book."

At once there was a clamor.

"Treasure Island—"

"Swallows and Amazons—"

"Coral Island—"

Ralph waved the conch.

"This is our island. It's a good island. Until the grownups come to fetch us we'll have fun."

Jack held out his hand for the conch.

"There's pigs," he said. "There's food; and bathing water in that little stream along there—and everything. Didn't anyone find anything else?"

He handed the conch back to Ralph and sat down. Apparently no one had found anything.

The older boys first noticed the child when he resisted. There was a group of little boys urging him forward and he did not want to go. He was a shrimp of a boy, about six years old, and one side of his face was blotted out by a mulberry-colored birthmark. He stood now, warped out of the perpendicular by the fierce light of publicity, and he bored into the coarse grass with one toe. He was muttering and about to cry.

The other little boys, whispering but serious, pushed him toward Ralph.

"All right," said Ralph, "come on then."

The small boy looked round in panic.

"Speak up!"

The small boy held out his hands for the conch and the assembly shouted with laughter; at once he snatched back his hands and started to cry.

"Let him have the conch!" shouted Piggy. "Let him have it!"

At last Ralph induced him to hold the shell but by then the blow of laughter had taken away the child's voice. Piggy knelt by him, one hand on the great shell, listening and interpreting to the assembly.

"He wants to know what you're going to do about the snake-thing."

Ralph laughed, and the other boys laughed with him. The small boy twisted further into himself.

"Tell us about the snake-thing."

"Now he says it was a beastie."

"Beastie?"

"A snake-thing. Ever so big. He saw it."

"Where?"

"In the woods."

Either the wandering breezes or perhaps the decline of the sun allowed a little coolness to lie under the trees. The boys felt it and stirred restlessly.

"You couldn't have a beastie, a snake-thing, on an island this size," Ralph explained kindly. "You only get them in big countries, like Africa, or India."

Murmur; and the grave nodding of heads.

"He says the beastie came in the dark."

"Then he couldn't see it!"

Laughter and cheers.

"Did you hear that? Says he saw the thing in the dark—"

"He still says he saw the beastie. It came and went away again an' came back and wanted to eat him—"

"He was dreaming."

Laughing, Ralph looked for confirmation round the ring of faces. The older boys agreed; but here and there among the little ones was the doubt that required more than rational assurance.

"He must have had a nightmare. Stumbling about among all those creepers."

More grave nodding; they knew about nightmares.

"He says he saw the beastie, the snake-thing, and will it come back tonight?"

"But there isn't a beastie!"

"He says in the morning it turned into them things like ropes in the trees and hung in the branches. He says will it come back tonight?"

"But there isn't a beastie!"

There was no laughter at all now and more grave watching. Ralph pushed both hands through his hair and looked at the little boy in mixed amusement and exasperation.

Jack seized the conch.

"Ralph's right of course. There isn't a snake-thing. But if there was a snake we'd hunt it and kill it. We're going to hunt pigs to get meat for everybody. And we'll look for the snake too—"

"But there isn't a snake!"

"We'll make sure when we go hunting."

Ralph was annoyed and, for the moment, defeated. He felt himself facing something ungraspable. The eyes that looked so intently at him were without humor.

"But there isn't a beast!"

Something he had not known was there rose in him and compelled him to make the point, loudly and again.

"But I tell you there isn't a beast!"

The assembly was silent.

Ralph lifted the conch again and his good humor came back as he thought of what he had to say next.

"Now we come to the most important thing. I've been thinking. I was thinking while we were climbing the mountain." He flashed a conspiratorial grin at the other two. "And on the beach just now. This is what I thought. We want to have fun. And we want to be rescued."

The passionate noise of agreement from the assembly hit him like a wave and he lost his thread. He thought again.

"We want to be rescued; and of course we shall be rescued."

Voices babbled. The simple statement, unbacked by any proof but the weight of Ralph's new authority, brought light and happiness. He had to wave the conch before he could make them hear him.

"My father's in the Navy. He said there aren't any unknown islands left. He says the Queen has a big room full of maps and all the islands in the world are drawn there. So the Queen's got a picture of this island."

Again came the sounds of cheerfulness and better heart.

"And sooner or later a ship will put in here. It might even be Daddy's ship. So you see, sooner or later, we shall be rescued."

He paused, with the point made. The assembly was lifted toward safety by his words. They liked and now respected him. Spontaneously they began to clap and presently the platform was loud with applause. Ralph flushed, looking sideways at Piggy's open admiration, and then the other way at Jack who was smirking and showing that he too knew how to clap.

Ralph waved the conch.

"Shut up! Wait! Listen!"

He went on in the silence, borne on his triumph.

"There's another thing. We can help them to find us. If a ship comes near the island they may not notice us. So we must make smoke on top of the mountain. We must make a fire."

"A fire! Make a fire!"

At once half the boys were on their feet. Jack clamored among them, the conch forgotten.

"Come on! Follow me!"

The space under the palm trees was full of noise and movement. Ralph was on his feet too, shouting for quiet, but no one heard him. All at once the crowd swayed toward the island and was gone—following Jack. Even the tiny children went and did their best among the leaves and broken branches. Ralph was left, holding the conch, with no one but Piggy.

Piggy's breathing was quite restored.

"Like kids!" he said scornfully. "Acting like a crowd of kids!"

Ralph looked at him doubtfully and laid the conch on the tree trunk.

"I bet it's gone tea-time," said Piggy. "What do they think they're going to do on that mountain?"

He caressed the shell respectfully, then stopped and looked up.

"Ralph! Hey! Where you going?"

Ralph was already clambering over the first smashed swathes of the scar. A long way ahead of him was crashing and laughter.

Piggy watched him in disgust.

"Like a crowd of kids—"

He sighed, bent, and laced up his shoes. The noise of the errant assembly faded up the mountain. Then, with the martyred expression of a parent who has to keep up with the senseless ebullience of the children, he picked up the conch, turned toward the forest, and began to pick his way over the tumbled scar.

Below the other side of the mountain top was a platform of forest. Once more Ralph found himself making the cupping gesture.

"Down there we could get as much wood as we want."

Jack nodded and pulled at his underlip. Starting perhaps a hundred feet below them on the steeper side of the mountain, the patch might have been designed expressly for fuel. Trees, forced by the damp heat, found too little soil for full growth, fell early and decayed: creepers cradled them, and new saplings searched a way up.

Jack turned to the choir, who stood ready. Their black caps of maintenance were slid over one ear like berets.

"We'll build a pile. Come on."

They found the likeliest path down and began tugging at the dead wood. And the small boys who had reached the top came sliding too till everyone but Piggy was busy. Most of the wood was so rotten that when they pulled, it broke up into a shower of fragments and woodlice and decay; but some trunks came out in one piece. The twins, Sam 'n Eric, were the first to get a likely log but they could do nothing till Ralph, Jack, Simon, Roger and Maurice found room for a hand-hold. Then they inched the grotesque dead thing up the rock and toppled it over on top. Each party of boys added a quota, less or more, and the pile grew. At the return Ralph found himself alone on a limb with Jack and they grinned at each other, sharing this burden. Once more, amid the breeze, the shouting, the slanting sunlight on the high mountain, was shed that glamour, that strange invisible light of friendship, adventure, and content.

"Almost too heavy."

Jack grinned back.

"Not for the two of us."

Together, joined in an effort by the burden, they staggered up the last steep of the mountain. Together, they chanted One! Two! Three! and crashed the log on to the great pile. Then they stepped back, laughing with triumphant pleasure, so that immediately Ralph had to stand on his head. Below them, boys were still laboring, though some of the small ones had lost interest and were searching this new forest for fruit. Now the twins, with unsuspected intelligence, came up the mountain with armfuls of dried leaves and dumped them against the pile. One by one, as they sensed that the pile was complete, the boys stopped going back for more and stood, with the pink, shattered top of the mountain around them. Breath came evenly by now, and sweat dried.

Ralph and Jack looked at each other while society paused about them. The shameful knowledge grew in them and they did not know how to begin confession.

Ralph spoke first, crimson in the face.

"Will you?"

He cleared his throat and went on.

"Will you light the fire?"

Now the absurd situation was open, Jack blushed too. He began to mutter vaguely.

"You rub two sticks. You rub—"

He glanced at Ralph, who blurted out the last confession of incompetence.

"Has anyone got any matches?"

"You make a bow and spin the arrow," said Roger. He rubbed his hands in mime. "Psss. Psss."

A little air was moving over the mountain. Piggy came with it, in shorts and shirt, laboring cautiously out of the forest with the evening sunlight gleaming from his glasses. He held the conch under his arm.

Ralph shouted at him.

"Piggy! Have you got any matches?"

The other boys took up the cry till the mountain rang. Piggy shook his head and came to the pile.

"My! You've made a big heap, haven't you?"

Jack pointed suddenly.

"His specs—use them as burning glasses!"

Piggy was surrounded before he could back away.

"Here—let me go!" His voice rose to a shriek of terror as Jack snatched the glasses off his face. "Mind out! Give 'em back! I can hardly see! You'll break the conch!"

Ralph elbowed him to one side and knelt by the pile.

"Stand out of the light."

There was pushing and pulling and officious cries. Ralph moved the lenses back and forth, this way and that, till a glossy white image of the declining sun lay on a piece of rotten wood. Almost at once a thin trickle of smoke rose up and made him cough. Jack knelt too and blew gently, so that the smoke drifted away, thickening, and a tiny flame appeared. The flame, nearly invisible at first in that bright sunlight, enveloped a small twig, grew, was enriched with color and reached up to a branch which exploded with a sharp crack. The flame flapped higher and the boys broke into a cheer.

"My specs!" howled Piggy. "Give me my specs!"

Ralph stood away from the pile and put the glasses into Piggy's groping hands. His voice subsided to a mutter.

"Jus' blurs, that's all. Hardly see my hand—"

The boys were dancing. The pile was so rotten, and now so tinder-dry, that whole limbs yielded passionately to the yellow flames that poured upwards and shook a great beard of flame twenty feet in the air. For yards round the fire the heat was like a blow, and the breeze was a river of sparks. Trunks crumbled to white dust.

Ralph shouted.

"More wood! All of you get more wood!"

Life became a race with the fire and the boys scattered through the upper forest. To keep a clean flag of flame flying on the mountain was the immediate end and no one looked further. Even the smallest boys, unless fruit claimed them, brought little pieces of wood and threw them in. The air moved a little faster and became a light wind, so that leeward and windward side were clearly differentiated. On one side the air was cool, but on the other the fire thrust out a savage arm of heat that crinkled hair on the instant. Boys who felt the evening wind on their damp faces paused to enjoy the freshness of it and then found they were exhausted. They flung themselves down in the shadows that lay among the shattered rocks. The beard of flame diminished quickly; then the pile fell inwards with a soft, cindery sound, and sent a great tree of sparks upwards that leaned away and drifted downwind. The boys lay, painting like dogs.

Ralph raised his head off his forearms.

"That was no good."

Roger spat efficiently into the hot dust.

"What d'you mean?"

"There wasn't any smoke. Only flame."

Piggy had settled himself in a space between two rocks, and sat with the conch on his knees.

"We haven't made a fire," he said, "what's any use. We couldn't keep a fire like that going, not if we tried."

"A fat lot you tried," said Jack contemptuously. "You just sat."

"We used his specs," said Simon, smearing a black cheek with his forearm. "He helped that way."

"I got the conch," said Piggy indignantly. "You let me speak!"

"The conch doesn't count on top of the mountain," said Jack, "so you shut up."

"I got the conch in my hand."

"Put on green branches," said Maurice. "That's the best way to make smoke."

"I got the conch——"

Jack turned fiercely.

"You shut up!"

Piggy wilted. Ralph took the conch from him and looked round the circle of boys.

"We've got to have special people for looking after the fire. Any day there may be a ship out there"——he waved his arm at the taut wire of the horizon——"and if we have a signal going they'll come and take us off. And another thing. We ought to have more rules. Where the conch is, that's a meeting. The same up here as down there."

They assented. Piggy opened his mouth to speak, caught Jack's eye and shut it again. Jack held out his hands for the conch and stood up, holding the delicate thing carefully in his sooty hands.

"I agree with Ralph. We've got to have rules and obey them. After all, we're not savages. We're English, and the English are best at everything. So we've got to do the right things."

He turned to Ralph.

"Ralph, I'll split up the choir—my hunters, that is—into groups, and we'll be responsible for keeping the fire going—"

This generosity brought a spatter of applause from the boys, so that Jack grinned at them, then waved the conch for silence.

"We'll let the fire burn out now. Who would see smoke at night-time, anyway? And we can start the fire again whenever we like. Altos, you can keep the fire going this week, and trebles the next—"

The assembly assented gravely.

"And we'll be responsible for keeping a lookout too. If we see a ship out there"—they followed the direction of his bony arm with their eyes—"we'll put green branches on. Then there'll be more smoke."

They gazed intently at the dense blue of the horizon, as if a little silhouette might appear there at any moment.

The sun in the west was a drop of burning gold that slid nearer and nearer the sill of the world. All at once they were aware of the evening as the end of light and warmth.

Roger took the conch and looked round at them gloomily.

"I've been watching the sea. There hasn't been the trace of a ship. Perhaps we'll never be rescued."

A murmur rose and swept away. Ralph took back the conch.

"I said before we'll be rescued sometime. We've just got to wait, that's all."

Daring, indignant, Piggy took the conch.

"That's what I said! I said about our meetings and things and then you said shut up—"

His voice lifted into the whine of virtuous recrimination. They stirred and began to shout him down.

"You said you wanted a small fire and you been and built a pile like a hayrick. If I say anything," cried Piggy, with bitter realism, "you say shut up; but if Jack or Maurice or Simon—"

He paused in the tumult, standing, looking beyond them and down the unfriendly side of the mountain to the great patch where they had found dead wood. Then he laughed so strangely that they were hushed, looking at the flash of his spectacles in astonishment. They followed his gaze to find the sour joke.

"You got your small fire all right."

Smoke was rising here and there among the creepers that festooned the dead or dying trees. As they watched, a flash of fire appeared at the root of one wisp, and then the smoke thickened. Small flames stirred at the trunk of a tree and crawled away through leaves and brushwood, dividing and increasing. One patch touched a tree trunk and scrambled up like a bright squirrel. The smoke increased, sifted, rolled outwards. The squirrel leapt on the wings of the wind and clung to another standing tree, eating downwards. Beneath the dark canopy of leaves and smoke the fire laid hold on the forest and began to gnaw. Acres of black and yellow smoke rolled steadily toward the sea. At the sight of the flames and the irresistible course of the fire, the boys broke into shrill, excited cheering. The flames, as though they were a kind of wild life, crept as a jaguar creeps on its belly toward a line of birch-like saplings that fledged an outcrop of the pink rock. They flapped at the first of the trees, and the branches grew a brief foliage of fire. The heart of flame leapt nimbly across the gap between the trees and then went swinging and flaring along the whole row of them. Beneath the capering boys a quarter of a mile square of forest was savage with smoke and flame. The separate noises of the fire merged into a drum-roll that seemed to shake the mountain.

"You got your small fire all right."

Startled, Ralph realized that the boys were falling still and silent, feeling the beginnings of awe at the power set free below them. The knowledge and the awe made him savage.

"Oh, shut up!"

"I got the conch," said Piggy, in a hurt voice. "I got a right to speak."

They looked at him with eyes that lacked interest in what they saw, and cocked ears at the drum-roll of the fire. Piggy glanced nervously into hell and cradled the conch.

"We got to let that burn out now. And that was our firewood."

He licked his lips.

"There ain't nothing we can do. We ought to be more careful. I'm scared—"

Jack dragged his eyes away from the fire.

"You're always scared. Yah—Fatty!"

"I got the conch," said Piggy bleakly. He turned to Ralph. "I got the conch, ain't I Ralph?"

Unwillingly Ralph turned away from the splendid, awful sight. "What's that?"

"The conch. I got a right to speak."

The twins giggled together.

"We wanted smoke—"

"Now look—!"

A pall stretched for miles away from the island. All the boys except Piggy started to giggle; presently they were shrieking with laughter.

Piggy lost his temper.

"I got the conch! Just you listen! The first thing we ought to have made was shelters down there by the beach. It wasn't half cold down there in the night. But the first time Ralph says 'fire' you goes howling and screaming up this here mountain. Like a pack of kids!"

By now they were listening to the tirade.

"How can you expect to be rescued if you don't put first things first and act proper?"

He took off his glasses and made as if to put down the conch; but the sudden motion toward it of most of the older boys changed his mind. He tucked the shell under his arm, and crouched back on a rock.

"Then when you get here you build a bonfire that isn't no use. Now you been and set the whole island on fire. Won't we look funny if the whole island burns up? Cooked fruit, that's what we'll have to eat, and roast pork. And that's nothing to laugh at! You said Ralph was chief and you don't give him time to think. Then when he says something you rush off, like, like—"

He paused for breath, and the fire growled at them.

"And that's not all. Them kids. The little 'uns. Who took any notice of 'em? Who knows how many we got?"

Ralph took a sudden step forward.

"I told you to. I told you to get a list of names!"

"How could I," cried Piggy indignantly, "all by myself? They waited for two minutes, then they fell in the sea; they went into the forest; they just scattered everywhere. How was I to know which was which?"

Ralph licked pale lips.

"Then you don't know how many of us there ought to be?"

"How could I with them little 'uns running round like insects? Then when you three came back, as soon as you said make a fire, they all ran away, and I never had a chance—"

"That's enough!" said Ralph sharply, and snatched back the conch. "If you didn't you didn't."

"—then you come up here an' pinch my specs—"

Jack turned on him.

"You shut up!"

"—and them little 'uns was wandering about down there where the fire is. How d'you know they aren't still there?"

Piggy stood up and pointed to the smoke and flames. A murmur rose among the boys and died away. Something strange was happening to Piggy, for he was gasping for breath.

"That little 'un—" gasped Piggy—"him with the mark on his face, I don't see him. Where is he now?"

The crowd was as silent as death.

"Him that talked about the snakes. He was down there—"

A tree exploded in the fire like a bomb. Tall swathes of creepers rose for a moment into view, agonized, and went down again. The little boys screamed at them.

"Snakes! Snakes! Look at the snakes!"

In the west, and unheeded, the sun lay only an inch or two above the sea. Their faces were lit redly from beneath. Piggy fell against a rock and clutched it with both hands.

"That little 'un that had a mark on his face—where is—he now? I tell you I don't see him."

The boys looked at each other fearfully, unbelieving.

"—where is he now?"

Ralph muttered the reply as if in shame.

"Perhaps he went back to the, the—"

Beneath them, on the unfriendly side of the mountain, the drum-roll continued.

three

HUTS ON THE BEACH

JACK WAS BENT DOUBLE. HE WAS DOWN LIKE A sprinter, his nose only a few inches from the humid earth. The tree trunks and the creepers that festooned them lost themselves in a green dusk thirty feet above him, and all about was the undergrowth. There was only the faintest indication of a trail here; a cracked twig and what might be the impression of one side of a hoof. He lowered his chin and stared at the traces as though he would force them to speak to him. Then dog-like, uncomfortably on all fours yet unheeding his discomfort, he stole forward five yards and stopped. Here was loop of creeper with a tendril pendant from a node. The tendril was polished on the underside; pigs, passing through the loop, brushed it with their bristly hide.

Jack crouched with his face a few inches away from this clue, then stared forward into the semi-darkness of the undergrowth. His sandy hair, considerably longer than it had been when they dropped in, was lighter now; and his bare back was a mass of dark freckles and peeling sunburn. A sharpened stick about five feet long trailed from his right hand, and except for a pair of tattered shorts held up by his knife-belt he was naked. He closed his eyes, raised his head and breathed in gently with flared nostrils, assessing the current of warm air for information. The forest and he were very still.

At length he let out his breath in a long sigh and opened his eyes. They were bright blue, eyes that in this frustration seemed bolting and nearly mad. He passed his tongue across dry lips and scanned the uncommunicative forest. Then again he stole forward and cast this way and that over the ground.

The silence of the forest was more oppressive than the heat, and at this hour of the day there was not even the whine of insects. Only when Jack himself roused a gaudy bird from a primitive nest of sticks was the silence shattered and echoes set ringing by a harsh cry that seemed to come out of the abyss of ages. Jack himself shrank at this cry with a hiss of indrawn breath, and for a minute became less a hunter than a furtive thing, ape-like among the tangle of trees. Then the trail, the frustration, claimed him again and he searched the ground avidly. By the trunk of a vast tree that grew pale flowers on its grey bark he checked, closed his eyes, and once more drew in the warm air; and this time his breath came short, there was even a passing pallor in his face, and then the surge of blood again. He passed like a shadow under the darkness of the tree and crouched, looking down at the trodden ground at his feet.

The droppings were warm. They lay piled among turned earth. They were olive green, smooth, and they steamed a little. Jack lifted his head and stared at the inscrutable masses of creeper that lay across the trail. Then he raised his spear and sneaked forward. Beyond the creeper, the trail joined a pig-run that was wide enough and trodden enough to be a path. The ground was hardened by an accustomed tread and as Jack rose to his full height he heard something moving on it. He swung back his right arm and hurled the spear with all his strength. From the pig-run came

the quick, hard patter of hoofs, a castanet sound, seductive, mad-
dening—the promise of meat. He rushed out of the undergrowth
and snatched up his spear. The pattering of pig's trotters died
away in the distance.

Jack stood there, streaming with sweat, streaked with brown
earth, stained by all the vicissitudes of a day's hunting. Swearing,
he turned off the trail and pushed his way through until the forest
opened a little and instead of bald trunks supporting a dark roof
there were light grey trunks and crowns of feathery palm. Beyond
these was the glitter of the sea and he could hear voices. Ralph
was standing by a contraption of palm trunks and leaves, a rude
shelter that faced the lagoon and seemed very near to falling
down. He did not notice when Jack spoke.

"Got any water?"

Ralph looked up, frowning, from the complication of leaves.
He did not notice Jack even when he saw him.

"I said have you got any water? I'm thirsty."

Ralph withdrew his attention from the shelter and realized Jack
with a start.

"Oh, hullo. Water? There by the tree. Ought to be some left."

Jack took up a coconut shell that brimmed with fresh water
from among a group that was arranged in the shade, and drank.
The water splashed over his chin and neck and chest. He breathed
noisily when he had finished.

"Needed that."

Simon spoke from inside the shelter.

"Up a bit."

Ralph turned to the shelter and lifted a branch with a whole
tiling of leaves.

The leaves came apart and fluttered down. Simon's contrite
face appeared in the hole.

"Sorry."

Ralph surveyed the wreck with distaste.

"Never get it done."

He flung himself down at Jack's feet. Simon remained, looking out of the hole in the shelter. Once down, Ralph explained.

"Been working for days now. And look!"

Two shelters were in position, but shaky. This one was a ruin.

"And they keep running off. You remember the meeting? How everyone was going to work hard until the shelters were finished?"

"Except me and my hunters—"

"Except the hunters. Well, the littluns are—"

He gesticulated, sought for a word.

"They're hopeless. The older ones aren't much better. D'you see? All day I've been working with Simon. No one else. They're off bathing, or eating, or playing."

Simon poked his head out carefully.

"You're chief. You tell 'em off."

Ralph lay flat and looked up at the palm trees and the sky.

"Meetings. Don't we love meetings? Every day. Twice a day. We talk." He got on one elbow. "I bet if I blew the conch this minute, they'd come running. Then we'd be, you know, very solemn, and someone would say we ought to build a jet, or a submarine, or a TV set. When the meeting was over they'd work for five minutes, then wander off or go hunting."

Jack flushed.

"We want meat."

"Well, we haven't got any yet. And we want shelters. Besides, the rest of your hunters came back hours ago. They've been swimming."

"I went on," said Jack. "I let them go. I had to go on. I—"

He tried to convey the compulsion to track down and kill that
was swallowing him up.

"I went on. I thought, by myself—"

The madness came into his eyes again.

"I thought I might kill."

"But you didn't."

"I thought I might."

Some hidden passion vibrated in Ralph's voice.

"But you haven't yet."

His invitation might have passed as casual, were it not for the
undertone.

"You wouldn't care to help with the shelters, I suppose?"

"We want meat—"

"And we don't get it."

Now the antagonism was audible.

"But I shall! Next time! I've got to get a barb on this spear!
We wounded a pig and the spear fell out. If we could only make
barbs—"

"We need shelters."

Suddenly Jack shouted in rage.

"Are you accusing—?"

"All I'm saying is we've worked dashed hard. That's all."

They were both red in the face and found looking at each
other difficult. Ralph rolled on his stomach and began to play
with the grass.

"If it rains like when we dropped in we'll need shelters all right.
And then another thing. We need shelters because of the—"

He paused for a moment and they both pushed their anger
away. Then he went on with the safe, changed subject.

"You've noticed, haven't you?"

Jack put down his spear and squatted.

"Noticed what?"

"Well. They're frightened."

He rolled over and peered into Jack's fierce, dirty face.

"I mean the way things are. They dream. You can hear 'em. Have you been awake at night?"

Jack shook his head.

"They talk and scream. The littluns. Even some of the others. As if—"

"As if it wasn't a good island."

Astonished at the interruption, they looked up at Simon's serious face.

"As if," said Simon, "the beastie, the beastie or the snake-thing, was real. Remember?"

The two older boys flinched when they heard the shameful syllable. Snakes were not mentioned now, were not mentionable.

"As if this wasn't a good island," said Ralph slowly. "Yes, that's right."

Jack sat up and stretched out his legs.

"They're batty."

"Crackers. Remember when we went exploring?"

They grinned at each other, remembering the glamour of the first day. Ralph went on.

"So we need shelters as a sort of—"

"Home."

"That's right."

Jack drew up his legs, clasped his knees, and frowned in an effort to attain clarity.

"All the same—in the forest. I mean when you're hunting, not when you're getting fruit, of course, but when you're on your own—"

He paused for a moment, not sure if Ralph would take him seriously.

"Go on."

"If you're hunting sometimes you catch yourself feeling as if—" He flushed suddenly. "There's nothing in it of course. Just a feeling. But you can feel as if you're not hunting, but—being hunted, as if something's behind you all the time in the jungle."

They were silent again: Simon intent, Ralph incredulous and faintly indignant. He sat up, rubbing one shoulder with a dirty hand.

"Well, I don't know."

Jack leapt to his feet and spoke very quickly.

"That's how you can feel in the forest. Of course there's nothing in it. Only—only—"

He took a few rapid steps toward the beach, then came back.

"Only I know how they feel. See? That's all."

"The best thing we can do is get ourselves rescued."

Jack had to think for a moment before he could remember what rescue was.

"Rescue? Yes, of course! All the same, I'd like to catch a pig first—" He snatched up his spear and dashed it into the ground. The opaque, mad look came into his eyes again. Ralph looked at him critically through his tangle of fair hair.

"So long as your hunters remember the fire—"

"You and your fire!"

The two boys trotted down the beach, and, turning at the water's edge, looked back at the pink mountain. The trickle of smoke sketched a chalky line up the solid blue of the sky, wavered high up and faded. Ralph frowned.

"I wonder how far off you could see that."

"Miles."

"We don't make enough smoke."

The bottom part of the trickle, as though conscious of their gaze, thickened to a creamy blur which crept up the feeble column.

"They've put on green branches," muttered Ralph. "I wonder!" He screwed up his eyes and swung round to search the horizon.

"Got it!"

Jack shouted so loudly that Ralph jumped.

"What? Where? Is it a ship?"

But Jack was pointing to the high declivities that led down from the mountain to the flatter part of the island.

"Of course! They'll lie up there—they must, when the sun's too hot—"

Ralph gazed bewildered at his rapt face.

"—they get up high. High up and in the shade, resting during the heat, like cows at home—"

"I thought you saw a ship!"

"We could steal up on one—paint our faces so they wouldn't see—perhaps surround them and then—"

Indignation took away Ralph's control.

"I was talking about smoke! Don't you want to be rescued? All you can talk about is pig, pig, pig!"

"But we want meat!"

"And I work all day with nothing but Simon and you come back and don't even notice the huts!"

"I was working too—"

"But you like it!" shouted Ralph. "You want to hunt! While I—"

They faced each other on the bright beach, astonished at the rub of feeling. Ralph looked away first, pretending interest in a group of littluns on the sand. From beyond the platform came the shouting of the hunters in the swimming pool. On the end of the platform, Piggy was lying flat, looking down into the brilliant water.

"People don't help much."

He wanted to explain how people were never quite what you thought they were.

"Simon. He helps." He pointed at the shelters.

"All the rest rushed off. He's done as much as I have. Only—"

"Simon's always about."

Ralph started back to the shelters with Jack by his side.

"Do a bit for you," muttered Jack, "before I have a bathe."

"Don't bother."

But when they reached the shelters Simon was not to be seen. Ralph put his head in the hole, withdrew it, and turned to Jack.

"He's buzzed off."

"Got fed up," said Jack, "and gone for a bathe."

Ralph frowned.

"He's queer. He's funny."

Jack nodded, as much for the sake of agreeing as anything, and by tacit consent they left the shelter and went toward the bathing pool.

"And then," said Jack, "when I've had a bathe and something to eat, I'll just trek over to the other side of the mountain and see if I can see any traces. Coming?"

"But the sun's nearly set!"

"I might have time—"

They walked along, two continents of experience and feeling, unable to communicate.

"If I could only get a pig!"

"I'll come back and go on with the shelter."

They looked at each other, baffled, in love and hate. All the warm salt water of the bathing pool and the shouting and splashing and laughing were only just sufficient to bring them together again.

Simon was not in the bathing pool as they had expected.

When the other two had trotted down the beach to look back at the mountain he had followed them for a few yards and then stopped. He had stood frowning down at a pile of sand on the beach where somebody had been trying to build a little house or hut. Then he turned his back on this and walked into the forest with an air of purpose. He was a small, skinny boy, his chin pointed, and his eyes so bright they had deceived Ralph into thinking him delightfully gay and wicked. The coarse mop of black hair was long and swung down, almost concealing a low, broad forehead. He wore the remains of shorts and his feet were bare like Jack's. Always darkish in color, Simon was burned by the sun to a deep tan that glistened with sweat.

He picked his way up the scar, passed the great rock where Ralph had climbed on the first morning, then turned off to his right among the trees. He walked with an accustomed tread through the acres of fruit trees, where the least energetic could find an easy if unsatisfying meal. Flower and fruit grew together on the same tree and everywhere was the scent of ripeness and the booming of a million bees at pasture. Here the littluns who had run after him caught up with him. They talked, cried out unintelligibly, lugged him toward the trees. Then, amid the roar of bees in the afternoon sunlight, Simon found for them the fruit they could not reach, pulled off the choicest from up in the foliage, passed them back down to the endless, outstretched hands. When he had satisfied them he paused and looked round.

The littluns watched him inscrutably over double handfuls of ripe fruit.

Simon turned away from them and went where the just perceptible path led him. Soon high jungle closed in. Tall trunks bore unexpected pale flowers all the way up to the dark canopy where life went on clamorously. The air here was dark too, and the creepers dropped their ropes like the rigging of foundered ships. His feet left prints in the soft soil and the creepers shivered throughout their lengths when he bumped them.

He came at last to a place where more sunshine fell. Since they had not so far to go for light the creepers had woven a great mat that hung at the side of an open space in the jungle; for here a patch of rock came close to the surface and would not allow more than little plants and ferns to grow. The whole space was walled with dark aromatic bushes, and was a bowl of heat and light. A great tree, fallen across one corner, leaned against the trees that still stood and a rapid climber flaunted red and yellow sprays right to the top.

Simon paused. He looked over his shoulder as Jack had done at the close ways behind him and glanced swiftly round to confirm that he was utterly alone. For a moment his movements were almost furtive. Then he bent down and wormed his way into the center of the mat. The creepers and the bushes were so close that he left his sweat on them and they pulled together behind him. When he was secure in the middle he was in a little cabin screened off from the open space by a few leaves. He squatted down, parted the leaves and looked out into the clearing. Nothing moved but a pair of gaudy butterflies that danced round each other in the hot air. Holding his breath he cocked a critical ear at the sounds of the island. Evening was advancing toward the island; the sounds of the bright fantastic birds, the bee-sounds, even the crying of the gulls that were returning to their roosts among the square rocks, were fainter. The deep sea breaking miles away on the reef made an undertone less perceptible than the susurration of the blood.

Simon dropped the screen of leaves back into place. The slope of the bars of honey-colored sunlight decreased; they slid up the bushes, passed over the green candle-like buds, moved up toward the canopy, and darkness thickened under the trees. With the fading of the light the riotous colors died and the heat and urgency cooled away. The candle-buds stirred. Their green sepals drew back a little and the white tips of the flowers rose delicately to meet the open air.

Now the sunlight had lifted clear of the open space and withdrawn from the sky. Darkness poured out, submerging the ways between the trees till they were dim and strange as the bottom of the sea. The candle-buds opened their wide white flowers glimmering under the light that pricked down from the first stars. Their scent spilled out into the air and took possession of the island.

four

PAINTED FACES
AND LONG HAIR

THE FIRST RHYTHM THAT THEY BECAME USED TO was the slow swing from dawn to quick dusk. They accepted the pleasures of morning, the bright sun, the whelming sea and sweet air, as a time when play was good and life so full that hope was not necessary and therefore forgotten. Toward noon, as the floods of light fell more nearly to the perpendicular, the stark colors of the morning were smoothed in pearl and opalescence; and the heat—as though the impending sun's height gave it momentum—became a blow that they ducked, running to the shade and lying there, perhaps even sleeping.

Strange things happened at midday. The glittering sea rose up, moved apart in planes of blatant impossibility; the coral reef and the few stunted palms that clung to the more elevated parts would float up into the sky, would quiver, be plucked apart, run like raindrops on a wire or be repeated as in an odd succession of mirrors. Sometimes land loomed where there was no land and flicked out like a bubble as the children watched. Piggy discounted all this learnedly as a "mirage"; and since no boy could reach even the reef over the stretch of water where the snapping sharks waited, they grew accustomed to these mysteries and ignored them, just as they ignored the miraculous, throbbing stars.

At midday the illusions merged into the sky and there the sun gazed down like an angry eye. Then, at the end of the afternoon, the mirage subsided and the horizon became level and blue and clipped as the sun declined. That was another time of comparative coolness but menaced by the coming of the dark. When the sun sank, darkness dropped on the island like an extinguisher and soon the shelters were full of restlessness, under the remote stars.

Nevertheless, the northern European tradition of work, play, and food right through the day, made it possible for them to adjust themselves wholly to this new rhythm. The littlun Percival had early crawled into a shelter and stayed there for two days, talking, singing, and crying, till they thought him batty and were faintly amused. Ever since then he had been peaked, red-eyed, and miserable; a littlun who played little and cried often.

The smaller boys were known now by the generic title of "littluns." The decrease in size, from Ralph down, was gradual; and though there was a dubious region inhabited by Simon and Robert and Maurice, nevertheless no one had any difficulty in recognizing biguns at one end and littluns at the other. The undoubted littluns, those aged about six, led a quite distinct, and at the same time intense, life of their own. They ate most of the day, picking fruit where they could reach it and not particular about ripeness and quality. They were used now to stomachaches and a sort of chronic diarrhoea. They suffered untold terrors in the dark and huddled together for comfort. Apart from food and sleep, they found time for play, aimless and trivial, in the white sand by the bright water. They cried for their mothers much less often than might have been expected; they were very brown, and filthily dirty. They obeyed the summons of the conch, partly because Ralph blew it, and he was big enough to be a link with the adult world of authority; and partly because they enjoyed the entertainment of the assemblies. But otherwise they seldom bothered with the biguns and their passionately emotional and corporate life was their own.

They had built castles in the sand at the bar of the little river. These castles were about one foot high and were decorated with shells, withered flowers, and interesting stones. Round the castles was a complex of marks, tracks, walls, railway lines, that were of significance only if inspected with the eye at beach-level. The littluns played here, if not happily at least with absorbed attention; and often as many as three of them would play the same game together.

Three were playing here now. Henry was the biggest of them. He was also a distant relative of that other boy whose mulberry-marked face had not been seen since the evening of the great fire; but he was not old enough to understand this, and if he had been told that the other boy had gone home in an aircraft, he would have accepted the statement without fuss or disbelief.

Henry was a bit of a leader this afternoon, because the other two were Percival and Johnny, the smallest boys on the island. Percival was mouse-colored and had not been very attractive even to his mother; Johnny was well built, with fair hair and a natural belligerence. Just now he was being obedient because he was interested; and the three children, kneeling in the sand, were at peace.

Roger and Maurice came out of the forest. They were relieved from duty at the fire and had come down for a swim. Roger led the way straight through the castles, kicking them over, burying the flowers, scattering the chosen stones. Maurice followed, laughing, and added to the destruction. The three littluns paused in their game and looked up. As it happened, the particular marks in which they were interested had not been touched, so they made no protest. Only Percival began to whimper with an eyeful of sand and Maurice hurried away. In his other life Maurice had received chastisement for filling a younger eye with sand. Now, though there was no parent to let fall a heavy hand, Maurice still felt the unease of wrongdoing. At the back of his mind formed the uncertain outlines of an excuse. He muttered something about a swim and broke into a trot.

Roger remained, watching the littluns. He was not noticeably darker than when he had dropped in, but the shock of black hair, down his nape and low on his forehead, seemed to suit his gloomy face and made what had seemed at first an unsociable remoteness into something forbidding. Percival finished his whimper and went on playing, for the tears had washed the sand away. Johnny watched him with china-blue eyes; then began to fling up sand in a shower, and presently Percival was crying again.

When Henry tired of his play and wandered off along the beach, Roger followed him, keeping beneath the palms and drifting casually in the same direction. Henry walked at a distance from the palms and the shade because he was too young to keep himself out of the sun. He went down the beach and busied himself at the water's edge. The great Pacific tide was coming in and every few seconds the relatively still water of the lagoon heaved forwards an inch. There were creatures that lived in this last fling of the sea, tiny transparencies that came questing in with the water over the hot, dry sand. With impalpable organs of sense they examined this new field. Perhaps food had appeared where at the last incursion there had been none; bird droppings, insects perhaps, any of the strewn detritus of landward life. Like a myriad of tiny teeth in a saw, the transparencies came scavenging over the beach.

This was fascinating to Henry. He poked about with a bit of stick, that itself was wave-worn and whitened and a vagrant, and tried to control the motions of the scavengers. He made little runnels that the tide filled and tried to crowd them with creatures. He became absorbed beyond mere happiness as he felt himself exercising control over living things. He talked to them, urging them, ordering them. Driven back by the tide, his footprints became bays in which they were trapped and gave him the illusion of mastery. He squatted on his hams at the water's edge, bowed, with a shock of hair falling over his forehead and past his eyes, and the afternoon sun emptied down invisible arrows.

Roger waited too. At first he had hidden behind a great palm; but Henry's absorption with the transparencies was so obvious that at last he stood out in full view. He looked along the beach. Percival had gone off, crying, and Johnny was left in triumphant possession of the castles. He sat there, crooning to himself and throwing sand at an imaginary Percival. Beyond him, Roger could see the platform and the glints of spray where Ralph and Simon and Piggy and Maurice were diving in the pool. He listened carefully but could only just hear them.

A sudden breeze shook the fringe of palm trees, so that the fronds tossed and fluttered. Sixty feet above Roger, several nuts, fibrous lumps as big as rugby balls, were loosed from their stems. They fell about him with a series of hard thumps and he was not touched. Roger did not consider his escape, but looked from the nuts to Henry and back again.

The subsoil beneath the palm trees was a raised beach, and generations of palms had worked loose in this the stones that had lain on the sands of another shore. Roger stooped, picked up a stone, aimed, and threw it at Henry—threw it to miss. The stone, that token of preposterous time, bounced five yards to

Henry's right and fell in the water. Roger gathered a handful of stones and began to throw them. Yet there was a space round Henry, perhaps six yards in diameter, into which he dare not throw. Here, invisible yet strong, was the taboo of the old life. Round the squatting child was the protection of parents and school and policemen and the law. Roger's arm was conditioned by a civilization that knew nothing of him and was in ruins.

Henry was surprised by the plopping sounds in the water. He abandoned the noiseless transparencies and pointed at the center of the spreading rings like a setter. This side and that the stones fell, and Henry turned obediently but always too late to see the stones in the air. At last he saw one and laughed, looking for the friend who was teasing him. But Roger had whipped behind the palm again, was leaning against it breathing quickly, his eyelids fluttering. Then Henry lost interest in stones and wandered off.

"Roger."

Jack was standing under a tree about ten yards away. When Roger opened his eyes and saw him, a darker shadow crept beneath the swarthiness of his skin; but Jack noticed nothing. He was eager, impatient, beckoning, so that Roger went to him.

There was a small pool at the end of the river, dammed back by sand and full of white water-lilies and needle-like reeds. Here Sam and Eric were waiting, and Bill. Jack, concealed from the sun, knelt by the pool and opened the two large leaves that he carried. One of them contained white clay, and the other red. By them lay a stick of charcoal brought down from the fire.

Jack explained to Roger as he worked.

"They don't smell me. They see me, I think. Something pink, under the trees."

He smeared on the clay.

"If only I'd some green!"

He turned a half-concealed face up to Roger and answered the incomprehension of his gaze.

"For hunting. Like in the war. You know—dazzle paint. Like things trying to look like something else—" He twisted in the urgency of telling. "—Like moths on a tree trunk."

Roger understood and nodded gravely. The twins moved toward Jack and began to protest timidly about something. Jack waved them away.

"Shut up."

He rubbed the charcoal stick between the patches of red and white on his face.

"No. You two come with me."

He peered at his reflection and disliked it. He bent down, took up a double handful of lukewarm water and rubbed the mess from his face. Freckles and sandy eyebrows appeared.

Roger smiled, unwillingly.

"You don't half look a mess."

Jack planned his new face. He made one cheek and one eye-socket white, then he rubbed red over the other half of his face and slashed a black bar of charcoal across from right ear to left jaw. He looked in the pool for his reflection, but his breathing troubled the mirror.

"Samneric. Get me a coconut. An empty one."

He knelt, holding the shell of water. A rounded patch of sunlight fell on his face and a brightness appeared in the depths of the water. He looked in astonishment, no longer at himself but at an awesome stranger. He split the water and leapt to his feet, laughing excitedly. Beside the pool his sinewy body held up a mask that drew their eyes and appalled them. He began to dance and his laughter became a bloodthirsty snarling. He capered toward Bill, and the mask was a thing on its own, behind which

Jack hid, liberated from shame and self-consciousness. The face of red and white and black swung through the air and jigged toward Bill. Bill started up laughing; then suddenly he fell silent and blundered away through the bushes.

Jack rushed toward the twins.

"The rest are making a line. Come on!"

"But—"

"—we—"

"Come on! I'll creep up and stab—"

The mask compelled them.

Ralph climbed out of the bathing pool and trotted up the beach and sat in the shade beneath the palms. His fair hair was plastered over his eyebrows and he pushed it back. Simon was floating in the water and kicking with his feet, and Maurice was practicing diving. Piggy was mooning about, aimlessly picking up things and discarding them. The rock-pools which so fascinated him were covered by the tide, so he was without an interest until the tide went back. Presently, seeing Ralph under the palms, he came and sat by him.

Piggy wore the remainders of a pair of shorts, his fat body was golden brown, and the glasses still flashed when he looked at anything. He was the only boy on the island whose hair never seemed to grow. The rest were shock-headed, but Piggy's hair still lay in wisps over his head as though baldness were his natural state and this imperfect covering would soon go, like the velvet on a young stag's antlers.

"I've been thinking," he said, "about a clock. We could make a sundial. We could put a stick in the sand, and then—"

The effort to express the mathematical processes involved was too great. He made a few passes instead.

"And an airplane, and a TV set," said Ralph sourly, "and a steam engine."

Piggy shook his head.

"You have to have a lot of metal things for that," he said, "and we haven't got no metal. But we got a stick."

Ralph turned and smiled involuntarily. Piggy was a bore; his fat, his ass-mar and his matter-of-fact ideas were dull, but there was always a little pleasure to be got out of pulling his leg, even if one did it by accident.

Piggy saw the smile and misinterpreted it as friendliness. There had grown up tacitly among the biguns the opinion that Piggy was an outsider, not only by accent, which did not matter, but by fat, and ass-mar, and specs, and a certain disinclination for manual labor. Now, finding that something he had said made Ralph smile, he rejoiced and pressed his advantage.

"We got a lot of sticks. We could have a sundial each. Then we should know what the time was."

"A fat lot of good that would be."

"You said you wanted things done. So as we could be rescued."

"Oh, shut up."

He leapt to his feet and trotted back to the pool, just as Maurice did a rather poor dive. Ralph was glad of a chance to change the subject. He shouted as Maurice came to the surface.

"Belly flop! Belly flop!"

Maurice flashed a smile at Ralph who slid easily into the water. Of all the boys, he was the most at home there; but today, irked by the mention of rescue, the useless, footling mention of rescue, even the green depths of water and the shattered, golden sun held no balm. Instead of remaining and playing, he swam with steady strokes under Simon and crawled out of the other side of the pool to lie there, sleek and streaming like a seal. Piggy, always clumsy, stood up and came to stand by him, so that Ralph rolled on his stomach and pretended not to see. The mirages had died away and gloomily he ran his eye along the taut blue line of the horizon.

The next moment he was on his feet and shouting.

"Smoke! Smoke!"

Simon tried to sit up in the water and got a mouthful. Maurice, who had been standing ready to dive, swayed back on his heels, made a bolt for the platform, then swerved back to the grass under the palms. There he started to pull on his tattered shorts, to be ready for anything.

Ralph stood, one hand holding back his hair, the other clenched. Simon was climbing out of the water. Piggy was rubbing his glasses on his shorts and squinting at the sea. Maurice had got both legs through one leg of his shorts. Of all the boys, only Ralph was still.

"I can't see no smoke," said Piggy incredulously. "I can't see no smoke, Ralph—where is it?"

Ralph said nothing. Now both his hands were clenched over his forehead so that the fair hair was kept out of his eyes. He was leaning forward and already the salt was whitening his body.

"Ralph—where's the ship?"

Simon stood by, looking from Ralph to the horizon. Maurice's trousers gave way with a sigh and he abandoned them as a wreck, rushed toward the forest, and then came back again.

The smoke was a tight little knot on the horizon and was uncoiling slowly. Beneath the smoke was a dot that might be a funnel. Ralph's face was pale as he spoke to himself.

"They'll see our smoke."

Piggy was looking in the right direction now.

"It don't look much."

He turned round and peered up at the mountain. Ralph continued to watch the ship, ravenously. Color was coming back into his face. Simon stood by him, silent.

"I know I can't see very much," said Piggy, "but have we got any smoke?"

Ralph moved impatiently, still watching the ship.

"The smoke on the mountain."

Maurice came running, and stared out to sea. Both Simon and Piggy were looking up at the mountain. Piggy screwed up his face but Simon cried out as though he had hurt himself.

"Ralph! Ralph!"

The quality of his speech twisted Ralph on the sand.

"You tell me," said Piggy anxiously. "Is there a signal?"

Ralph looked back at the dispersing smoke in the horizon, then up at the mountain.

"Ralph—please! Is there a signal?"

Simon put out his hand, timidly, to touch Ralph; but Ralph started to run, splashing through the shallow end of the bathing pool, across the hot, white sand and under the palms. A moment later he was battling with the complex undergrowth that was already engulfing the scar. Simon ran after him, then Maurice. Piggy shouted.

"Ralph! Please—Ralph!"

Then he too started to run, stumbling over Maurice's discarded shorts before he was across the terrace. Behind the four boys, the smoke moved gently along the horizon; and on the beach, Henry and Johnny were throwing sand at Percival who was crying quietly again; and all three were in complete ignorance of the excitement.

By the time Ralph had reached the landward end of the scar he was using precious breath to swear. He did desperate violence to his naked body among the rasping creepers so that blood was sliding over him. Just where the steep ascent of the mountain began, he stopped. Maurice was only a few yards behind him.

"Piggy's specs!" shouted Ralph. "If the fire's all out, we'll need them—"

He stopped shouting and swayed on his feet. Piggy was only just visible, bumbling up from the beach. Ralph looked at the horizon, then up to the mountain. Was it better to fetch Piggy's glasses, or would the ship have gone? Or if they climbed on, supposing the fire was all out, and they had to watch Piggy crawling nearer and the ship sinking under the horizon? Balanced on a high peak of need, agonized by indecision, Ralph cried out:

"Oh God, oh God!"

Simon, struggling with the bushes, caught his breath. His face was twisted. Ralph blundered on, savaging himself, as the wisp of smoke moved on.

The fire was dead. They saw that straight away; saw what they had really known down on the beach when the smoke of home had beckoned. The fire was out, smokeless and dead; the watchers were gone. A pile of unused fuel lay ready.

Ralph turned to the sea. The horizon stretched, impersonal once more, barren of all but the faintest trace of smoke. Ralph ran stumbling along the rocks, saved himself on the edge of the pink cliff, and screamed at the ship.

"Come back! Come back!"

He ran backwards and forwards along the cliff, his face always to the sea, and his voice rose insanely.

"Come back! Come back!"

Simon and Maurice arrived. Ralph looked at them with un-winking eyes. Simon turned away, smearing the water from his cheeks. Ralph reached inside himself for the worst word he knew.

"They let the bloody fire go out."

He looked down the unfriendly side of the mountain. Piggy arrived, out of breath and whimpering like a littlun. Ralph clenched his fist and went very red. The intentness of his gaze, the bitterness of his voice, pointed for him.

"There they are."

A procession had appeared, far down among the pink stones that lay near the water's edge. Some of the boys wore black caps but otherwise they were almost naked. They lifted sticks in the air together whenever they came to an easy patch. They were chanting, something to do with the bundle that the errant twins carried so carefully. Ralph picked out Jack easily, even at that distance, tall, red-haired, and inevitably leading the procession.

Simon looked now, from Ralph to Jack, as he had looked from Ralph to the horizon, and what he saw seemed to make him afraid. Ralph said nothing more, but waited while the procession came nearer. The chant was audible but at that distance still wordless. Behind Jack walked the twins, carrying a great stake on their shoulders. The gutted carcass of a pig swung from the stake, swinging heavily as the twins toiled over the uneven ground. The pig's head hung down with gaping neck and seemed to search for something on the ground. At last the words of the chant floated up to them, across the bowl of blackened wood and ashes.

"*Kill the pig. Cut her throat. Spill her blood.*"

Yet as the words became audible, the procession reached the steepest part of the mountain, and in a minute or two the chant had died away. Piggy sniveled and Simon shushed him quickly as though he had spoken too loudly in church.

Jack, his face smeared with clays, reached the top first and hailed Ralph excitedly, with lifted spear.

"Look! We've killed a pig—we stole up on them—we got in a circle—"

Voices broke in from the hunters.

"We got in a circle—"

"We crept up—"

"The pig squealed—"

The twins stood with the pig swinging between them, dropping black gouts on the rock. They seemed to share one wide, ecstatic grin. Jack had too many things to tell Ralph at once. Instead, he danced a step or two, then remembered his dignity and stood still, grinning. He noticed blood on his hands and grimaced distastefully, looked for something on which to clean them, then wiped them on his shorts and laughed.

Ralph spoke.

"You let the fire go out."

Jack checked, vaguely irritated by this irrelevance but too happy to let it worry him.

"We can light the fire again. You should have been with us, Ralph. We had a smashing time. The twins got knocked over—"

"We hit the pig—"

"—I fell on top—"

"I cut the pig's throat," said Jack, proudly, and yet twitched as he said it. "Can I borrow yours, Ralph, to make a nick in the hilt?"

The boys chattered and danced. The twins continued to grin.

"There was lashings of blood," said Jack, laughing and shuddering, "you should have seen it!"

"We'll go hunting every day—"

Ralph spoke again, hoarsely. He had not moved.

"You let the fire go out."

This repetition made Jack uneasy. He looked at the twins and then back at Ralph.

"We had to have them in the hunt," he said, "or there wouldn't have been enough for a ring."

He flushed, conscious of a fault.

"The fire's only been out an hour or two. We can light up again—"

He noticed Ralph's scarred nakedness, and the sombre silence of all four of them. He sought, charitable in his happiness, to include them in the thing that had happened. His mind was crowded with memories; memories of the knowledge that had come to them when they closed in on the struggling pig, knowledge that they had outwitted a living thing, imposed their will upon it, taken away its life like a long satisfying drink.

He spread his arms wide.

"You should have seen the blood!"

The hunters were more silent now, but at this they buzzed again. Ralph flung back his hair. One arm pointed at the empty horizon. His voice was loud and savage, and struck them into silence.

"There was a ship."

Jack, faced at once with too many awful implications, ducked away from them. He laid a hand on the pig and drew his knife. Ralph brought his arm down, fist clenched, and his voice shook.

"There was a ship. Out there. You said you'd keep the fire going and you let it out!" He took a step toward Jack, who turned and faced him.

"They might have seen us. We might have gone home—"

This was too bitter for Piggy, who forgot his timidity in the agony of his loss. He began to cry out, shrilly:

"You and your blood, Jack Merridew! You and your hunting! We might have gone home—"

Ralph pushed Piggy to one side.

"I was chief, and you were going to do what I said. You talk. But you can't even build huts—then you go off hunting and let out the fire—"

He turned away, silent for a moment. Then his voice came again on a peak of feeling.

"There was a ship—"

One of the smaller hunters began to wail. The dismal truth was filtering through to everybody. Jack went very red as he hacked and pulled at the pig.

"The job was too much. We needed everyone."

Ralph turned.

"You could have had everyone when the shelters were finished. But you had to hunt—"

"We needed meat."

Jack stood up as he said this, the bloodied knife in his hand. The two boys faced each other. There was the brilliant world of hunting, tactics, fierce exhilaration, skill; and there was the world of longing and baffled commonsense. Jack transferred the knife to his left hand and smudged blood over his forehead as he pushed down the plastered hair.

Piggy began again.

"You didn't ought to have let that fire out. You said you'd keep the smoke going—"

This from Piggy, and the wails of agreement from some of the hunters, drove Jack to violence. The bolting look came into his blue eyes. He took a step, and able at last to hit someone, stuck his fist into Piggy's stomach. Piggy sat down with a grunt. Jack stood over him. His voice was vicious with humiliation.

"You would, would you? Fatty!"

Ralph made a step forward and Jack smacked Piggy's head. Piggy's glasses flew off and tinkled on the rocks. Piggy cried out in terror:

"My specs!"

He went crouching and feeling over the rocks but Simon, who got there first, found them for him. Passions beat about Simon on the mountain-top with awful wings.

"One side's broken."

Piggy grabbed and put on the glasses. He looked malevolently at Jack.

"I got to have them specs. Now I only got one eye. Jus' you wait—"

Jack made a move toward Piggy who scrambled away till a great rock lay between them. He thrust his head over the top and glared at Jack through his one flashing glass.

"Now I only got one eye. Just you wait—"

Jack mimicked the whine and scramble.

"Jus' you wait—yah!"

Piggy and the parody were so funny that the hunters began to laugh. Jack felt encouraged. He went on scrambling and the laughter rose to a gale of hysteria. Unwillingly Ralph felt his lips twitch; he was angry with himself for giving way.

He muttered.

"That was a dirty trick."

Jack broke out of his gyration and stood facing Ralph. His words came in a shout.

"All right, all right!"

He looked at Piggy, at the hunters, at Ralph.

"I'm sorry. About the fire, I mean. There. I—"

He drew himself up.

"—I apologize."

The buzz from the hunters was one of admiration at this handsome behavior. Clearly they were of the opinion that Jack had done the decent thing, had put himself in the right by his generous apology and Ralph, obscurely, in the wrong. They waited for an appropriately decent answer.

Yet Ralph's throat refused to pass one. He resented, as an addition to Jack's misbehavior, this verbal trick. The fire was dead, the ship was gone. Could they not see? Anger instead of decency passed his throat.

"That was a dirty trick."

They were silent on the mountain-top while the opaque look appeared in Jack's eyes and passed away.

Ralph's final word was an ingracious mutter.

"All right. Light the fire."

With some positive action before them, a little of the tension died. Ralph said no more, did nothing, stood looking down at the ashes round his feet. Jack was loud and active. He gave orders, sang, whistled, threw remarks at the silent Ralph—remarks that did not need an answer, and therefore could not invite a snub; and still Ralph was silent. No one, not even Jack, would ask him to move and in the end they had to build the fire three yards away and in a place not really as convenient.

So Ralph asserted his chieftainship and could not have chosen a better way if he had thought for days. Against his weapon, so indefinable and so effective, Jack was powerless and raged without knowing why. By the time the pile was built, they were on different sides of a high barrier.

When they had dealt with the fire another crisis arose. Jack had no means of lighting it. Then to his surprise, Ralph went to Piggy and took the glasses from him. Not even Ralph knew how a link between him and Jack had been snapped and fastened elsewhere.

"I'll bring 'em back."

"I'll come too."

Piggy stood behind him, islanded in a sea of meaningless color, while Ralph knelt and focused the glossy spot. Instantly the fire was alight, Piggy held out his hands and grabbed the glasses back.

Before these fantastically attractive flowers of violet and red and yellow, unkindness melted away. They became a circle of boys round a camp fire and even Piggy and Ralph were half-drawn in. Soon some of the boys were rushing down the slope for more wood while Jack hacked the pig. They tried holding the whole carcass on a stake over the fire, but the stake burnt more quickly than the pig roasted. In the end they skewered bits of meat on branches and held them in the flames: and even then almost as much boy was roasted as meat.

Ralph's mouth watered. He meant to refuse meat, but his past diet of fruit and nuts, with an odd crab or fish, gave him too little resistance. He accepted a piece of half-raw meat and gnawed it like a wolf.

Piggy spoke, also dribbling.

"Aren't I having none?"

Jack had meant to leave him in doubt, as an assertion of power; but Piggy by advertising his omission made more cruelty necessary.

"You didn't hunt."

"No more did Ralph," said Piggy wetly, "nor Simon." He amplified. "There isn't more than a ha'porth of meat in a crab."

Ralph stirred uneasily. Simon, sitting between the twins and Piggy, wiped his mouth and shoved his piece of meat over the rocks to Piggy, who grabbed it. The twins giggled and Simon lowered his face in shame.

Then Jack leapt to his feet, slashed off a great hunk of meat, and flung it down at Simon's feet.

"Eat! Damn you!"

He glared at Simon.

"Take it!"

He spun on his heel, center of a bewildered circle of boys.

"I got you meat!"

Numberless and inexpressible frustrations combined to make his rage elemental and awe-inspiring.

"I painted my face—I stole up. Now you eat—all of you— and I—"

Slowly the silence on the mountain-top deepened till the click of the fire and the soft hiss of roasting meat could be heard clearly. Jack looked round for understanding but found only respect. Ralph stood among the ashes of the signal fire, his hands full of meat, saying nothing.

Then at last Maurice broke the silence. He changed the subject to the only one that could bring the majority of them together.

"Where did you find the pig?"

Roger pointed down the unfriendly side. "They were there— by the sea."

Jack, recovering, could not bear to have his story told. He broke in quickly.

"We spread round. I crept, on hands and knees. The spears fell out because they hadn't barbs on. The pig ran away and made an awful noise—"

"It turned back and ran into the circle, bleeding—"

All the boys were talking at once, relieved and excited.

"We closed in—"

The first blow had paralyzed its hind quarters, so then the circle could close in and beat and beat—

"I cut the pig's throat—"

The twins, still sharing their identical grin, jumped up and ran round each other. Then the rest joined in, making pig-dying noises and shouting.

"One for his nob!"

"Give him a fourpenny one!"

Then Maurice pretended to be the pig and ran squealing into the center, and the hunters, circling still, pretended to beat him. As they danced, they sang.

"Kill the pig. Cut her throat. Bash her in."

Ralph watched them, envious and resentful. Not till they flagged and the chant died away, did he speak.

"I'm calling an assembly."

One by one, they halted, and stood watching him.

"With the conch. I'm calling a meeting even if we have to go on into the dark. Down on the platform. When I blow it. Now."

He turned away and walked off, down the mountain.

five

BEAST FROM
WATER

HE TIDE WAS COMING IN AND THERE WAS ONLY
a narrow strip of firm beach between the water and the
white, stumbling stuff near the palm terrace. Ralph chose the firm
strip as a path because he needed to think, and only here could
he allow his feet to move without having to watch them. Suddenly, pacing by the water, he was overcome with astonishment.
He found himself understanding the wearisomeness of this life,
where every path was an improvisation and a considerable part
of one's waking life was spent watching one's feet. He stopped,
facing the strip; and remembering that first enthusiastic exploration as though it were part of a brighter childhood, he smiled
jeeringly. He turned then and walked back toward the platform
with the sun in his face. The time had come for the assembly
and as he walked into the concealing splendors of the sunlight
he went carefully over the points of his speech. There must be
no mistake about this assembly, no chasing imaginary....

He lost himself in a maze of thoughts that were rendered vague
by his lack of words to express them. Frowning, he tried again.

This meeting must not be fun, but business.

At that he walked faster, aware all at once of urgency and the
declining sun and a little wind created by his speed that breathed

about his face. This wind pressed his grey shirt against his chest so that he noticed—in this new mood of comprehension—how the folds were stiff like cardboard, and unpleasant; noticed too how the frayed edges of his shorts were making an uncomfortable, pink area on the front of his thighs. With a convulsion of the mind, Ralph discovered dirt and decay, understood how much he disliked perpetually flicking the tangled hair out of his eyes, and at last, when the sun was gone, rolling noisily to rest among dry leaves. At that he began to trot.

The beach near the bathing pool was dotted with groups of boys waiting for the assembly. They made way for him silently, conscious of his grim mood and the fault at the fire.

The place of assembly in which he stood was roughly a triangle; but irregular and sketchy, like everything they made. First there was the log on which he himself sat; a dead tree that must have been quite exceptionally big for the platform. Perhaps one of those legendary storms of the Pacific had shifted it here. This palm trunk lay parallel to the beach, so that when Ralph sat he faced the island but to the boys was a darkish figure against the shimmer of the lagoon. The two sides of the triangle of which the log was base were less evenly defined. On the right was a log polished by restless seats along the top, but not so large as the chief's and not so comfortable. On the left were four small logs, one of them—the farthest—lamentably springy. Assembly after assembly had broken up in laughter when someone had leaned too far back and the log had whipped and thrown half a dozen boys backwards into the grass. Yet now, he saw, no one had had the wit—not himself nor Jack, nor Piggy—to bring a stone and wedge the thing. So they would continue enduring the ill-balanced twister, because, because.... Again he lost himself in deep waters.

Grass was worn away in front of each trunk but grew tall and untrodden in the center of the triangle. Then, at the apex, the grass was thick again because no one sat there. All round the place of assembly the grey trunks rose, straight or leaning, and supported the low roof of leaves. On two sides was the beach; behind, the lagoon; in front, the darkness of the island.

Ralph turned to the chief's seat. They had never had an assembly as late before. That was why the place looked so different. Normally the underside of the green roof was lit by a tangle of golden reflections, and their faces were lit upside down—like, thought Ralph, when you hold an electric torch in your hands. But now the sun was slanting in at one side, so that the shadows were where they ought to be.

Again he fell into that strange mood of speculation that was so foreign to him. If faces were different when lit from above or below—what was a face? What was anything?

Ralph moved impatiently. The trouble was, if you were a chief you had to think, you had to be wise. And then the occasion slipped by so that you had to grab at a decision. This made you think; because thought was a valuable thing, that got results....

Only, decided Ralph as he faced the chief's seat, I can't think. Not like Piggy.

Once more that evening Ralph had to adjust his values. Piggy could think. He could go step by step inside that fat head of his, only Piggy was no chief. But Piggy, for all his ludicrous body, had brains. Ralph was a specialist in thought now, and could recognize thought in another.

The sun in his eyes reminded him how time was passing, so he took the conch down from the tree and examined the surface. Exposure to the air had bleached the yellow and pink to near-white, and transparency. Ralph felt a kind of affectionate reverence for the conch, even though he had fished the thing out of the lagoon himself. He faced the place of assembly and put the conch to his lips.

The others were waiting for this and came straight away. Those who were aware that a ship had passed the island while the fire was out were subdued by the thought of Ralph's anger; while those, including the littluns who did not know, were impressed by the general air of solemnity. The place of assembly filled quickly; Jack, Simon, Maurice, most of the hunters, on Ralph's right; the rest on the left, under the sun. Piggy came and stood outside the triangle. This indicated that he wished to listen, but would not speak; and Piggy intended it as a gesture of disapproval.

"The thing is: we need an assembly."

No one said anything but the faces turned to Ralph were intent. He flourished the conch. He had learnt as a practical business that fundamental statements like this had to be said at least twice, before everyone understood them. One had to sit, attracting all eyes to the conch, and drop words like heavy round stones among the little groups that crouched or squatted. He was searching his mind for simple words so that even the littluns would understand what the assembly was about. Later perhaps, practiced debaters—Jack, Maurice, Piggy—would use their whole art to twist the meeting: but now at the beginning the subject of the debate must be laid out clearly.

"We need an assembly. Not for fun. Not for laughing and falling off the log"—the group of littluns on the twister giggled and looked at each other—"not for making jokes, or for"—he lifted the conch in an effort to find the compelling word—"for cleverness. Not for these things. But to put things straight."

He paused for a moment.

"I've been alone. By myself I went, thinking what's what. I know what we need. An assembly to put things straight. And first of all, I'm speaking."

He paused for a moment and automatically pushed back his hair. Piggy tiptoed to the triangle, his ineffectual protest made, and joined the others.

Ralph went on.

"We have lots of assemblies. Everybody enjoys speaking and being together. We decide things. But they don't get done. We were going to have water brought from the stream and left in those coconut shells under fresh leaves. So it was, for a few days. Now there's no water. The shells are dry. People drink from the river."

There was a murmur of assent.

"Not that there's anything wrong with drinking from the river. I mean I'd sooner have water from that place—you know, the pool where the waterfall is—then out of an old coconut shell. Only we said we'd have the water brought. And now not. There were only two full shells there this afternoon."

He licked his lips.

"Then there's huts. Shelters."

The murmur swelled again and died away.

"You mostly sleep in shelters. Tonight, except for Samneric up by the fire, you'll all sleep there. Who built the shelters?"

Clamor rose at once. Everyone had built the shelters. Ralph had to wave the conch once more.

"Wait a minute! I mean, who built all three? We all built the first one, four of us the second one, and me 'n Simon built the last one over there. That's why it's so tottery. No. Don't laugh. That shelter might fall down if the rain comes back. We'll need those shelters then."

He paused and cleared his throat.

"There's another thing. We chose those rocks right along beyond the bathing pool as a lavatory. That was sensible too. The
tide cleans the place up. You littluns know about that."

There were sniggers here and there and swift glances.

"Now people seem to use anywhere. Even near the shelters and
the platform. You littluns, when you're getting fruit; if you're
taken short—"

The assembly roared.

"I said if you're taken short you keep away from the fruit.
That's dirty!"

Laughter rose again.

"I said that's dirty!"

He plucked at his stiff, grey shirt.

"That's really dirty. If you're taken short you go right along
the beach to the rocks. See?"

Piggy held out his hands for the conch but Ralph shook his
head. His speech was planned, point by point.

"We've all got to use the rocks again. This place is getting
dirty." He paused. The assembly, sensing a crisis, was tensely
expectant. "And then: about the fire."

Ralph let out his spare breath with a little gasp that was echoed
by his audience. Jack started to chip a piece of wood with his
knife and whispered something to Robert, who looked away.

"The fire is the most important thing on the island. How can
we ever be rescued except by luck, if we don't keep a fire going?
Is a fire too much for us to make?"

He flung out an arm.

"Look at us! How many are we? And yet we can't keep a fire
going to make smoke. Don't you understand? Can't you see we
ought to—ought to die before we let the fire out?"

There was a self-conscious giggling among the hunters. Ralph turned on them passionately.

"You hunters! You can laugh! But I tell you the smoke is more important than the pig, however often you kill one. Do all of you see?" He spread his arms wide and turned to the whole triangle.

"We've got to make smoke up there—or die."

He paused, feeling for his next point.

"And another thing."

Someone called out.

"Too many things."

There came a mutter of agreement. Ralph overrode them.

"And another thing. We nearly set the whole island on fire. And we waste time, rolling rocks, and making little cooking fires. Now I say this and make it a rule, because I'm chief. We won't have a fire anywhere but on the mountain. Ever."

There was a row immediately. Boys stood up and shouted and Ralph shouted back.

"Because if you want a fire to cook fish or crab, you can jolly well go up the mountain. That way we'll be certain."

Hands were reaching for the conch in the light of the setting sun. He held on and leapt on the trunk.

"All this I meant to say. Now I've said it. You voted me for chief. Now you do what I say."

They quieted, slowly, and at last were seated again. Ralph dropped down and spoke in his ordinary voice.

"So remember. The rocks for a lavatory. Keep the fire going and smoke showing as a signal. Don't take fire from the mountain. Take your food up there."

Jack stood up, scowling in the gloom, and held out his hands.

"I haven't finished yet."

"But you've talked and talked!"

"I've got the conch."

Jack sat down, grumbling.

"Then the last thing. This is what people can talk about."

He waited till the platform was very still.

"Things are breaking up. I don't understand why. We began well; we were happy. And then—"

He moved the conch gently, looking beyond them at nothing, remembering the beastie, the snake, the fire, the talk of fear.

"Then people started getting frightened."

A murmur, almost a moan, rose and passed away. Jack had stopped whittling. Ralph went on, abruptly.

"But that's littluns' talk. We'll get that straight. So the last part, the bit we can all talk about, is kind of deciding on the fear."

The hair was creeping into his eyes again.

"We've got to talk about this fear and decide there's nothing in it. I'm frightened myself, sometimes; only that's nonsense! Like bogies. Then, when we've decided, we can start again and be careful about things like the fire." A picture of three boys walking along the bright beach flitted through his mind. "And be happy."

Ceremonially, Ralph laid the conch on the trunk beside him as a sign that the speech was over. What sunlight reached them was level.

Jack stood up and took the conch.

"So this is a meeting to find out what's what. I'll tell you what's what. You littluns started all this, with the fear talk. Beasts! Where from? Of course we're frightened sometimes but we put up with being frightened. Only Ralph says you scream in the night. What does that mean but nightmares? Anyway, you don't hunt or build or help—you're a lot of cry-babies and sissies.

That's what. And as for the fear—you'll have to put up with that like the rest of us."

Ralph looked at Jack open-mouthed, but Jack took no notice.

"The thing is—fear can't hurt you any more than a dream. There aren't any beasts to be afraid of on this island." He looked along the row of whispering littluns. "Serve you right if something did get you, you useless lot of cry-babies! But there *is* no animal—"

Ralph interrupted him testily.

"What is all this? Who said anything about an animal?"

"You did, the other day. You said they dream and cry out. Now they talk—not only the littluns, but my hunters sometimes—talk of a thing, a dark thing, a beast, some sort of animal. I've heard. You thought not, didn't you? Now listen. You don't get big animals on small islands. Only pigs. You only get lions and tigers in big countries like Africa and India—"

"And the Zoo—"

"I've got the conch. I'm not talking about the fear. I'm talking about the beast. Be frightened if you like. But as for the beast—"

Jack paused, cradling the conch, and turned to his hunters with their dirty black caps.

"Am I a hunter or am I not?"

They nodded, simply. He was a hunter all right. No one doubted that.

"Well then—I've been all over this island. By myself. If there were a beast I'd have seen it. Be frightened because you're like that—but there is no beast in the forest."

Jack handed back the conch and sat down. The whole assembly applauded him with relief. Then Piggy held out his hand.

"I don't agree with all Jack said, but with some. 'Course there isn't a beast in the forest. How could there be? What would a beast eat?"

"Pig."

"We eat pig."

"Piggy!"

"I got the conch!" said Piggy indignantly. "Ralph—they ought to shut up, oughtn't they? You shut up, you littluns! What I mean is that I don't agree about this here fear. Of course there isn't nothing to be afraid of in the forest. Why—I been there myself! You'll be talking about ghosts and such things next. We know what goes on and if there's something wrong, there's someone to put it right."

He took off his glasses and blinked at them. The sun had gone as if the light had been turned off.

He proceeded to explain.

"If you get a pain in your stomach, whether it's a little one or a big one—"

"Yours is a big one."

"When you done laughing perhaps we can get on with the meeting. And if them littluns climb back on the twister again they'll only fall off in a sec. So they might as well sit on the ground and listen. No. You have doctors for everything, even the inside of your mind. You don't really mean that we got to be frightened all the time of nothing? Life," said Piggy expansively, "is scientific, that's what it is. In a year or two when the war's over they'll be traveling to Mars and back. I know there isn't no beast—not with claws and all that, I mean—but I know there isn't no fear, either."

Piggy paused.

"Unless—"

Ralph moved restlessly.

"Unless what?"

"Unless we get frightened of people."

A sound, half-laugh, half-jeer, rose among the seated boys. Piggy ducked his head and went on hastily.

"So let's hear from that littlun who talked about a beast and perhaps we can show him how silly he is."

The littluns began to jabber among themselves, then one stood forward.

"What's your name?"

"Phil."

For a littlun he was self-confident, holding out his hands, cradling the conch as Ralph did, looking round at them to collect their attention before he spoke.

"Last night I had a dream, a horrid dream, fighting with things. I was outside the shelter by myself, fighting with things, those twisty things in the trees."

He paused, and the other littluns laughed in horrified sympathy.

"Then I was frightened and I woke up. And I was outside the shelter by myself in the dark and the twisty things had gone away."

The vivid horror of this, so possible and so nakedly terrifying, held them all silent. The child's voice went piping on from behind the white conch.

"And I was frightened and started to call out for Ralph and then I saw something moving among the trees, something big and horrid."

He paused, half-frightened by the recollection yet proud of the sensation he was creating.

"That was a nightmare," said Ralph. "He was walking in his sleep."

The assembly murmured in subdued agreement.

The littlun shook his head stubbornly.

"I was asleep when the twisty things were fighting and when they went away I was awake, and I saw something big and horrid moving in the trees."

Ralph held out his hands for the conch and the littlun sat down.

"You were asleep. There wasn't anyone there. How could anyone be wandering about in the forest at night? Was anyone? Did anyone go out?"

There was a long pause while the assembly grinned at the thought of anyone going out in the darkness. Then Simon stood up and Ralph looked at him in astonishment.

"You! What were you mucking about in the dark for?"

Simon grabbed the conch convulsively.

"I wanted—to go to a place—a place I know."

"What place?"

"Just a place I know. A place in the jungle."

He hesitated.

Jack settled the question for them with that contempt in his voice that could sound so funny and so final.

"He was taken short."

With a feeling of humiliation on Simon's behalf, Ralph took back the conch, looking Simon sternly in the face as he did so.

"Well, don't do it again. Understand? Not at night. There's enough silly talk about beasts, without the littluns seeing you gliding about like a—"

The derisive laughter that rose had fear in it and condemnation. Simon opened his mouth to speak but Ralph had the conch, so he backed to his seat.

When the assembly was silent Ralph turned to Piggy.

"Well, Piggy?"

"There was another one. Him."

The littluns pushed Percival forward, then left him by himself. He stood knee-deep in the central grass, looking at his hidden feet, trying to pretend he was in a tent. Ralph remembered another small boy who had stood like this and he flinched away from the memory. He had pushed the thought down and out of sight, where only some positive reminder like this could bring it to the surface. There had been no further numberings of the littluns, partly because there was no means of insuring that all of them were accounted for and partly because Ralph knew the answer to at least one question Piggy had asked on the mountaintop. There were little boys, fair, dark, freckled, and all dirty, but their faces were all dreadfully free of major blemishes. No one had seen the mulberry-colored birthmark again. But that time Piggy had coaxed and bullied. Tacitly admitting that he remembered the unmentionable, Ralph nodded to Piggy.

"Go on. Ask him."

Piggy knelt, holding the conch.

"Now then. What's your name?"

The small boy twisted away into his tent. Piggy turned helplessly to Ralph, who spoke sharply.

"What's your name?"

Tormented by the silence and the refusal the assembly broke into a chant.

"What's your name? What's your name?"

"Quiet!"

Ralph peered at the child in the twilight.

"Now tell us. What's your name?"

"Percival Wemys Madison. The Vicarage, Harcourt St. Anthony, Hants, telephone, telephone, tele—"

As if this information was rooted far down in the springs of sorrow, the littlun wept. His face puckered, the tears leapt from his eyes, his mouth opened till they could see a square black hole. At first he was a silent effigy of sorrow; but then the lamentation rose out of him, loud and sustained as the conch.

"Shut up, you! Shut up!"

Percival Wemys Madison would not shut up. A spring had been tapped, far beyond the reach of authority or even physical intimidation. The crying went on, breath after breath, and seemed to sustain him upright as if he were nailed to it.

"Shut up! Shut up!"

For now the littluns were no longer silent. They were reminded of their personal sorrows; and perhaps felt themselves to share in a sorrow that was universal. They began to cry in sympathy, two of them almost as loud as Percival.

Maurice saved them. He cried out.

"Look at me!"

He pretended to fall over. He rubbed his rump and sat on the twister so that he fell in the grass. He clowned badly; but Percival and the others noticed and sniffed and laughed. Presently they were all laughing so absurdly that the biguns joined in.

Jack was the first to make himself heard. He had not got the conch and thus spoke against the rules; but nobody minded.

"And what about the beast?"

Something strange was happening to Percival. He yawned and staggered, so that Jack seized and shook him.

"Where does the beast live?"

Percivel sagged in Jack's grip.

"That's a clever beast," said Piggy, jeering, "if it can hide on this island."

"Jack's been everywhere—"

"Where could a beast live?"

"Beast my foot!"

Percival muttered something and the assembly laughed again. Ralph leaned forward.

"What does he say?"

Jack listened to Percival's answer and then let go of him. Percival, released, surrounded by the comfortable presence of humans, fell in the long grass and went to sleep.

Jack cleared his throat, then reported casually.

"He says the beast comes out of the sea."

The last laugh died away. Ralph turned involuntarily, a black, humped figure against the lagoon. The assembly looked with him, considered the vast stretches of water, the high sea beyond, unknown indigo of infinite possibility, heard silently the sough and whisper from the reef.

Maurice spoke, so loudly that they jumped.

"Daddy said they haven't found all the animals in the sea yet."

Argument started again. Ralph held out the glimmering conch and Maurice took it obediently. The meeting subsided.

"I mean when Jack says you can be frightened because people are frightened anyway that's all right. But when he says there's only pigs on this island I expect he's right but he doesn't know, not really, not certainly I mean—" Maurice took a breath. "My daddy says there's things, what d'you call 'em that make ink— squids—that are hundreds of yards long and eat whales whole." He paused again and laughed gaily. "I don't believe in the beast of course. As Piggy says, life's scientific, but we don't know, do we? Not certainly, I mean—"

Someone shouted.

"A squid couldn't come up out of the water!"

"Could!"

"Couldn't!"

97

In a moment the platform was full of arguing, gesticulating shadows. To Ralph, seated, this seemed the breaking up of sanity. Fear, beasts, no general agreement that the fire was all-important: and when one tried to get the thing straight the argument sheered off, bringing up fresh, unpleasant matter.

He could see a whiteness in the gloom near him so he grabbed it from Maurice and blew as loudly as he could. The assembly was shocked into silence. Simon was close to him, laying hands on the conch. Simon felt a perilous necessity to speak; but to speak in assembly was a terrible thing to him.

"Maybe," he said hesitantly, "maybe there is a beast."

The assembly cried out savagely and Ralph stood up in amazement.

"You, Simon? You believe in this?"

"I don't know," said Simon. His heartbeats were choking him. "But. . . ."

The storm broke.

"Sit down!"

"Shut up!"

"Take the conch!"

"Sod you!"

"Shut up!"

Ralph shouted.

"Hear him! He's got the conch!"

"What I mean is . . . maybe it's only us."

"Nuts!"

That was from Piggy, shocked out of decorum. Simon went on.

"We could be sort of. . . ."

Simon became inarticulate in his effort to express mankind's essential illness. Inspiration came to him.

"What's the dirtiest thing there is?"

As an answer Jack dropped into the uncomprehending silence that followed it the one crude expressive syllable. Release was immense. Those littluns who had climbed back on the twister fell off again and did not mind. The hunters were screaming with delight.

Simon's effort fell about him in ruins; the laughter beat him cruelly and he shrank away defenseless to his seat.

At last the assembly was silent again. Someone spoke out of turn.

"Maybe he means it's some sort of ghost."

Ralph lifted the conch and peered into the gloom. The lightest thing was the pale beach. Surely the littluns were nearer? Yes—there was no doubt about it, they were huddled into a tight knot of bodies in the central grass. A flurry of wind made the palms talk and the noise seemed very loud now that darkness and silence made it so noticeable. Two grey trunks rubbed each other with an evil speaking that no one had noticed by day.

Piggy took the conch out of his hands. His voice was indignant.

"I don't believe in no ghosts—ever!"

Jack was up too, unaccountably angry.

"Who cares what you believe—Fatty!"

"I got the conch!"

There was the sound of a brief tussle and the conch moved to and fro.

"You gimme the conch back!"

Ralph pushed between them and got a thump on the chest. He wrestled the conch from someone and sat down breathlessly.

"There's too much talk about ghosts. We ought to have left all this for daylight."

A hushed and anonymous voice broke in.

"Perhaps that's what the beast is—a ghost."

The assembly was shaken as by a wind.

"There's too much talking out of turn," Ralph said, "because we can't have proper assemblies if you don't stick to the rules."

He stopped again. The careful plan of this assembly had broken down.

"What d'you want me to say then? I was wrong to call this assembly so late. We'll have a vote on them; on ghosts I mean; and then go to the shelters because we're all tired. No—Jack is it?—wait a minute. I'll say here and now that I don't believe in ghosts. Or I don't think I do. But I don't like the thought of them. Not now that is, in the dark. But we were going to decide what's what."

He raised the conch for a moment.

"Very well then. I suppose what's what is whether there are ghosts or not—"

He thought for a moment, formulating the question.

"Who thinks there may be ghosts?"

For a long time there was silence and no apparent movement. Then Ralph peered into the gloom and made out the hands. He spoke flatly.

"I see."

The world, that understandable and lawful world, was slipping away. Once there was this and that; and now—and the ship had gone.

The conch was snatched from his hands and Piggy's voice shrilled.

"I didn't vote for no ghosts!"

He whirled round on the assembly.

"Remember that, all of you!"

They heard him stamp.

"What are we? Humans? Or animals? Or savages? What's grownups going to think? Going off—hunting pigs—letting fires out—and now!"

A shadow fronted him tempestuously.

"You shut up, you fat slug!"

There was a moment's struggle and the glimmering conch jigged up and down. Ralph leapt to his feet.

"Jack! Jack! You haven't got the conch! Let him speak."

Jack's face swam near him.

"And you shut up! Who are you, anyway? Sitting there telling people what to do. You can't hunt, you can't sing—"

"I'm chief. I was chosen."

"Why should choosing make any difference? Just giving orders that don't make any sense—"

"Piggy's got the conch."

"That's right—favor Piggy as you always do—"

"Jack!"

Jack's voice sounded in bitter mimicry.

"Jack! Jack!"

"The rules!" shouted Ralph. "You're breaking the rules!"

"Who cares?"

Ralph summoned his wits.

"Because the rules are the only thing we've got!"

But Jack was shouting against him.

"Bollocks to the rules! We're strong—we hunt! If there's a beast, we'll hunt it down! We'll close in and beat and beat and beat—!"

He gave a wild whoop and leapt down to the pale sand. At once the platform was full of noise and excitement, scramblings, screams and laughter. The assembly shredded away and became a discursive and random scatter from the palms to the water and away along the beach, beyond night-sight. Ralph found his cheek touching the conch and took it from Piggy.

"What's grownups going to say?" cried Piggy again. "Look at 'em!"

The sound of mock hunting, hysterical laughter and real terror came from the beach.

"Blow the conch, Ralph."

Piggy was so close that Ralph could see the glint of his one glass.

"There's the fire. Can't they see?"

"You got to be tough now. Make 'em do what you want."

Ralph answered in the cautious voice of one who rehearses a theorem.

"If I blow the conch and they don't come back; then we've had it. We shan't keep the fire going. We'll be like animals. We'll never be rescued."

"If you don't blow, we'll soon be animals anyway. I can't see what they're doing but I can hear."

The dispersed figures had come together on the sand and were a dense black mass that revolved. They were chanting something and littluns that had had enough were staggering away, howling. Ralph raised the conch to his lips and then lowered it.

"The trouble is: Are there ghosts, Piggy? Or beasts?"

"Course there aren't."

"Why not?"

"'Cos things wouldn't make sense. Houses an' streets, an'— TV—they wouldn't work."

The dancing, chanting boys had worked themselves away till their sound was nothing but a wordless rhythm.

"But s'pose they don't make sense? Not here, on this island? Supposing things are watching us and waiting?"

Ralph shuddered violently and moved closer to Piggy, so that they bumped frighteningly.

"You stop talking like that! We got enough trouble, Ralph, an' I've had as much as I can stand. If there is ghosts—"

"I ought to give up being chief. Hear 'em."

"Oh lord! Oh no!"

Piggy gripped Ralph's arm.

"If Jack was chief he'd have all hunting and no fire. We'd be here till we died."

His voice ran up to a squeak.

"Who's that sitting there?"

"Me. Simon."

"Fat lot of good we are," said Ralph. "Three blind mice. I'll give up."

"If you give up," said Piggy, in an appalled whisper, "what 'ud happen to me?"

"Nothing."

"He hates me. I dunno why. If he could do what he wanted— you're all right, he respects you. Besides—you'd hit him."

"You were having a nice fight with him just now."

"I had the conch," said Piggy simply. "I had a right to speak."

Simon stirred in the dark.

"Go on being chief."

"You shut up, young Simon! Why couldn't you say there wasn't a beast?"

"I'm scared of him," said Piggy, "and that's why I know him. If you're scared of someone you hate him but you can't stop thinking about him. You kid yourself he's all right really, an' then when you see him again; it's like asthma an' you can't breathe. I tell you what. He hates you too, Ralph—"

"Me? Why me?"

"I dunno. You got him over the fire; an' you're chief an' he isn't."

"But he's, he's, Jack Merridew!"

"I been in bed so much I done some thinking. I know about people. I know about me. And him. He can't hurt you: but if you stand out of the way he'd hurt the next thing. And that's me."

"Piggy's right, Ralph. There's you and Jack. Go on being chief."

"We're all drifting and things are going rotten. At home there was always a grownup. Please, sir; please, miss; and then you got an answer. How I wish!"

"I wish my auntie was here."

"I wish my father . . . Oh, what's the use?"

"Keep the fire going."

The dance was over and the hunters were going back to the shelters.

"Grownups know things," said Piggy. "They ain't afraid of the dark. They'd meet and have tea and discuss. Then things 'ud be all right—"

"They wouldn't set fire to the island. Or lose—"

"They'd build a ship—"

The three boys stood in the darkness, striving unsuccessfully to convey the majesty of adult life.

"They wouldn't quarrel—"

"Or break my specs—"

"Or talk about a beast—"

"If only they could get a message to us," cried Ralph desperately. "If only they could send us something grownup... a sign or something."

A thin wail out of the darkness chilled them and set them grabbing for each other. Then the wail rose, remote and unearthly, and turned to an inarticulate gibbering. Percival Wemys Madison, of the Vicarage, Harcourt St. Anthony, lying in the long grass, was living through circumstances in which the incantation of his address was powerless to help him.

six

BEAST FROM
AIR

HERE WAS NO LIGHT LEFT SAVE THAT OF THE stars. When they had understood what made this ghostly noise and Percival was quiet again, Ralph and Simon picked him up unhandily and carried him to a shelter. Piggy hung about near for all his brave words, and the three bigger boys went together to the next shelter. They lay restlessly and noisily among the dry leaves, watching the patch of stars that was the opening toward the lagoon. Sometimes a littlun cried out from the other shelters and once a bigun spoke in the dark. Then they too fell asleep.

A sliver of moon rose over the horizon, hardly large enough to make a path of light even when it sat right down on the water; but there were other lights in the sky, that moved fast, winked, or went out, though not even a faint popping came down from the battle fought at ten miles' eight. But a sign came down from the world of grown-ups, though at the time there was no child awake to read it. There was a sudden bright explosion and cork-screw trail across the sky; then darkness again and stars. There was a speck above the island, a figure dropping swiftly beneath a parachute, a figure that hung with dangling limbs. The changing winds of various altitudes took the figure where they would. Then, three miles up, the wind steadied and bore it in a descending curve round the sky and swept it in a great slant across the reef and the lagoon toward the mountain. The figure fell and crumpled among the blue flowers of the mountain-side, but now there was a gentle breeze at this height too and the parachute flopped and banged and pulled. So the figure, with feet that dragged behind it, slid up the mountain. Yard by yard, puff by puff, the breeze hauled the figure through the blue flowers, over the boulders and red stones, till it lay huddled among the shattered rocks of the mountain-top. Here the breeze was fitful and allowed the strings of the parachute to tangle and festoon; and the figure sat, its helmeted head between its knees, held by a complication of lines. When the breeze blew, the lines would strain taut and some accident of this pull lifted the head and chest upright so that the figure seemed to peer across the brow of the mountain. Then, each time the wind dropped, the lines would slacken and the figure bow forward again, sinking its head between its knees. So as the stars moved across the sky, the figure sat on the mountain-top and bowed and sank and bowed again.

In the darkness of early morning there were noises by a rock a little way down the side of the mountain. Two boys rolled out a pile of brushwood and dead leaves, two dim shadows talking sleepily to each other. They were the twins, on duty at the fire. In theory one should have been asleep and one on watch. But they could never manage to do things sensibly if that meant acting independently, and since staying awake all night was impossible, they had both gone to sleep. Now they approached the darker smudge that had been the signal fire, yawning, rubbing their eyes, treading with practiced feet. When they reached it they stopped yawning, and one ran quickly back for brushwood and leaves.

The other knelt down.

"I believe it's out."

He fiddled with the sticks that were pushed into his hands. "No."

He lay down and put his lips close to the smudge and blew softly. His face appeared, lit redly. He stopped blowing for a moment.

"Sam—give us—"

"—tinder wood."

Eric bent down and blew softly again till the patch was bright. Sam poked the piece of tinder wood into the hot spot, then a branch. The glow increased and the branch took fire. Sam piled on more branches.

"Don't burn the lot," said Eric, "you're putting on too much."

"Let's warm up."

"We'll only have to fetch more wood."

"I'm cold."

"So'm I."

"Besides, it's—"

"—dark. All right, then."

Eric squatted back and watched Sam make up the fire. He built a little tent of dead wood and the fire was safely alight.

"That was near."

"He'd have been—"

"Waxy."

"Huh."

For a few moments the twins watched the fire in silence. Then Eric sniggered.

"Wasn't he waxy?"

"About the—"

"Fire and the pig."

"Lucky he went for Jack, 'stead of us."

"Huh. Remember old Waxy at school?"

" 'Boy—you-are-driving-me-slowly-insane!' "

The twins shared their identical laughter, then remembered the darkness and other things and glanced round uneasily. The flames, busy about the tent, drew their eyes back again. Eric watched the scurrying woodlice that were so frantically unable to avoid the flames, and thought of the first fire—just down there, on the steeper side of the mountain, where now was complete darkness. He did not like to remember it, and looked away at the mountain-top.

Warmth radiated now, and beat pleasantly on them. Sam amused himself by fitting branches into the fire as closely as possible. Eric spread out his hands, searching for the distance at which the heat was just bearable. Idly looking beyond the fire, he resettled the scattered rocks from their flat shadows into daylight contours. Just there was the big rock, and the three stones there, that split rock, and there beyond was a gap—just there—

"Sam."

"Huh?"

"Nothing."

The flames were mastering the branches, the bark was curling and falling away, the wood exploding. The tent fell inwards and flung a wide circle of light over the mountain-top.

"Sam—"

"Huh?"

"Sam! Sam!"

Sam looked at Eric irritably. The intensity of Eric's gaze made the direction in which he looked terrible, for Sam had his back to it. He scrambled round the fire, squatted by Eric, and looked to see. They became motionless, gripped in each other's arms, four unwinking eyes aimed and two mouths open.

Far beneath them, the trees of the forest sighed, then roared. The hair on their foreheads fluttered and flames blew out sideways from the fire. Fifteen yards away from them came the plopping noise of fabric blown open.

Neither of the boys screamed but the grip of their arms tightened and their mouths grew peaked. For perhaps ten seconds they crouched like that while the flailing fire sent smoke and sparks and waves of inconstant light over the top of the mountain.

Then as though they had but one terrified mind between them they scrambled away over the rocks and fled.

Ralph was dreaming. He had fallen asleep after what seemed hours of tossing and turning noisily among the dry leaves. Even the sounds of nightmare from the other shelters no longer reached him, for he was back to where he came from, feeding the ponies with sugar over the garden wall. Then someone was shaking his arm, telling him that it was time for tea.

"Ralph! Wake up!"

The leaves were roaring like the sea.

"Ralph, wake up!"

"What's the matter?"

"We saw—"

"—the beast—"

"—plain!"

"Who are you? The twins?"

"We saw the beast—"

"Quiet. Piggy!"

The leaves were roaring still. Piggy bumped into him and a twin grabbed him as he made for the oblong of paling stars.

"You can't go out—it's horrible!"

"Piggy—where are the spears?"

"I can hear the—"

"Quiet then. Lie still."

They lay there listening, at first with doubt but then with terror to the description the twins breathed at them between bouts of extreme silence. Soon the darkness was full of claws, full of the awful unknown and menace. An interminable dawn faded the stars out, and at last light, sad and grey, filtered into the shelter. They began to stir though still the world outside the shelter was impossibly dangerous. The maze of the darkness sorted into near and far, and at the high point of the sky the cloudlets were warmed with color. A single sea bird flapped upwards with a hoarse cry that was echoed presently, and something squawked in the forest. Now streaks of cloud near the horizon began to glow rosily, and the feathery tops of the palms were green.

Ralph knelt in the entrance to the shelter and peered cautiously round him.

"Sam 'n Eric. Call them to an assembly. Quietly. Go on."

The twins, holding tremulously to each other, dared the few yards to the next shelter and spread the dreadful news. Ralph stood up and walked for the sake of dignity, though with his back pricking, to the platform. Piggy and Simon followed him and the other boys came sneaking after.

Ralph took the conch from where it lay on the polished seat and held it to his lips; but then he hesitated and did not blow. He held the shell up instead and showed it to them and they understood.

The rays of the sun that were fanning upwards from below the horizon swung downwards to eye-level. Ralph looked for a moment at the growing slice of gold that lit them from the right hand and seemed to make speech possible. The circle of boys before him bristled with hunting spears.

He handed the conch to Eric, the nearest of the twins.

"We've seen the beast with our own eyes. No—we weren't asleep—"

Sam took up the story. By custom now one conch did for both twins, for their substantial unity was recognized.

"It was furry. There was something moving behind its head—wings. The beast moved too—"

"That was awful. It kind of sat up—"

"The fire was bright—"

"We'd just made it up—"

"—more sticks on—"

"There were eyes—"

"Teeth—"

"Claws—"

"We ran as fast as we could—"

"Bashed into things—"

"The beast followed us—"

"I saw it slinking behind the trees—"

"Nearly touched me—"

Ralph pointed fearfully at Eric's face, which was striped with scars where the bushes had torn him.

"How did you do that?"

Eric felt his face.

"I'm all rough. Am I bleeding?"

The circle of boys shrank away in horror. Johnny, yawning still, burst into noisy tears and was slapped by Bill till he choked on them. The bright morning was full of threats and the circle began to change. It faced out, rather than in, and the spears of sharpened wood were like a fence. Jack called them back to the center.

"This'll be a real hunt! Who'll come?"

Ralph moved impatiently.

"These spears are made of wood. Don't be silly."

Jack sneered at him.

"Frightened?"

" 'Course I'm frightened. Who wouldn't be?"

He turned to the twins, yearning but hopeless.

"I suppose you aren't pulling our legs?"

The reply was too emphatic for anyone to doubt them.

Piggy took the conch.

"Couldn't we—kind of—stay here? Maybe the beast won't come near us."

But for the sense of something watching them, Ralph would have shouted at him.

"Stay here? And be cramped into this bit of the island, always on the lookout? How should we get our food? And what about the fire?"

"Let's be moving," said Jack relentlessly, "we're wasting time."

"No we're not. What about the littluns?"

"Sucks to the littluns!"

"Someone's got to look after them."

"Nobody has so far."

"There was no need! Now there is. Piggy'll look after them."

"That's right. Keep Piggy out of danger."

"Have some sense. What can Piggy do with only one eye?"

The rest of the boys were looking from Jack to Ralph, curiously.

"And another thing. You can't have an ordinary hunt because the beast doesn't leave tracks. If it did you'd have seen them. For all we know, the beast may swing through the trees like what's its name."

They nodded.

"So we've got to think."

Piggy took off his damaged glasses and cleaned the remaining lens.

"How about us, Ralph?"

"You haven't got the conch. Here."

"I mean—how about us? Suppose the beast comes when you're all away. I can't see proper, and if I get scared—"

Jack broke in, contemptuously.

"You're always scared."

"I got the conch—"

"Conch! Conch!" shouted Jack. "We don't need the conch any more. We know who ought to say things. What good did Simon do speaking, or Bill, or Walter? It's time some people knew they've got to keep quiet and leave deciding things to the rest of us."

Ralph could no longer ignore his speech. The blood was hot in his cheeks.

"You haven't got the conch," he said. "Sit down."

Jack's face went so white that the freckles showed as clear, brown flecks. He licked his lips and remained standing.

"This is a hunter's job."

The rest of the boys watched intently. Piggy, finding himself uncomfortably embroiled, slid the conch to Ralph's knees and sat down. The silence grew oppressive and Piggy held his breath.

"This is more than a hunter's job," said Ralph at last, "because you can't track the beast. And don't you want to be rescued?"

He turned to the assembly.

"Don't you all want to be rescued?"

He looked back at Jack.

"I said before, the fire is the main thing. Now the fire must be out—"

The old exasperation saved him and gave him the energy to attack.

"Hasn't anyone got any sense? We've got to relight that fire. You never thought of that, Jack, did you? Or don't any of you want to be rescued?"

Yes, they wanted to be rescued, there was no doubt about that; and with a violent swing to Ralph's side, the crisis passed. Piggy let out his breath with a gasp, reached for it again and failed. He lay against a log, his mouth gaping, blue shadows creeping round his lips. Nobody minded him.

"Now think, Jack. Is there anywhere on the island you haven't been?"

Unwillingly Jack answered.

"There's only—but of course! You remember? The tail-end part, where the rocks are all piled up. I've been near there. The rock makes a sort of bridge. There's only one way up."

"And the thing might live there."

All the assembly talked at once.

"Quite! All right. That's where we'll look. If the beast isn't there we'll go up the mountain and look; and light the fire."

"Let's go."

"We'll eat first. Then go." Ralph paused. "We'd better take spears."

After they had eaten, Ralph and the biguns set out along the beach. They left Piggy propped up on the platform. This day promised, like the others, to be a sunbath under a blue dome. The beach stretched away before them in a gentle curve till perspective drew it into one with the forest; for the day was not advanced enough to be obscured by the shifting veils of mirage. Under Ralph's direction, they picked up a careful way along the palm terrace, rather than dare the hot sand down by the water. He let Jack lead the way; and Jack trod with theatrical caution though they could have seen an enemy twenty yards away. Ralph walked in the rear, thankful to have escaped responsibility for a time.

Simon, walking in front of Ralph, felt a flicker of incredulity—a beast with claws that scratched, that sat on a mountain-top, that left no tracks and yet was not fast enough to catch Samneric. However Simon thought of the beast, there rose before his inward sight the picture of a human at once heroic and sick.

He sighed. Other people could stand up and speak to an assembly, apparently, without that dreadful feeling of the pressure of personality; could say what they would as though they were speaking to only one person. He stepped aside and looked back. Ralph was coming along, holding his spear over his shoulder. Diffidently, Simon allowed his pace to slacken until he was walking side by side with Ralph and looking up at him through the coarse black hair that now fell to his eyes. Ralph glanced sideways, smiled constrainedly as though he had forgotten that Simon had made a fool of himself, then looked away again at nothing. For a moment or two Simon was happy to be accepted and then he ceased to think about himself. When he bashed into a tree Ralph looked sideways impatiently and Robert sniggered. Simon reeled and a white spot on his forehead turned red and trickled. Ralph dismissed Simon and returned to his personal hell. They would reach the castle some time; and the chief would have to go forward.

Jack came trotting back.

"We're in sight now."

"All right. We'll get as close as we can."

He followed Jack toward the castle where the ground rose slightly. On their left was an impenetrable tangle of creepers and trees.

"Why couldn't there be something in that?"

"Because you can see. Nothing goes in or out."

"What about the castle then?"

"Look."

Ralph parted the screen of grass and looked out. There were only a few more yards of stony ground and then the two sides of the island came almost together so that one expected a peak of headland. But instead of this a narrow ledge of rock, a few yards wide and perhaps fifteen long, continued the island out into the sea. There lay another of those pieces of pink squareness that underlay the structure of the island. This side of the castle, perhaps a hundred feet high, was the pink bastion they had seen from the mountain-top. The rock of the cliff was split and the top littered with great lumps that seemed to totter.

Behind Ralph the tall grass had filled with silent hunters. Ralph looked at Jack.

"You're a hunter."

Jack went red.

"I know. All right."

Something deep in Ralph spoke for him.

"I'm chief. I'll go. Don't argue."

He turned to the others.

"You. Hide here. Wait for me."

He found his voice tended either to disappear or to come out too loud. He looked at Jack.

"Do you—think?"

Jack muttered.

"I've been all over. It must be here."

"I see."

Simon mumbled confusedly: "I don't believe in the beast."

Ralph answered him politely, as if agreeing about the weather.

"No. I suppose not."

His mouth was tight and pale. He put back his hair very slowly.

"Well. So long."

He forced his feet to move until they had carried him out on to the neck of land.

He was surrounded on all sides by chasms of empty air. There was nowhere to hide, even if one did not have to go on. He paused on the narrow neck and looked down. Soon, in a matter of centuries, the sea would make an island of the castle. On the right hand was the lagoon, troubled by the open sea; and on the left—

Ralph shuddered. The lagoon had protected them from the Pacific: and for some reason only Jack had gone right down to the water on the other side. Now he saw the landsman's view of the swell and it seemed like the breathing of some stupendous creature. Slowly the waters sank among the rocks, revealing pink tables of granite, strange growths of coral, polyp, and weed. Down, down, the waters went, whispering like the wind among the heads of the forest. There was one flat rock there, spread like a table, and the waters sucking down on the four weedy sides made them seem like cliffs. Then the sleeping leviathan breathed out, the waters rose, the weed streamed, and the water boiled over the table rock with a roar. There was no sense of the passage of waves; only this minute-long fall and rise and fall.

Ralph turned away to the red cliff. They were waiting behind him in the long grass, waiting to see what he would do. He noticed that the sweat in his palm was cool now; realized with surprise that he did not really expect to meet any beast and didn't know what he would do about it if he did.

He saw that he could climb the cliff but this was not necessary. The squareness of the rock allowed a sort of plinth round it, so that to the right, over the lagoon, one could inch along a ledge and turn the corner out of sight. It was easy going, and soon he was peering round the rock.

Nothing but what you might expect: pink, tumbled boulders with guano layered on them like icing; and a steep slope up to the shattered rocks that crowned the bastion.

A sound behind him made him turn. Jack was edging along the ledge.

"Couldn't let you do it on your own."

Ralph said nothing. He led the way over the rocks, inspected a sort of half-cave that held nothing more terrible than a clutch of rotten eggs, and at last sat down, looking round him and tapping the rock with the butt of his spear.

Jack was excited.

"What a place for a fort!"

A column of spray wetted them.

"No fresh water."

"What's that then?"

There was indeed a long green smudge half-way up the rock. They climbed up and tasted the trickle of water.

"You could keep a coconut shell there, filling all the time."

"Not me. This is a rotten place."

Side by side they scaled the last height to where the diminishing pile was crowned by the last broken rock. Jack struck the near one with his fist and it grated slightly.

"Do you remember—?"

Consciousness of the bad times in between came to them both. Jack talked quickly.

"Shove a palm trunk under that and if an enemy came—look!"

A hundred feet below them was the narrow causeway, then the stony ground, then the grass dotted with heads, and behind that the forest.

"One heave," cried Jack, exulting, "and—wheee—!"

He made a sweeping movement with his hand. Ralph looked toward the mountain.

"What's the matter?"

Ralph turned.

"Why?"

"You were looking—I don't know why."

"There's no signal now. Nothing to show."

"You're nuts on the signal."

The taut blue horizon encircled them, broken only by the mountain-top.

"That's all we've got."

He leaned his spear against the rocking stone and pushed back two handfuls of hair.

"We'll have to go back and climb the mountain. That's where they saw the beast."

"The beast won't be there."

"What else can we do?"

The others, waiting in the grass, saw Jack and Ralph unharmed and broke cover into the sunlight. They forgot the beast in the excitement of exploration. They swarmed across the bridge and soon were climbing and shouting. Ralph stood now, one hand against an enormous red block, a block large as a mill wheel that had been split off and hung, tottering. Somberly he watched the mountain. He clenched his fist and beat hammer-wise on the red wall at his right. His lips were tightly compressed and his eyes yearned beneath the fringe of hair.

"Smoke."

He sucked his bruised fist.

"Jack! Come on."

But Jack was not there. A knot of boys, making a great noise that he had not noticed, were heaving and pushing at a rock. As he turned, the base cracked and the whole mass toppled into the sea so that a thunderous plume of spray leapt half-way up the cliff.

"Stop it! Stop it!"

His voice struck a silence among them.

"Smoke."

A strange thing happened in his head. Something flittered there in front of his mind like a bat's wing, obscuring his idea.

"Smoke."

At once the ideas were back, and the anger.

"We want smoke. And you go wasting your time. You roll rocks."

Roger shouted.

"We've got plenty of time!"

Ralph shook his head.

"We'll go to the mountain."

The clamor broke out. Some of the boys wanted to go back to the beach. Some wanted to roll more rocks. The sun was bright and danger had faded with the darkness.

"Jack. The beast might be on the other side. You can lead again. You've been."

"We could go by the shore. There's fruit."

Bill came up to Ralph.

"Why can't we stay here for a bit?"

"That's right."

"Let's have a fort."

"There's no food here," said Ralph, "and no shelter. Not much fresh water."

"This would make a wizard fort."

"We can roll rocks—"

"Right onto the bridge—"

"I say we'll go on!" shouted Ralph furiously. "We've got to make certain. We'll go now."

"Let's stay here—"

"Back to the shelter—"

"I'm tired—"

"No!"

Ralph struck the skin off his knuckles. They did not seem to hurt.

"I'm chief. We've got to make certain. Can't you see the mountain? There's no signal showing. There may be a ship out there. Are you all off your rockers?"

Mutinously, the boys fell silent or muttering.

Jack led the way down the rock and across the bridge.

seven

SHADOWS AND TALL TREES

THE PIG-RUN KEPT CLOSE TO THE JUMBLE OF rocks that lay down by the water on the other side and Ralph was content to follow Jack along it. If you could shut your ears to the slow suck down of the sea and boil of the return, if you could forget how dun and unvisited were the ferny coverts on either side, then there was a chance that you might put the beast out of mind and dream for a while. The sun had swung over the vertical and the afternoon heat was closing in on the island. Ralph passed a message forward to Jack and when they next came to fruit the whole party stopped and ate.

Sitting, Ralph was aware of the heat for the first time that day. He pulled distastefully at his grey shirt and wondered whether he might undertake the adventure of washing it. Sitting under what seemed an unusual heat, even for this island, Ralph planned his toilet. He would like to have a pair of scissors and cut this hair—he flung the mass back—cut this filthy hair right back to half an inch. He would like to have a bath, a proper wallow with soap. He passed his tongue experimentally over his teeth and decided that a toothbrush would come in handy too. Then there were his nails—

Ralph turned his hand over and examined them. They were bitten down to the quick though he could not remember when he had restarted this habit nor any time when he indulged it.

"Be sucking my thumb next—"

He looked round, furtively. Apparently no one had heard. The hunters sat, stuffing themselves with this easy meal, trying to convince themselves that they got sufficient kick out of bananas and that other olive-grey, jelly-like fruit. With the memory of his sometime clean self as a standard, Ralph looked them over. They were dirty, not with the spectacular dirt of boys who have fallen into mud or been brought down hard on a rainy day. Not one of them was an obvious subject for a shower, and yet—hair, much too long, tangled here and there, knotted round a dead leaf or a twig; faces cleaned fairly well by the process of eating and sweating but marked in the less accessible angles with a kind of shadow; clothes, worn away, stiff like his own with sweat, put on, not for decorum or comfort but out of custom; the skin of the body, scurfy with brine—

He discovered with a little fall of the heart that these were the conditions he took as normal now and that he did not mind. He sighed and pushed away the stalk from which he had stripped the fruit. Already the hunters were stealing away to do their business in the woods or down by the rocks. He turned and looked out to sea.

Here, on the other side of the island, the view was utterly different. The filmy enchantments of mirage could not endure the cold ocean water and the horizon was hard, clipped blue. Ralph wandered down to the rocks. Down here, almost on a level with the sea, you could follow with your eye the ceaseless, bulging passage of the deep sea waves. They were miles wide, apparently not breakers or the banked ridges of shallow water. They traveled

the length of the island with an air of disregarding it and being set on other business; they were less a progress than a momentous rise and fall of the whole ocean. Now the sea would suck down, making cascades and waterfalls of retreating water, would sink past the rocks and plaster down the seaweed like shining hair: then, pausing, gather and rise with a roar, irresistibly swelling over point and outcrop, climbing the little cliff, sending at last an arm of surf up a gully to end a yard or so from him in fingers of spray.

Wave after wave, Ralph followed the rise and fall until something of the remoteness of the sea numbed his brain. Then gradually the almost infinite size of this water forced itself on his attention. This was the divider, the barrier. On the other side of the island, swathed at midday with mirage, defended by the shield of the quiet lagoon, one might dream of rescue; but here, faced by the brute obtuseness of the ocean, the miles of division, one was clamped down, one was helpless, one was condemned, one was—

Simon was speaking almost in his ear. Ralph found that he had rock painfully gripped in both hands, found his body arched, the muscles of his neck stiff, his mouth strained open.

"You'll get back to where you came from."

Simon nodded as he spoke. He was kneeling on one knee, looking down from a higher rock which he held with both hands; his other leg stretched down to Ralph's level.

Ralph was puzzled and searched Simon's face for a clue.

"It's so big, I mean—"

Simon nodded.

"All the same. You'll get back all right. I think so, anyway."

Some of the strain had gone from Ralph's body. He glanced at the sea and then smiled bitterly at Simon.

"Got a ship in your pocket?"

Simon grinned and shook his head.

"How do you know, then?"

When Simon was still silent Ralph said curtly, "You're batty."

Simon shook his head violently till the coarse black hair flew backwards and forwards across his face.

"No, I'm not. I just *think you'll get back all right.*"

For a moment nothing more was said. And then they suddenly smiled at each other.

Roger called from the coverts.

"Come and see!"

The ground was turned over near the pig-run and there were droppings that steamed. Jack bent down to them as though he loved them.

"Ralph—we need meat even if we are hunting the other thing."

"If you mean going the right way, we'll hunt."

They set off again, the hunters bunched a little by fear of the mentioned beast, while Jack quested ahead. They went more slowly than Ralph had bargained for; yet in a way he was glad to loiter, cradling his spear. Jack came up against some emergency of his craft and soon the procession stopped. Ralph leaned against a tree and at once the daydreams came swarming up. Jack was in charge of the hunt and there would be time to get to the mountain—

Once, following his father from Chatham to Devonport, they had lived in a cottage on the edge of the moors. In the succession of houses that Ralph had known, this one stood out with particular clarity because after that house he had been sent away to school. Mummy had still been with them and Daddy had come home every day. Wild ponies came to the stone wall at the bottom of the garden, and it had snowed. Just behind the cottage there was a sort of shed and you could lie up there, watching the flakes swirl past. You could see the damp spot where each flake died, then you could mark the first flake that lay down without melting and watch the whole ground turn white. You could go indoors when you were cold and look out of the window, past the bright copper kettle and the plate with the little blue men.

When you went to bed there was a bowl of cornflakes with sugar and cream. And the books—they stood on the shelf by the bed, leaning together with always two or three laid flat on top because he had not bothered to put them back properly. They were dog-eared and scratched. There was the bright, shining one about Topsy and Mopsy that he never read because it was about two girls; there was the one about the magician which you read with a kind of tied-down terror, skipping page twenty-seven with the awful picture of the spider; there was a book about people who had dug things up, Egyptian things; there was *The Boy's Book of Trains, The Boy's Book of Ships.* Vividly they came before him; he could have reached up and touched them, could feel the weight and slow slide with which *The Mammoth Book for Boys* would come out and slither down. . . . Everything was all right; everything was good-humored and friendly.

The bushes crashed ahead of them. Boys flung themselves wildly from the pig track and scrabbled in the creepers, screaming. Ralph saw Jack nudged aside and fall. Then there was a creature bounding along the pig track toward him, with tusks gleaming and an intimidating grunt. Ralph found he was able to measure the distance coldly and take aim. With the boar only five yards away, he flung the foolish wooden stick that he carried, saw it hit the great snout and hang there for a moment. The boar's note changed to a squeal and it swerved aside into the covert. The pig-run filled with shouting boys again, Jack came running back, and poked about in the undergrowth.

"Through here—"

"But he'd do us!"

"Through here, I said—"

The boar was floundering away from them. They found another pig-run parallel to the first and Jack raced away. Ralph was full of fright and apprehension and pride.

"I hit him! The spear stuck in—"

Now they came, unexpectedly, to an open space by the sea. Jack cast about on the bare rock and looked anxious.

"He's gone."

"I hit him," said Ralph again, "and the spear stuck in a bit."

He felt the need of witnesses.

"Didn't you see me?"

Maurice nodded.

"I saw you. Right bang on his snout—Wheee!"

Ralph talked on, excitedly.

"I hit him all right. The spear stuck in. I wounded him!"

He sunned himself in their new respect and felt that hunting was good after all.

"I walloped him properly. That was the beast, I think!" Jack came back.

"That wasn't the beast. That was a boar."

"I hit him."

"Why didn't you grab him? I tried—"

Ralph's voice ran up.

"But a boar!"

Jack flushed suddenly.

"You said he'd do us. What did you want to throw for? Why didn't you wait?

He held out his arm.

"Look."

He turned his left forearm for them all to see. On the outside was a rip; not much, but bloody.

"He did that with his tusks. I couldn't get my spear down in time."

Attention focused on Jack.

"That's a wound," said Simon, "and you ought to suck it. Like Berengaria."

Jack sucked.

"I hit him," said Ralph indignantly. "I hit him with my spear, I wounded him."

He tried for their attention.

"He was coming along the path. I threw, like this—"

Robert snarled at him. Ralph entered into the play and everybody laughed. Presently they were all jabbing at Robert who made mock rushes.

Jack shouted.

"Make a ring!"

The circle moved in and round. Robert squealed in mock terror, then in real pain.

"Ow! Stop it! You're hurting!"

The butt end of a spear fell on his back as he blundered among them.

"Hold him!"

They got his arms and legs. Ralph, carried away by a sudden thick excitement, grabbed Eric's spear and jabbed at Robert with it.

"Kill him! Kill him!"

All at once, Robert was screaming and struggling with the strength of frenzy. Jack had him by the hair and was brandishing his knife. Behind him was Roger, fighting to get close. The chant rose ritually, as at the last moment of a dance or a hunt.

"*Kill the pig! Cut his throat! Kill the pig! Bash him in!*"

Ralph too was fighting to get near, to get a handful of that brown, vulnerable flesh. The desire to squeeze and hurt was over-mastering.

Jack's arm came down; the heaving circle cheered and made pig-dying noises. Then they lay quiet, panting, listening to Robert's frightened snivels. He wiped his face with a dirty arm, and made an effort to retrieve his status.

"Oh, my bum!"

He rubbed his rump ruefully. Jack rolled over.

"That was a good game."

"Just a game," said Ralph uneasily. "I got jolly badly hurt at rugger once."

"We ought to have a drum," said Maurice, "then we could do it properly."

Ralph looked at him.

"How properly?"

"I dunno. You want a fire, I think, and a drum, and you keep time to the drum."

"You want a pig," said Roger, "like a real hunt."

"Or someone to pretend," said Jack. "You could get someone to dress up as a pig and then he could act—you know, pretend to knock me over and all that."

"You want a real pig," said Robert, still caressing his rump, "because you've got to kill him."

"Use a littlun," said Jack, and everybody laughed.

Ralph sat up.

"Well. We shan't find what we're looking for at this rate."

One by one they stood up, twitching rags into place.

Ralph looked at Jack.

"Now for the mountain."

"Shouldn't we go back to Piggy," said Maurice, "before dark?"

The twins nodded like one boy.

"Yes, that's right. Let's go up there in the morning."

Ralph looked out and saw the sea.

"We've got to start the fire again."

"You haven't got Piggy's specs," said Jack, "so you can't."

"Then we'll find out if the mountain's clear."

Maurice spoke, hesitating, not wanting to seem a funk.

"Supposing the beast's up there?"

Jack brandished his spear.

"We'll kill it."

The sun seemed a little cooler. He slashed with the spear.

"What are we waiting for?"

"I suppose," said Ralph, "if we keep on by the sea this way, we'll come out below the burnt bit and then we can climb the mountain.

Once more Jack led them along by the suck and heave of the blinding sea.

Once more Ralph dreamed, letting his skillful feet deal with the difficulties of the path. Yet here his feet seemed less skillful than before. For most of the way they were forced right down to the bare rock by the water and had to edge along between that and the dark luxuriance of the forest. There were little cliffs to be scaled, some to be used as paths, lengthy traverses where one used hands as well as feet. Here and there they could clamber over wave-wet rock, leaping across clear pools that the tide had left. They came to a gully that split the narrow foreshore like a defense. This seemed to have no bottom and they peered awe-

stricken into the gloomy crack where water gurgled. Then the
wave came back, the gully boiled before them and spray dashed
up to the very creeper so that the boys were wet and shrieking.
They tried the forest but it was thick and woven like a bird's
nest. In the end they had to jump one by one, waiting till the
water sank; and even so, some of them got a second drenching.
After that the rocks seemed to be growing impassable so they sat
for a time, letting their rags dry and watching the clipped outlines
of the rollers that moved so slowly past the island. They found
fruit in a haunt of bright little birds that hovered like insects.
Then Ralph said they were going too slowly. He himself climbed
a tree and parted the canopy, and saw the square head of the
mountain seeming still a great way off. Then they tried to hurry
along the rocks and Robert cut his knee quite badly and they
had to recognize that this path must be taken slowly if they were
to be safe. So they proceeded after that as if they were climbing
a dangerous mountain, until the rocks became an uncompromis-
ing cliff, overhung with impossible jungle and falling sheer into
the sea.

Ralph looked at the sun critically.

"Early evening. After tea-time, at any rate."

"I don't remember this cliff," said Jack, crestfallen, "so this
must be the bit of the coast I missed."

Ralph nodded.

"Let me think."

By now, Ralph had no self-consciousness in public thinking
but would treat the day's decisions as though he were playing
chess. The only trouble was that he would never be a very good
chess player. He thought of the littluns and Piggy. Vividly he
imagined Piggy by himself, huddled in a shelter that was silent
except for the sounds of nightmare.

"We can't leave the littluns alone with Piggy. Not all night."

The other boys said nothing but stood round, watching him.

"If we went back we should take hours."

Jack cleared his throat and spoke in a queer, tight voice.

"We mustn't let anything happen to Piggy, must we?"

Ralph tapped his teeth with the dirty point of Eric's spear.

"If we go across—"

He glanced round him.

"Someone's got to go across the island and tell Piggy we'll be back after dark."

Bill spoke, unbelieving.

"Through the forest by himself? Now?"

"We can't spare more than one."

Simon pushed his way to Ralph's elbow.

"I'll go if you like. I don't mind, honestly."

Before Ralph had time to reply, he smiled quickly, turned and climbed into the forest.

Ralph looked back at Jack, seeing him, infuriatingly, for the first time.

"Jack—that time you went the whole way to the castle rock."

Jack glowered.

"Yes?"

"You came along part of this shore—below the mountain, beyond there."

"Yes."

"And then?"

"I found a pig-run. It went for miles."

"So the pig-run must be somewhere in there."

Ralph nodded. He pointed at the forest.

Everybody agreed, sagely.

"All right then. We'll smash a way through till we find the pig-run."

He took a step and halted.

"Wait a minute though! Where does the pig-run go to?"

"The mountain," said Jack, "I told you." He sneered. "Don't you want to go to the mountain?"

Ralph sighed, sensing the rising antagonism, understanding that this was how Jack felt as soon as he ceased to lead.

"I was thinking of the light. We'll be stumbling about."

"We were going to look for the beast."

"There won't be enough light."

"I don't mind going," said Jack hotly. "I'll go when we get there. Won't you? Would you rather go back to the shelters and tell Piggy?"

Now it was Ralph's turn to flush but he spoke despairingly, out of the new understanding that Piggy had given him.

"Why do you hate me?"

The boys stirred uneasily, as though something indecent had been said. The silence lengthened.

Ralph, still hot and hurt, turned away first.

"Come on."

He led the way and set himself as by right to hack at the tangles. Jack brought up the rear, displaced and brooding.

The pig-track was a dark tunnel, for the sun was sliding quickly toward the edge of the world and in the forest shadows were never far to seek. The track was broad and beaten and they ran along at a swift trot. Then the roof of leaves broke up and they halted, breathing quickly, looking at the few stars that pricked round the head of the mountain.

"There you are."

The boys peered at each other doubtfully. Ralph made a decision.

"We'll go straight across to the platform and climb tomorrow."

They murmured agreement; but Jack was standing by his shoulder.

"If you're frightened of course—"

Ralph turned on him.

"Who went first on the castle rock?"

"I went too. And that was daylight."

"All right. Who wants to climb the mountain now?"

Silence was the only answer.

"Samneric? What about you?"

"We ought to go an' tell Piggy—"

"—yes, tell Piggy that—"

"But Simon went!"

"We ought to tell Piggy—in case—"

"Robert? Bill?"

They were going straight back to the platform now. Not, of course, that they were afraid—but tired.

Ralph turned back to Jack.

"You see?"

"I'm going up the mountain." The words came from Jack viciously, as though they were a curse. He looked at Ralph, his thin body tensed, his spear held as if he threatened him.

"I'm going up the mountain to look for the beast—now." Then the supreme sting, the casual, bitter word. "Coming?"

At that word the other boys forgot their urge to be gone and turned back to sample this fresh rub of two spirits in the dark. The word was too good, too bitter, too successfully daunting to be repeated. It took Ralph at low water when his nerve was relaxed for the return to the shelter and the still, friendly waters of the lagoon.

"I don't mind."

Astonished, he heard his voice come out, cool and casual, so that the bitterness of Jack's taunt fell powerless.

"If you don't mind, of course."

"Oh, not at all."

Jack took a step.

"Well then—"

Side by side, watched by silent boys, the two started up the mountain.

Ralph stopped.

"We're silly. Why should only two go? If we find anything, two won't be enough."

There came the sound of boys scuttling away. Astonishingly, a dark figure moved against the tide.

"Roger?"

"Yes."

"That's three, then."

Once more they set out to climb the slope of the mountain. The darkness seemed to flow round them like a tide. Jack, who had said nothing, began to choke and cough, and a gust of wind set all three spluttering. Ralph's eyes were blinded with tears.

"Ashes. We're on the edge of the burnt patch."

Their footsteps and the occasional breeze were stirring up small devils of dust. Now that they stopped again, Ralph had time while he coughed to remember how silly they were. If there was no beast—and almost certainly there was no beast—in that case, well and good; but if there was something waiting on top of the mountain—what was the use of three of them, handicapped by the darkness and carrying only sticks?

"We're being fools."

Out of the darkness came the answer.

"Windy?"

Irritably Ralph shook himself. This was all Jack's fault.

" 'Course I am. But we're still being fools."

"If you don't want to go on," said the voice sarcastically, "I'll go up by myself."

Ralph heard the mockery and hated Jack. The sting of ashes in his eyes, tiredness, fear, enraged him.

"Go on then! We'll wait here."

There was silence.

"Why don't you go? Are you frightened?"

A stain in the darkness, a stain that was Jack, detached itself and began to draw away.

"All right. So long."

The stain vanished. Another took its place.

Ralph felt his knee against something hard and rocked a charred trunk that was edgy to the touch. He felt the sharp cinders that had been bark push against the back of his knee and knew that Roger had sat down. He felt with his hands and lowered himself beside Roger, while the trunk rocked among invisible ashes. Roger, uncommunicative by nature, said nothing. He offered no opinion on the beast nor told Ralph why he had chosen to come on this mad expedition. He simply sat and rocked the trunk gently. Ralph noticed a rapid and infuriating tapping noise and realized that Roger was banging his silly wooden stick against something.

So they sat, the rocking, tapping, impervious Roger and Ralph, fuming; round them the close sky was loaded with stars, save where the mountain punched up a hole of blackness.

There was a slithering noise high above them, the sound of someone taking giant and dangerous strides on rock or ash. Then Jack found them, and was shivering and croaking in a voice they could just recognize as his.

"I saw a thing on top."

They heard him blunder against the trunk which rocked violently. He lay silent for a moment, then muttered.

"Keep a good lookout. It may be following."

A shower of ash pattered round them. Jack sat up.

"I saw a thing bulge on the mountain."

"You only imagined it," said Ralph shakily, "because nothing would bulge. Not any sort of creature."

Roger spoke; they jumped, for they had forgotten him.

"A frog."

Jack giggled and shuddered.

"Some frog. There was a noise too. A kind of 'plop' noise. Then the thing bulged."

Ralph surprised himself, not so much by the quality of his voice, which was even, but by the bravado of its intention.

"We'll go and look."

For the first time since he had first known Jack, Ralph could feel him hesitate.

"Now—?"

His voice spoke for him.

"Of course."

He got off the trunk and led the way across the clinking cinders up into the dark, and the others followed.

Now that his physical voice was silent the inner voice of reason, and other voices too, made themselves heard. Piggy was calling him a kid. Another voice told him not to be a fool; and the

darkness and desperate enterprise gave the night a kind of den-
tist's chair unreality.

As they came to the last slope, Jack and Roger drew near,
changed from the ink-stains to distinguishable figures. By common consent they stopped and crouched together. Behind them,
on the horizon, was a patch of lighter sky where in a moment
the moon would rise. The wind roared once in the forest and
pushed their rags against them.

Ralph stirred.

"Come on."

They crept forward, Roger lagging a little. Jack and Ralph
turned the shoulder of the mountain together. The glittering
lengths of the lagoon lay below them and beyond that a long
white smudge that was the reef. Roger joined them.

Jack whispered.

"Let's creep forward on hands and knees. Maybe it's asleep."

Roger and Ralph moved on, this time leaving Jack in the rear,
for all his brave words. They came to the flat top where the rock
was hard to hands and knees.

A creature that bulged.

Ralph put his hand in the cold, soft ashes of the fire and
smothered a cry. His hand and shoulder were twitching from the
unlooked-for contact. Green lights of nausea appeared for a moment and ate into the darkness. Roger lay behind him and Jack's
mouth was at his ear.

"Over there, where there used to be a gap in the rock. A sort
of hump—see?"

Ashes blew into Ralph's face from the dead fire. He could not
see the gap or anything else, because the green lights were opening
again and growing, and the top of the mountain was sliding
sideways.

Once more, from a distance, he heard Jack's whisper.

"Scared?"

Not scared so much as paralyzed; hung up there immovable on the top of a diminishing, moving mountain. Jack slid away from him, Roger bumped, fumbled with a hiss of breath, and passed onwards. He heard them whispering.

"Can you see anything?"

"There—"

In front of them, only three or four yards away, was a rock-like hump where no rock should be. Ralph could hear a tiny chattering noise coming from somewhere—perhaps from his own mouth. He bound himself together with his will, fused his fear and loathing into a hatred, and stood up. He took two leaden steps forward.

Behind them the sliver of moon had drawn clear of the horizon. Before them, something like a great ape was sitting asleep with its head between its knees. Then the wind roared in the forest, there was confusion in the darkness and the creature lifted its head, holding toward them the ruin of a face.

Ralph found himself taking giant strides among the ashes, heard other creatures crying out and leaping and dared the impossible on the dark slope; presently the mountain was deserted, save for the three abandoned sticks and the thing that bowed.

eight

GIFT FOR THE DARKNESS

Piggy looked up miserably from the dawn-pale beach to the dark mountain.

"Are you sure? Really sure, I mean?"

"I told you a dozen times now," said Ralph, "we saw it."

"D'you think we're safe down here?"

"How the hell should I know?"

Ralph jerked away from him and walked a few paces along the beach. Jack was kneeling and drawing a circular pattern in the sand with his forefinger. Piggy's voice came to them, hushed.

"Are you sure? Really?"

"Go up and see," said Jack contemptuously, "and good riddance."

"No fear."

"The beast had teeth," said Ralph, "and big black eyes."

He shuddered violently. Piggy took off his one round of glass and polished the surface.

"What we going to do?"

Ralph turned toward the platform. The conch glimmered among the trees, a white blob against the place where the sun would rise. He pushed back his mop.

"I don't know."

He remembered the panic flight down the mountainside.

"I don't think we'd ever fight a thing that size, honestly, you know. We'd talk but we wouldn't fight a tiger. We'd hide. Even Jack 'ud hide."

Jack still looked at the sand.

"What about my hunters?"

Simon came stealing out of the shadows by the shelters. Ralph ignored Jack's question. He pointed to the touch of yellow above the sea.

"As long as there's light we're brave enough. But then? And now that thing squats by the fire as though it didn't want us to be rescued—"

He was twisting his hands now, unconsciously. His voice rose.

"So we can't have a signal fire.... We're beaten."

A point of gold appeared above the sea and at once all the sky lightened.

"What about my hunters?"

"Boys armed with sticks."

Jack got to his feet. His face was red as he marched away. Piggy put on his one glass and looked at Ralph.

"Now you done it. You been rude about his hunters."

"Oh shut up!"

The sound of the inexpertly blown conch interrupted them. As though he were serenading the rising sun, Jack went on blowing till the shelters were astir and the hunters crept to the platform and the littluns whimpered as now they so frequently did. Ralph rose obediently, and Piggy, and they went to the platform.

"Talk," said Ralph bitterly, "talk, talk, talk."

He took the conch from Jack.

"This meeting—"

Jack interrupted him.

"I called it."

"If you hadn't called it I should have. You just blew the conch."

"Well, isn't that calling it?"

"Oh, take it! Go on—talk!"

Ralph thrust the conch into Jack's arms and sat down on the trunk.

"I've called an assembly," said Jack, "because of a lot of things. First, you know now, we've seen the beast. We crawled up. We were only a few feet away. The beast sat up and looked at us. I don't know what it does. We don't even know what it is—"

"The beast comes out of the sea—"

"Out of the dark—"

"Trees—"

"Quiet!" shouted Jack. "You, listen. The beast is sitting up there, whatever it is—"

"Perhaps it's waiting—"

"Hunting—"

"Yes, hunting."

"Hunting," said Jack. He remembered his age-old tremors in the forest. "Yes. The beast is a hunter. Only—shut up! The next thing is that we couldn't kill it. And the next is that Ralph said my hunters are no good."

"I never said that!"

"I've got the conch. Ralph thinks you're cowards, running away from the boar and the beast. And that's not all."

There was a kind of sigh on the platform as if everyone knew what was coming. Jack's voice went up, tremulous yet determined, pushing against the unco-operative silence.

"He's like Piggy. He says things like Piggy. He isn't a proper chief."

Jack clutched the conch to him.

"He's a coward himself."

For a moment he paused and then went on.

"On top, when Roger and me went on—he stayed back."

"I went too!"

"After."

The two boys glared at each other through screens of hair.

"I went on too," said Ralph, "then I ran away. So did you."

"Call me a coward then."

Jack turned to the hunters.

"He's not a hunter. He'd never have got us meat. He isn't a prefect and we don't know anything about him. He just gives orders and expects people to obey for nothing. All this talk—"

"All this talk!" shouted Ralph. "Talk, talk! Who wanted it? Who called the meeting?"

Jack turned, red in the face, his chin sunk back. He glowered up under his eyebrows.

"All right then," he said in tones of deep meaning, and menace, "all right."

He held the conch against his chest with one hand and stabbed the air with his index finger.

"Who thinks Ralph oughtn't to be chief?"

He looked expectantly at the boys ranged round, who had frozen. Under the palms there was deadly silence.

"Hands up," said Jack strongly, "whoever wants Ralph not to be chief?"

The silence continued, breathless and heavy and full of shame. Slowly the red drained from Jack's cheeks, then came back with a painful rush. He licked his lips and turned his head at an angle,

so that his gaze avoided the embarrassment of linking with another's eye.

"How many think——"

His voice tailed off. The hands that held the conch shook. He
cleared his throat, and spoke loudly.

"All right then."

He laid the conch with great care in the grass at his feet. The
humiliating tears were running from the corner of each eye.

"I'm not going to play any longer. Not with you."

Most of the boys were looking down now, at the grass or their
feet. Jack cleared his throat again.

"I'm not going to be a part of Ralph's lot——"

He looked along the right-hand logs, numbering the hunters
that had been a choir.

"I'm going off by myself. He can catch his own pigs. Anyone
who wants to hunt when I do can come too."

He blundered out of the triangle toward the drop to the white
sand.

"Jack!"

Jack turned and looked back at Ralph. For a moment he
paused and then cried out, high-pitched, enraged.

"——No!"

He leapt down from the platform and ran along the beach,
paying no heed to the steady fall of his tears; and until he dived
into the forest Ralph watched him.

Piggy was indignant.

"I been talking, Ralph, and you just stood there like——"

Softly, looking at Piggy and not seeing him, Ralph spoke to
himself.

"He'll come back. When the sun goes down he'll come." He looked at the conch in Piggy's hand.

"What?"

"Well there!"

Piggy gave up the attempt to rebuke Ralph. He polished his glass again and went back to his subject.

"We can do without Jack Merridew. There's others besides him on this island. But now we really got a beast, though I can't hardly believe it, we'll need to stay close to the platform; there'll be less need of him and his hunting. So now we can really decide on what's what."

"There's no help, Piggy. Nothing to be done."

For a while they sat in depressed silence. Then Simon stood up and took the conch from Piggy, who was so astonished that he remained on his feet. Ralph looked up at Simon.

"Simon? What is it this time?"

A half-sound of jeering ran round the circle and Simon shrank from it.

"I thought there might be something to do. Something we—"

Again the pressure of the assembly took his voice away. He sought for help and sympathy and chose Piggy. He turned half toward him, clutching the conch to his brown chest.

"I think we ought to climb the mountain."

The circle shivered with dread. Simon broke off and turned to Piggy who was looking at him with an expression of derisive incomprehension.

"What's the good of climbing up to this here beast when Ralph and the other two couldn't do nothing?"

Simon whispered his answer.

"What else is there to do?"

His speech made, he allowed Piggy to lift the conch out of his hands. Then he retired and sat as far away from the others as possible.

Piggy was speaking now with more assurance and with what, if the circumstances had not been so serious, the others would have recognized as pleasure.

"I said we could all do without a certain person. Now I say we got to decide on what can be done. And I think I could tell you what Ralph's going to say next. The most important thing on the island is the smoke and you can't have no smoke without a fire."

Ralph made a restless movement.

"No go, Piggy. We've got no fire. That thing sits up there—we'll have to stay here."

Piggy lifted the conch as though to add power to his next words.

"We got no fire on the mountain. But what's wrong with a fire down here? A fire could be built on them rocks. On the sand, even. We'd make smoke just the same."

"That's right!"

"Smoke!"

"By the bathing pool!"

The boys began to babble. Only Piggy could have the intellectual daring to suggest moving the fire from the mountain.

"So we'll have the fire down here," said Ralph. He looked about him. "We can build it just here between the bathing pool and the platform. Of course—"

He broke off, frowning, thinking the thing out, unconsciously tugging at the stub of a nail with his teeth.

"Of course the smoke won't show so much, not be seen so far away. But we needn't go near, near the—"

The others nodded in perfect comprehension. There would be no need to go near.

"We'll build the fire now."

The greatest ideas are the simplest. Now there was something to be done they worked with passion. Piggy was so full of delight and expanding liberty in Jack's departure, so full of pride in his contribution to the good of society, that he helped to fetch wood. The wood he fetched was close at hand, a fallen tree on the platform that they did not need for the assembly, yet to the others the sanctity of the platform had protected even what was useless there. Then the twins realized they would have a fire near them as a comfort in the night and this set a few littluns dancing and clapping hands.

The wood was not so dry as the fuel they had used on the mountain. Much of it was damply rotten and full of insects that scurried; logs had to be lifted from the soil with care or they crumbled into sodden powder. More than this, in order to avoid going deep into the forest the boys worked near at hand on any fallen wood no matter how tangled with new growth. The skirts of the forest and the scar were familiar, near the conch and the shelters and sufficiently friendly in daylight. What they might become in darkness nobody cared to think. They worked therefore with great energy and cheerfulness, though as time crept by there was a suggestion of panic in the energy and hysteria in the cheerfulness. They built a pyramid of leaves and twigs, branches and logs, on the bare sand by the platform. For the first time on the island, Piggy himself removed his one glass, knelt down and focused the sun on tinder. Soon there was a ceiling of smoke and a bush of yellow flame.

The littluns who had seen few fires since the first catastrophe became wildly excited. They danced and sang and there was a partyish air about the gathering.

At last Ralph stopped work and stood up, smudging the sweat from his face with a dirty forearm.

"We'll have to have a small fire. This one's too big to keep up."

Piggy sat down carefully on the sand and began to polish his glass.

"We could experiment. We could find out how to make a small hot fire and then put green branches on to make smoke. Some of them leaves must be better for that than the others."

As the fire died down so did the excitement. The littluns stopped singing and dancing and drifted away toward the sea or the fruit trees or the shelters.

Ralph dropped down in the sand.

"We'll have to make a new list of who's to look after the fire."

"If you can find 'em."

He looked round. Then for the first time he saw how few biguns there were and understood why the work had been so hard.

"Where's Maurice?"

Piggy wiped his glass again.

"I expect ... no, he wouldn't go into the forest by himself, would he?"

Ralph jumped up, ran swiftly round the fire and stood by Piggy, holding up his hair.

"But we've got to have a list! There's you and me and Samneric and—"

He would not look at Piggy but spoke casually.

"Where's Bill and Roger?"

Piggy leaned forward and put a fragment of wood on the fire.

"I expect they've gone. I expect they won't play either."

Ralph sat down and began to poke little holes in the sand. He was surprised to see that one had a drop of blood by it. He examined his bitten nail closely and watched the little globe of blood that gathered where the quick was gnawed away.

Piggy went on speaking.

"I seen them stealing off when we was gathering wood. They went that way. The same way as he went himself."

Ralph finished his inspection and looked up into the air. The sky, as if in sympathy with the great changes among them, was different today and so misty that in some places the hot air seemed white. The disc of the sun was dull silver as though it were nearer and not so hot, yet the air stifled.

"They always been making trouble, haven't they?"

The voice came near his shoulder and sounded anxious.

"We can do without 'em. We'll be happier now, won't we?"

Ralph sat. The twins came, dragging a great log and grinning in their triumph. They dumped the log among the embers so that sparks flew.

"We can do all right on our own, can't we?"

For a long time while the log dried, caught fire and turned red hot, Ralph sat in the sand and said nothing. He did not see Piggy go to the twins and whisper to them, nor how the three boys went together into the forest.

"Here you are."

He came to himself with a jolt. Piggy and the other two were by him. They were laden with fruit.

"I thought perhaps," said Piggy, "we ought to have a feast, kind of."

The three boys sat down. They had a great mass of the fruit with them and all of it properly ripe. They grinned at Ralph as he took some and began to eat.

"Thanks," he said. Then with an accent of pleased surprise—
"Thanks!"

"Do all right on our own," said Piggy. "It's them that haven't
no common sense that make trouble on this island. We'll make
a little hot fire—"

Ralph remembered what had been worrying him.

"Where's Simon?"

"I don't know."

"You don't think he's climbing the mountain?"

Piggy broke into noisy laughter and took more fruit.

"He might be." He gulped his mouthful. "He's cracked."

Simon had passed through the area of fruit trees but today the
littluns had been too busy with the fire on the beach and they
had not pursued him there. He went on among the creepers until
he reached the great mat that was woven by the open space and
crawled inside. Beyond the screen of leaves the sunlight pelted
down and the butterflies danced in the middle their unending
dance. He knelt down and the arrow of the sun fell on him. That
other time the air had seemed to vibrate with heat; but now it
threatened. Soon the sweat was running from his long coarse hair.
He shifted restlessly but there was no avoiding the sun. Presently
he was thirsty, and then very thirsty. He continued to sit.

Far off along the beach, Jack was standing before a small group
of boys. He was looking brilliantly happy.

"Hunting," he said. He sized them up. Each of them wore the
remains of a black cap and ages ago they had stood in two demure
rows and their voices had been the song of angels.

"We'll hunt. I'm going to be chief."

They nodded, and the crisis passed easily.

"And then—about the beast."

They moved, looked at the forest.

"I say this. We aren't going to bother about the beast."

He nodded at them.

"We're going to forget the beast."

"That's right!"

"Yes!"

"Forget the beast!"

If Jack was astonished by their fervor he did not show it.

"And another thing. We shan't dream so much down here. This is near the end of the island."

They agreed passionately out of the depths of their tormented private lives.

"Now listen. We might go later to the castle rock. But now I'm going to get more of the biguns away from the conch and all that. We'll kill a pig and give a feast." He paused and went on more slowly. "And about the beast. When we kill we'll leave some of the kill for it. Then it won't bother us, maybe."

He stood up abruptly.

"We'll go into the forest now and hunt."

He turned and trotted away and after a moment they followed him obediently.

They spread out, nervously, in the forest. Almost at once Jack found the dung and scattered roots that told of pig and soon the track was fresh. Jack signaled the rest of the hunt to be quiet and went forward by himself. He was happy and wore the damp darkness of the forest like his old clothes. He crept down a slope to rocks and scattered trees by the sea.

The pigs lay, bloated bags of fat, sensuously enjoying the shadows under the trees. There was no wind and they were unsuspicious; and practice had made Jack silent as the shadows. He stole away again and instructed his hidden hunters. Presently they all began to inch forward sweating in the silence and heat. Under the trees an ear flapped idly. A little apart from the rest, sunk in deep maternal bliss, lay the largest sow of the lot. She was black and pink; and the great bladder of her belly was fringed with a row of piglets that slept or burrowed and squeaked.

Fifteen yards from the drove Jack stopped, and his arm, straightening, pointed at the sow. He looked round in inquiry to make sure that everyone understood and the other boys nodded at him. The row of right arms slid back.

"Now!"

The drove of pigs started up; and at a range of only ten yards the wooden spears with fire-hardened points flew toward the chosen pig. One piglet, with a demented shriek, rushed into the sea trailing Roger's spear behind it. The sow gave a gasping squeal and staggered up, with two spears sticking in her fat flank. The boys shouted and rushed forward, the piglets scattered and the sow burst the advancing line and went crashing away through the forest.

"After her!"

They raced along the pig-track, but the forest was too dark and tangled so that Jack, cursing, stopped them and cast among the trees. Then he said nothing for a time but breathed fiercely so that they were awed by him and looked at each other in uneasy admiration. Presently he stabbed down at the ground with his finger.

"There—"

Before the others could examine the drop of blood, Jack had swerved off, judging a trace, touching a bough that gave. So he followed, mysteriously right and assured, and the hunters trod behind him.

He stopped before a covert.

"In there."

They surrounded the covert but the sow got away with the sting of another spear in her flank. The trailing butts hindered her and the sharp, cross-cut points were a torment. She blundered into a tree, forcing a spear still deeper; and after that any of the hunters could follow her easily by the drops of vivid blood. The afternoon wore on, hazy and dreadful with damp heat; the sow staggered her way ahead of them, bleeding and mad, and the hunters followed, wedded to her in lust, excited by the long chase and the dropped blood. They could see her now, nearly got up with her, but she spurted with her last strength and held ahead of them again. They were just behind her when she staggered into an open space where bright flowers grew and butterflies danced round each other and the air was hot and still.

Here, struck down by the heat, the sow fell and the hunters hurled themselves at her. This dreadful eruption from an unknown world made her frantic; she squealed and bucked and the air was full of sweat and noise and blood and terror. Roger ran round the heap, prodding with his spear whenever pigflesh appeared. Jack was on top of the sow, stabbing downward with his knife. Roger found a lodgment for his point and began to push till he was leaning with his whole weight. The spear moved forward inch by inch and the terrified squealing became a high-pitched scream. Then Jack found the throat and the hot blood spouted over his hands. The sow collapsed under them and they were heavy and fulfilled upon her. The butterflies still danced, preoccupied in the center of the clearing.

At last the immediacy of the kill subsided. The boys drew back, and Jack stood up, holding out his hands.

"Look."

He giggled and flicked them while the boys laughed at his reeking palms. Then Jack grabbed Maurice and rubbed the stuff over his cheeks. Roger began to withdraw his spear and boys noticed it for the first time. Robert stabilized the thing in a phrase which was received uproariously.

"Right up her ass!"

"Did you hear?"

"Did you hear what he said?"

"Right up her ass!"

This time Robert and Maurice acted the two parts; and Maurice's acting of the pig's efforts to avoid the advancing spear was so funny that the boys cried with laughter.

At length even this palled. Jack began to clean his bloody hands on the rock. Then he started work on the sow and paunched her, lugging out the hot bags of colored guts, pushing them into a pile on the rock while the others watched him. He talked as he worked.

"We'll take the meat along the beach. I'll go back to the platform and invite them to a feast. That should give us time."

Roger spoke.

"Chief—"

"Uh—?"

"How can we make a fire?"

Jack squatted back and frowned at the pig.

"We'll raid them and take fire. There must be four of you; Henry and you, Robert and Maurice. We'll put on paint and sneak up; Roger can snatch a branch while I say what I want. The rest of you can get this back to where we were. We'll build the fire there. And after that—"

He paused and stood up, looking at the shadows under the trees. His voice was lower when he spoke again.

"But we'll leave part of the kill for ..."

He knelt down again and was busy with his knife. The boys crowded round him. He spoke over his shoulder to Roger.

"Sharpen a stick at both ends."

Presently he stood up, holding the dripping sow's head in his hands.

"Where's that stick?"

"Here."

"Ram one end in the earth. Oh—it's rock. Jam it in that crack. There."

Jack held up the head and jammed the soft throat down on the pointed end of the stick which pierced through into the mouth. He stood back and the head hung there, a little blood dribbling down the stick.

Instinctively the boys drew back too; and the forest was very still. They listened, and the loudest noise was the buzzing of flies over the spilled guts.

Jack spoke in a whisper.

"Pick up the pig."

Maurice and Robert skewered the carcass, lifted the dead weight, and stood ready. In the silence, and standing over the dry blood, they looked suddenly furtive.

Jack spoke loudly.

"This head is for the beast. It's a gift."

The silence accepted the gift and awed them. The head remained there, dim-eyed, grinning faintly, blood blackening between the teeth. All at once they were running away, as fast as they could, through the forest toward the open beach.

Simon stayed where he was, a small brown image, concealed by the leaves. Even if he shut his eyes the sow's head still remained like an after-image. The half-shut eyes were dim with the infinite cynicism of adult life. They assured Simon that everything was a bad business.

"I know that."

Simon discovered that he had spoken aloud. He opened his eyes quickly and there was the head grinning amusedly in the strange daylight, ignoring the flies, the spilled guts, even ignoring the indignity of being spiked on a stick.

He looked away, licking his dry lips.

A gift for the beast. Might not the beast come for it? The head, he thought, appeared to agree with him. Run away, said the head silently, go back to the others. It was a joke really— why should you bother? You were just wrong, that's all. A little headache, something you ate, perhaps. Go back, child, said the head silently.

Simon looked up, feeling the weight of his wet hair, and gazed at the sky. Up there, for once, were clouds, great bulging towers that sprouted away over the island, grey and cream and copper-colored. The clouds were sitting on the land; they squeezed, produced moment by moment this close, tormenting heat. Even the butterflies deserted the open space where the obscene thing grinned and dripped. Simon lowered his head, carefully keeping his eyes shut, then sheltered them with his hand. There were no shadows under the trees but everywhere a pearly stillness, so that what was real seemed illusive and without definition. The pile of guts was a black blob of flies that buzzed like a saw. After a while these flies found Simon. Gorged, they alighted by his runnels of sweat and drank. They tickled under his nostrils and played leapfrog on his thighs. They were black and iridescent green and without number; and in front of Simon, the Lord of the Flies hung on his stick and grinned. At last Simon gave up

and looked back; saw the white teeth and dim eyes, the blood—
and his gaze was held by that ancient, inescapable recognition. In
Simon's right temple, a pulse began to beat on the brain.

Ralph and Piggy lay in the sand, gazing at the fire and idly
flicking pebbles into its smokeless heart.

"That branch is gone."

"Where's Samneric?"

"We ought to get some more wood. We're out of green
branches."

Ralph sighed and stood up. There were no shadows under the
palms on the platform; only this strange light that seemed to
come from everywhere at once. High up among the bulging
clouds thunder went off like a gun.

"We're going to get buckets of rain."

"What about the fire?"

Ralph trotted into the forest and returned with a wide spray
of green which he dumped on the fire. The branch crackled, the
leaves curled and the yellow smoke expanded.

Piggy made an aimless little pattern in the sand with his fingers.

"Trouble is, we haven't got enough people for a fire. You got
to treat Samneric as one turn. They do everything together—"

"Of course."

"Well, that isn't fair. Don't you see? They ought to do two
turns."

Ralph considered this and understood. He was vexed to find
how little he thought like a grownup and sighed again. The island
was getting worse and worse.

Piggy looked at the fire.

"You'll want another green branch soon."

Ralph rolled over.

"Piggy. What are we going to do?"

"Just have to get on without 'em."

"But—the fire."

He frowned at the black and white mess in which lay the unburnt ends of branches. He tried to formulate.

"I'm scared."

He saw Piggy look up; and blundered on.

"Not of the beast. I mean I'm scared of that too. But nobody else understands about the fire. If someone threw you a rope when you were drowning. If a doctor said take this because if you don't take it you'll die—you would, wouldn't you? I mean?"

" 'Course I would."

"Can't they see? Can't they understand? Without the smoke signal we'll die here? Look at that!"

A wave of heated air trembled above the ashes but without a trace of smoke.

"We can't keep one fire going. And they don't care. And what's more—" He looked intensely into Piggy's streaming face.

"What's more, *I* don't sometimes. Supposing I got like the others—not caring. What 'ud become of us?"

Piggy took off his glasses, deeply troubled.

"I dunno, Ralph. We just got to go on, that's all. That's what grownups would do."

Ralph, having begun the business of unburdening himself, continued.

"Piggy, what's wrong?"

Piggy looked at him in astonishment.

"Do you mean the—?"

"No, not it . . . I mean . . . what makes things break up like they do?"

Piggy rubbed his glasses slowly and thought. When he understood how far Ralph had gone toward accepting him he flushed pinkly with pride.

"I dunno, Ralph. I expect it's him."

"Jack?"

"Jack." A taboo was evolving round that word too. Ralph nodded solemnly.

"Yes," he said, "I suppose it must be."

The forest near them burst into uproar. Demoniac figures with faces of white and red and green rushed out howling, so that the littluns fled screaming. Out of the corner of his eyes, Ralph saw Piggy running. Two figures rushed at the fire and he prepared to defend himself but they grabbed half-burnt branches and raced away along the beach. The three others stood still, watching Ralph; and he saw that the tallest of them, stark naked save for the paint and a belt, was Jack.

Ralph had his breath back and spoke.

"Well?"

Jack ignored him, lifted his spear and began to shout.

"Listen all of you. Me and my hunters, we're living along the beach by a flat rock. We hunt and feast and have fun. If you want to join my tribe come and see us. Perhaps I'll let you join. Perhaps not."

He paused and looked round. He was safe from shame or self-consciousness behind the mask of his paint and could look at each of them in turn. Ralph was kneeling by the remains of the fire like a sprinter at his mark and his face was half-hidden by hair and smut. Samneric peered together round a palm tree at the edge of the forest. A littlun howled, creased and crimson, by the bathing pool and Piggy stood on the platform, the white conch gripped in his hands.

"Tonight we're having a feast. We've killed a pig and we've got meat. You can come and eat with us if you like."

Up in the cloud canyons the thunder boomed again. Jack and the two anonymous savages with him swayed, looking up, and then recovered. The littlun went on howling. Jack was waiting for something. He whispered urgently to the others.

"Go on—now!"

The two savages murmured. Jack spoke sharply.

"Go on!"

The two savages looked at each other, raised their spears together and spoke in time.

"The Chief has spoken."

Then the three of them turned and trotted away.

Presently Ralph rose to his feet, looking at the place where the savages had vanished. Samneric came, talking in an awed whisper.

"I thought it was—"

"—and I was—"

"—scared."

Piggy stood above them on the platform, still holding the conch.

"That was Jack and Maurice and Robert," said Ralph. "Aren't they having fun?"

"I thought I was going to have asthma."

"Sucks to your ass-mar."

"When I saw Jack I was sure he'd go for the conch. Can't think why."

The group of boys looked at the white shell with affectionate respect. Piggy placed it in Ralph's hand and the littluns, seeing the familiar symbol, started to come back.

"Not here."

He turned toward the platform, feeling the need for ritual. First went Ralph, the white conch cradled, then Piggy very grave, then the twins, then the littluns and the others.

"Sit down all of you. They raided us for fire. They're having fun. But the—"

Ralph was puzzled by the shutter that flickered in his brain. There was something he wanted to say; then the shutter had come down.

"But the—"

They were regarding him gravely, not yet troubled by any doubts about his sufficiency. Ralph pushed the idiot hair out of his eyes and looked at Piggy.

"But the . . . oh . . . the fire! Of course, the fire!"

He started to laugh, then stopped and became fluent instead.

"The fire's the most important thing. Without the fire we can't be rescued. I'd like to put on war-paint and be a savage. But we must keep the fire burning. The fire's the most important thing on the island, because, because—"

He paused again and the silence became full of doubt and wonder.

Piggy whispered urgently. "Rescue."

"Oh yes. Without the fire we can't be rescued. So we must stay by the fire and make smoke."

When he stopped no one said anything. After the many brilliant speeches that had been made on this very spot Ralph's remarks seemed lame, even to the littluns.

At last Bill held out his hands for the conch.

"Now we can't have the fire up there—because we can't have the fire up there—we need more people to keep it going. Let's go to this feast and tell them the fire's hard on the rest of us. And the hunting and all that, being savages I mean—it must be jolly good fun."

Samneric took the conch.

"That must be fun like Bill says—and as he's invited us—"

"—to a feast—"

"—meat—"

"—crackling—"

"—I could do with some meat—"

Ralph held up his hand.

"Why shouldn't we get our own meat?"

The twins looked at each other. Bill answered.

"We don't want to go in the jungle."

Ralph grimaced.

"He—you know—goes."

"He's a hunter. They're all hunters. That's different."

No one spoke for a moment, then Piggy muttered to the sand.

"Meat—"

The littluns sat, solemnly thinking of meat, and dribbling. Overhead the cannon boomed again and the dry palm fronds clattered in a sudden gust of hot wind.

"You are a silly little boy," said the Lord of the Flies, "just an ignorant, silly little boy."

Simon moved his swollen tongue but said nothing.

"Don't you agree?" said the Lord of the Flies. "Aren't you just a silly little boy?"

Simon answered him in the same silent voice.

"Well then," said the Lord of the Flies, "you'd better run off and play with the others. They think you're batty. You don't want Ralph to think you're batty, do you? You like Ralph a lot, don't you? And Piggy, and Jack?"

Simon's head was tilted slightly up. His eyes could not break away and the Lord of the Flies hung in space before him.

"What are you doing out here all alone? Aren't you afraid of me?"

Simon shook.

"There isn't anyone to help you. Only me. And I'm the Beast."

Simon's mouth labored, brought forth audible words.

"Pig's head on a stick."

"Fancy thinking the Beast was something you could hunt and kill!" said the head. For a moment or two the forest and all the other dimly appreciated places echoed with the parody of laughter. "You knew, didn't you? I'm part of you? Close, close, close! I'm the reason why it's no go? Why things are what they are?"

The laughter shivered again.

"Come now," said the Lord of the Flies. "Get back to the others and we'll forget the whole thing."

Simon's head wobbled. His eyes were half closed as though he were imitating the obscene thing on the stick. He knew that one of his times was coming on. The Lord of the Flies was expanding like a balloon.

"This is ridiculous. You know perfectly well you'll only meet me down there—so don't try to escape!"

Simon's body was arched and stiff. The Lord of the Flies spoke in the voice of a schoolmaster.

"This has gone quite far enough. My poor, misguided child, do you think you know better than I do?"

There was a pause.

"I'm warning you. I'm going to get angry. D'you see? You're not wanted. Understand? We are going to have fun on this island. Understand? We are going to have fun on this island! So don't try it on, my poor misguided boy, or else—"

Simon found he was looking into a vast mouth. There was blackness within, a blackness that spread.

"—Or else," said the Lord of the Flies, "we shall do you? See? Jack and Roger and Maurice and Robert and Bill and Piggy and Ralph. Do you. See?"

Simon was inside the mouth. He fell down and lost consciousness.

nine

A VIEW TO A
DEATH

OVER THE ISLAND THE BUILD-UP OF CLOUDS CON-
tinued. A steady current of heated air rose all day from
the mountain and was thrust to ten thousand feet; revolving
masses of gas piled up the static until the air was ready to explode.
By early evening the sun had gone and a brassy glare had taken
the place of clear daylight. Even the air that pushed in from the
sea was hot and held no refreshment. Colors drained from water
and trees and pink surfaces of rock, and the white and brown
clouds brooded. Nothing prospered but the flies who blackened
their lord and made the spilt guts look like a heap of glistening
coal. Even when the vessel broke in Simon's nose and the blood
gushed out they left him alone, preferring the pig's high flavor.

With the running of the blood Simon's fit passed into the
weariness of sleep. He lay in the mat of creepers while the evening
advanced and the cannon continued to play. At last he woke and
saw dimly the dark earth close by his cheek. Still he did not move
but lay there, his face sideways on the earth, his eyes looking
dully before him. Then he turned over, drew his feet under him
and laid hold of the creepers to pull himself up. When the creepers shook the flies exploded from the guts with a vicious note
and clamped back on again. Simon got to his feet. The light was

unearthly. The Lord of the Flies hung on his stick like a black ball.

Simon spoke aloud to the clearing.

"What else is there to do?"

Nothing replied. Simon turned away from the open space and crawled through the creepers till he was in the dusk of the forest. He walked drearily between the trunks, his face empty of expression, and the blood was dry round his mouth and chin. Only sometimes as he lifted the ropes of creeper aside and chose his direction from the trend of the land, he mouthed words that did not reach the air.

Presently the creepers festooned the trees less frequently and there was a scatter of pearly light from the sky down through the trees. This was the backbone of the island, the slightly higher land that lay beneath the mountain where the forest was no longer deep jungle. Here there were wide spaces interspersed with thickets and huge trees and the trend of the ground led him up as the forest opened. He pushed on, staggering sometimes with his weariness but never stopping. The usual brightness was gone from his eyes and he walked with a sort of glum determination like an old man.

A buffet of wind made him stagger and he saw that he was out in the open, on rock, under a brassy sky. He found his legs were weak and his tongue gave him pain all the time. When the wind reached the mountain-top he could see something happen, a flicker of blue stuff against brown clouds. He pushed himself forward and the wind came again, stronger now, cuffing the forest heads till they ducked and roared. Simon saw a humped thing suddenly sit up on the top and look down at him. He hid his face, and toiled on.

The flies had found the figure too. The life-like movement would scare them off for a moment so that they made a dark cloud round the head. Then as the blue material of the parachute collapsed the corpulent figure would bow forward, sighing, and the flies settle once more.

Simon felt his knees smack the rock. He crawled forward and soon he understood. The tangle of lines showed him the mechanics of this parody; he examined the white nasal bones, the teeth, the colors of corruption. He saw how pitilessly the layers of rubber and canvas held together the poor body that should be rotting away. Then the wind blew again and the figure lifted, bowed, and breathed foully at him. Simon knelt on all fours and was sick till his stomach was empty. Then he took the lines in his hands; he freed them from the rocks and the figure from the wind's indignity.

At last he turned away and looked down at the beaches. The fire by the platform appeared to be out, or at least making no smoke. Further along the beach, beyond the little river and near a great slab of rock, a thin trickle of smoke was climbing into the sky. Simon, forgetful of the flies, shaded his eyes with both hands and peered at the smoke. Even at that distance it was possible to see that most of the boys—perhaps all of the boys— were there. So they had shifted camp then, away from the beast. As Simon thought this, he turned to the poor broken thing that sat stinking by his side. The beast was harmless and horrible; and the news must reach the others as soon as possible. He started down the mountain and his legs gave beneath him. Even with great care the best he could do was a stagger.

"Bathing," said Ralph, "that's the only thing to do."

Piggy was inspecting the looming sky through his glass.

"I don't like them clouds. Remember how it rained just after we landed?"

"Going to rain again."

Ralph dived into the pool. A couple of littluns were playing at the edge, trying to extract comfort from a wetness warmer than blood. Piggy took off his glasses, stepped primly into the water and then put them on again. Ralph came to the surface and squirted a jet of water at him.

"Mind my specs," said Piggy. "If I get water on the glass I got to get out and clean 'em."

Ralph squirted again and missed. He laughed at Piggy, expecting him to retire meekly as usual and in pained silence. Instead, Piggy beat the water with his hands.

"Stop it!" he shouted. "D'you hear?"

Furiously he drove the water into Ralph's face.

"All right, all right," said Ralph. "Keep your hair on."

Piggy stopped beating the water.

"I got a pain in my head. I wish the air was cooler."

"I wish the rain would come."

"I wish we could go home."

Piggy lay back against the sloping sand side of the pool. His stomach protruded and the water dried on it. Ralph squinted up at the sky. One could guess at the movement of the sun by the progress of a light patch among the clouds. He knelt in the water and looked round.

"Where's everybody?"

Piggy sat up.

"P'raps they're lying in the shelter."

"Where's Samneric?"

"And Bill?"

Piggy pointed beyond the platform.

"That's where they've gone. Jack's party."

"Let them go," said Ralph, uneasily, "I don't care."

"Just for some meat—"

"And for hunting," said Ralph, wisely, "and for pretending to be a tribe, and putting on war-paint."

Piggy stirred the sand under water and did not look at Ralph.

"P'raps we ought to go too."

Ralph looked at him quickly and Piggy blushed.

"I mean—to make sure nothing happens."

Ralph squirted water again.

Long before Ralph and Piggy came up with Jack's lot, they could hear the party. There was a stretch of grass in a place where the palms left a wide band of turf between the forest and the shore. Just one step down from the edge of the turf was the white, blown sand of above high water, warm, dry, trodden. Below that again was a rock that stretched away toward the lagoon. Beyond was a short stretch of sand and then the edge of the water. A fire burned on the rock and fat dripped from the roasting pigmeat into the invisible flames. All the boys of the island, except Piggy, Ralph, Simon, and the two tending the pig, were grouped on the turf. They were laughing, singing, lying, squatting, or standing on the grass, holding food in their hands. But to judge by the greasy faces, the meat eating was almost done; and some held coconut shells in their hands and were drinking from them. Before the party had started a great log had been dragged into the center of the lawn and Jack, painted and garlanded, sat there like an idol. There were piles of meat on green leaves near him, and fruit, and coconut shells full of drink.

Piggy and Ralph came to the edge of the grassy platform; and the boys, as they noticed them, fell silent one by one till only the boy next to Jack was talking. Then the silence intruded even there and Jack turned where he sat. For a time he looked at them and the crackle of the fire was the loudest noise over the droning of the reef. Ralph looked away; and Sam, thinking that Ralph had turned to him accusingly, put down his gnawed bone with a nervous giggle. Ralph took an uncertain step, pointed to a palm tree, and whispered something inaudible to Piggy; and they both giggled like Sam. Lifting his feet high out of the sand, Ralph started to stroll past. Piggy tried to whistle.

At this moment the boys who were cooking at the fire suddenly hauled off a great chunk of meat and ran with it toward the grass. They bumped Piggy, who was burnt, and yelled and danced. Immediately, Ralph and the crowd of boys were united and relieved by a storm of laughter. Piggy once more was the center of social derision so that everyone felt cheerful and normal.

Jack stood up and waved his spear.

"Take them some meat."

The boys with the spit gave Ralph and Piggy each a succulent chunk. They took the gift, dribbling. So they stood and ate beneath a sky of thunderous brass that rang with the storm-coming.

Jack waved his spear again.

"Has everybody eaten as much as they want?"

There was still food left, sizzling on the wooden spits, heaped on the green platters. Betrayed by his stomach, Piggy threw a picked bone down on the beach and stooped for more.

Jack spoke again, impatiently.

"Has everybody eaten as much as they want?"

His tone conveyed a warning, given out of the pride of ownership, and the boys ate faster while there was still time. Seeing there was no immediate likelihood of a pause, Jack rose from the log that was his throne and sauntered to the edge of the grass. He looked down from behind his paint at Ralph and Piggy. They moved a little farther off over the sand and Ralph watched the fire as he ate. He noticed, without understanding, how the flames were visible now against the dull light. Evening was come, not with calm beauty but with the threat of violence.

Jack spoke.

"Give me a drink."

Henry brought him a shell and he drank, watching Piggy and Ralph over the jagged rim. Power lay in the brown swell of his forearms: authority sat on his shoulder and chattered in his ear like an ape.

"All sit down."

The boys ranged themselves in rows on the grass before him but Ralph and Piggy stayed a foot lower, standing on the soft sand. Jack ignored them for the moment, turned his mask down to the seated boys and pointed at them with the spear.

"Who's going to join my tribe?"

Ralph made a sudden movement that became a stumble. Some of the boys turned toward him.

"I gave you food," said Jack, "and my hunters will protect you from the beast. Who will join my tribe?"

"I'm chief," said Ralph, "because you chose me. And we were going to keep the fire going. Now you run after food—"

"You ran yourself!" shouted Jack. "Look at that bone in your hands!"

Ralph went crimson.

"I said you were hunters. That was your job."

Jack ignored him again.

"Who'll join my tribe and have fun?"

"I'm chief," said Ralph tremulously. "And what about the fire? And I've got the conch—"

"You haven't got it with you," said Jack, sneering. "You left it behind. See, clever? And the conch doesn't count at this end of the island—"

All at once the thunder struck. Instead of the dull boom there was a point of impact in the explosion.

"The conch counts here too," said Ralph, "and all over the island."

"What are you going to do about it then?"

Ralph examined the ranks of boys. There was no help in them and he looked away, confused and sweating. Piggy whispered.

"The fire—rescue."

"Who'll join my tribe?"

"I will."

"Me."

"I will."

"I'll blow the conch," said Ralph breathlessly, "and call an assembly."

"We shan't hear it."

Piggy touched Ralph's wrist.

"Come away. There's going to be trouble. And we've had our meat."

There was a blink of bright light beyond the forest and the thunder exploded again so that a littlun started to whine. Big drops of rain fell among them making individual sounds when they struck.

"Going to be a storm," said Ralph, "and you'll have rain like when we dropped here. Who's clever now? Where are your shelters? What are you going to do about that?"

The hunters were looking uneasily at the sky, flinching from the stroke of the drops. A wave of restlessness set the boys swaying and moving aimlessly. The flickering light became brighter and the blows of the thunder were only just bearable. The littluns began to run about, screaming.

Jack leapt on to the sand.

"Do our dance! Come on! Dance!"

He ran stumbling through the thick sand to the open space of rock beyond the fire. Between the flashes of lightning the air was dark and terrible; and the boys followed him, clamorously. Roger became the pig, grunting and charging at Jack, who side-stepped. The hunters took their spears, the cooks took spits, and the rest clubs of firewood. A circling movement developed and a chant. While Roger mimed the terror of the pig, the littluns ran and jumped on the outside of the circle. Piggy and Ralph, under the threat of the sky, found themselves eager to take a place in this demented but partly secure society. They were glad to touch the brown backs of the fence that hemmed in the terror and made it governable.

"Kill the beast! Cut his throat! Spill his blood!"

The movement became regular while the chant lost its first superficial excitement and began to beat like a steady pulse. Roger ceased to be a pig and became a hunter, so that the center of the ring yawned emptily. Some of the littluns started a ring on their own; and the complementary circles went round and round as though repetition would achieve safety of itself. There was the throb and stamp of a single organism.

The dark sky was shattered by a blue-white scar. An instant later the noise was on them like the blow of a gigantic whip. The chant rose a tone in agony.

"Kill the beast! Cut his throat! Spill his blood!"

Now out of the terror rose another desire, thick, urgent, blind.

"Kill the beast! Cut his throat! Spill his blood!"

Again the blue-white scar jagged above them and the sulphurous explosion beat down. The littluns screamed and blundered about, fleeing from the edge of the forest, and one of them broke the ring of biguns in his terror.

"Him! Him!"

The circle became a horseshoe. A thing was crawling out of the forest. It came darkly, uncertainly. The shrill screaming that rose before the beast was like a pain. The beast stumbled into the horseshoe.

"Kill the beast! Cut his throat! Spill his blood!"

The blue-white scar was constant, the noise unendurable. Simon was crying out something about a dead man on a hill.

"Kill the beast! Cut his throat! Spill his blood! Do him in!"

The sticks fell and the mouth of the new circle crunched and screamed. The beast was on its knees in the center, its arms folded over its face. It was crying out against the abominable noise something about a body on the hill. The beast struggled forward, broke the ring and fell over the steep edge of the rock to the sand by the water. At once the crowd surged after it, poured down the rock, leapt on to the beast, screamed, struck, bit, tore. There were no words, and no movements but the tearing of teeth and claws.

Then the clouds opened and let down the rain like a waterfall. The water bounded from the mountain-top, tore leaves and branches from the trees, poured like a cold shower over the struggling heap on the sand. Presently the heap broke up and figures staggered away. Only the beast lay still, a few yards from the sea. Even in the rain they could see how small a beast it was; and already its blood was staining the sand.

Now a great wind blew the rain sideways, cascading the water from the forest trees. On the mountain-top the parachute filled and moved; the figure slid, rose to its feet, spun, swayed down through a vastness of wet air and trod with ungainly feet the tops of the high trees; falling, still falling, it sank toward the beach and the boys rushed screaming into the darkness. The parachute took the figure forward, furrowing the lagoon, and bumped it over the reef and out to sea.

Toward midnight the rain ceased and the clouds drifted away, so that the sky was scattered once more with the incredible lamps of stars. Then the breeze died too and there was no noise save the drip and trickle of water that ran out of clefts and spilled down, leaf by leaf, to the brown earth of the island. The air was cool, moist, and clear; and presently even the sound of the water was still. The beast lay huddled on the pale beach and the stains spread, inch by inch.

The edge of the lagoon became a streak of phosphorescence which advanced minutely, as the great wave of the tide flowed. The clear water mirrored the clear sky and the angular bright constellations. The line of phosphorescence bulged about the sand grains and little pebbles; it held them each in a dimple of tension, then suddenly accepted them with an inaudible syllable and moved on.

Along the shoreward edge of the shallows the advancing clearness was full of strange, moonbeam-bodied creatures with fiery eyes. Here and there a larger pebble clung to its own air and was covered with a coat of pearls. The tide swelled in over the rain-pitted sand and smoothed everything with a layer of silver. Now it touched the first of the stains that seeped from the broken body and the creatures made a moving patch of light as they gathered at the edge. The water rose farther and dressed Simon's coarse hair with brightness. The line of his cheek silvered and the turn of his shoulder became sculptured marble. The strange attendant creatures, with their fiery eyes and trailing vapors, busied themselves round his head. The body lifted a fraction of an inch from the sand and a bubble of air escaped from the mouth with a wet plop. Then it turned gently in the water.

Somewhere over the darkened curve of the world the sun and moon were pulling, and the film of water on the earth planet was held, bulging slightly on one side while the solid core turned. The great wave of the tide moved farther along the island and the water lifted. Softly, surrounded by a fringe of inquisitive bright creatures, itself a silver shape beneath the steadfast constellations, Simon's dead body moved out toward the open sea.

THE SHELL AND
THE GLASSES

PIGGY EYED THE ADVANCING FIGURE CAREFULLY. Nowadays he sometimes found that he saw more clearly if he removed his glasses and shifted the one lens to the other eye; but even through the good eye, after what had happened, Ralph remained unmistakably Ralph. He came now out of the coconut trees, limping, dirty, with dead leaves hanging from his shock of yellow hair. One eye was a slit in his puffy cheek and a great scab had formed on his right knee. He paused for a moment and peered at the figure on the platform.

"Piggy? Are you the only one left?"

"There's some littluns."

"They don't count. No biguns?"

"Oh—Samneric. They're collecting wood."

"Nobody else?"

"Not that I know of."

Ralph climbed on to the platform carefully. The coarse grass was still worn away where the assembly used to sit; the fragile white conch still gleamed by the polished seat. Ralph sat down in the grass facing the chief's seat and the conch. Piggy knelt at his left, and for a long minute there was silence.

At last Ralph cleared his throat and whispered something.

Piggy whispered back.

"What you say?"

Ralph spoke up.

"Simon."

Piggy said nothing but nodded, solemnly. They continued to sit, gazing with impaired sight at the chief's seat and the glittering lagoon. The green light and the glossy patches of sunshine played over their befouled bodies.

At length Ralph got up and went to the conch. He took the shell caressingly with both hands and knelt, leaning against the trunk.

"Piggy."

"Uh?"

"What we going to do?"

Piggy nodded at the conch.

"You could—"

"Call an assembly?"

Ralph laughed sharply as he said the word and Piggy frowned.

"You're still chief."

Ralph laughed again.

"You are. Over us."

"I got the conch."

"Ralph! Stop laughing like that. Look, there ain't no need, Ralph! What's the others going to think?"

At last Ralph stopped. He was shivering.

"Piggy."

"Uh?"

"That was Simon."

"You said that before."

"Piggy."

"Uh?"

"That was murder."

"You stop it!" said Piggy, shrilly. "What good're you doing talking like that?"

He jumped to his feet and stood over Ralph.

"It was dark. There was that—that bloody dance. There was lightning and thunder and rain. We was scared!"

"I wasn't scared," said Ralph slowly, "I was—I don't know what I was."

"We was scared!" said Piggy excitedly. "Anything might have happened. It wasn't—what you said."

He was gesticulating, searching for a formula.

"Oh, Piggy!"

Ralph's voice, low and stricken, stopped Piggy's gestures. He bent down and waited. Ralph, cradling the conch, rocked himself to and fro.

"Don't you understand, Piggy? The things we did—"

"He may still be—"

"No."

"P'raps he was only pretending—"

Piggy's voice trailed off at the sight of Ralph's face.

"You were outside. Outside the circle. You never really came in. Didn't you see what we—what they did?"

There was loathing, and at the same time a kind of feverish excitement, in his voice.

"Didn't you see, Piggy?"

"Not all that well. I only got one eye now. You ought to know that, Ralph."

Ralph continued to rock to and fro.

"It was an accident," said Piggy suddenly, "that's what it was. An accident." His voice shrilled again. "Coming in the dark—he hadn't no business crawling like that out of the dark. He was batty. He asked for it." He gesticulated widely again. "It was an accident."

"You didn't see what they did—"

"Look, Ralph. We got to forget this. We can't do no good thinking about it, see?"

"I'm frightened. Of us. I want to go home. Oh God, I want to go home."

"It was an accident," said Piggy stubbornly, "and that's that."

He touched Ralph's bare shoulder and Ralph shuddered at the human contact.

"And look, Ralph"—Piggy glanced round quickly, then leaned close—"don't let on we was in that dance. Not to Samneric."

"But we were! All of us!"

Piggy shook his head.

"Not us till last. They never noticed in the dark. Anyway you said I was only on the outside."

"So was I," muttered Ralph, "I was on the outside too."

Piggy nodded eagerly.

"That's right. We was on the outside. We never done nothing, we never seen nothing."

Piggy paused, then went on.

"We'll live on our own, the four of us—"

"Four of us. We aren't enough to keep the fire burning."

"We'll try. See? I lit it."

Samneric came dragging a great log out of the forest. They dumped it by the fire and turned to the pool. Ralph jumped to his feet.

"Hi! You two!"

The twins checked a moment, then walked on.

"They're going to bathe, Ralph."

"Better get it over."

The twins were very surprised to see Ralph. They flushed and looked past him into the air.

"Hullo. Fancy meeting you, Ralph."

"We just been in the forest—"

"—to get wood for the fire—"

"—we got lost last night."

Ralph examined his toes.

"You got lost after the..."

Piggy cleaned his lens.

"After the feast," said Sam in a stifled voice. Eric nodded. "Yes, after the feast."

"We left early," said Piggy quickly, "because we were tired."

"So did we—"

"—very early—"

"—we were very tired."

Sam touched a scratch on his forehead and then hurriedly took his hand away. Eric fingered his split lip.

"Yes. We were very tired," repeated Sam, "so we left early. Was it a good—"

The air was heavy with unspoken knowledge. Sam twisted and the obscene word shot out of him. "—dance?"

Memory of the dance that none of them had attended shook all four boys convulsively.

"We left early."

When Roger came to the neck of land that joined the Castle Rock to the mainland he was not surprised to be challenged. He had reckoned, during the terrible night, on finding at least some of the tribe holding out against the horrors of the island in the safest place.

The voice rang out sharply from on high, where the diminishing crags were balanced one on another.

"Halt! Who goes there?"

"Roger."

"Advance, friend."

Roger advanced.

"You could see who I was."

"The chief said we got to challenge everyone."

Roger peered up.

"You couldn't stop me coming if I wanted."

"Couldn't I? Climb up and see."

Roger clambered up the ladder-like cliff.

"Look at this."

A log had been jammed under the topmost rock and another lever under that. Robert leaned lightly on the lever and the rock groaned. A full effort would send the rock thundering down to the neck of land. Roger admired.

"He's a proper chief, isn't he?"

Robert nodded.

"He's going to take us hunting."

He jerked his head in the direction of the distant shelters where a thread of white smoke climbed up the sky. Roger, sitting on the very edge of the cliff, looked somberly back at the island as he worked with his fingers at a loose tooth. His gaze settled on the top of the distant mountain and Robert changed the unspoken subject.

"He's going to beat Wilfred."

"What for?"

Robert shook his head doubtfully.

"I don't know. He didn't say. He got angry and made us tie Wilfred up. He's been"—he giggled excitedly—"he's been tied for hours, waiting—"

"But didn't the chief say why?"

"I never heard him."

Sitting on the tremendous rock in the torrid sun, Roger received this news as an illumination. He ceased to work at his tooth and sat still, assimilating the possibilities of irresponsible authority. Then, without another word, he climbed down the back of the rocks toward the cave and the rest of the tribe.

The chief was sitting there, naked to the waist, his face blocked out in white and red. The tribe lay in a semicircle before him. The newly beaten and untied Wilfred was sniffing noisily in the background. Roger squatted with the rest.

"Tomorrow," went on the chief, "we shall hunt again."

He pointed at this savage and that with his spear.

"Some of you will stay here to improve the cave and defend the gate. I shall take a few hunters with me and bring back meat. The defenders of the gate will see that the others don't sneak in."

A savage raised his hand and the chief turned a bleak, painted face toward him.

"Why should they try to sneak in, Chief?"

The chief was vague but earnest.

"They will. They'll try to spoil things we do. So the watchers at the gate must be careful. And then—"

The chief paused. They saw a triangle of startling pink dart out, pass along his lips and vanish again.

"—and then, the beast might try to come in. You remember how he crawled—"

The semicircle shuddered and muttered in agreement.

"He came—disguised. He may come again even though we gave him the head of our kill to eat. So watch; and be careful."

Stanley lifted his forearm off the rock and held up an inter-rogative finger.

"Well?"

"But didn't we, didn't we—?"

He squirmed and looked down.

"No!"

In the silence that followed, each savage flinched away from his individual memory.

"No! How could we—kill—it?"

Half-relieved, half-daunted by the implication of further ter-rors, the savages murmured again.

"So leave the mountain alone," said the chief, solemnly, "and give it the head if you go hunting."

Stanley flicked his finger again.

"I expect the beast disguised itself."

"Perhaps," said the chief. A theological speculation presented itself. "We'd better keep on the right side of him, anyhow. You can't tell what he might do."

The tribe considered this; and then were shaken, as if by a flow of wind. The chief saw the effect of his words and stood abruptly.

"But tomorrow we'll hunt and when we've got meat we'll have a feast—"

Bill put up his hand.

"Chief."

"Yes?"

"What'll we use for lighting the fire?"

The chief's blush was hidden by the white and red clay. Into his uncertain silence the tribe spilled their murmur once more. Then the chief held up his hand.

"We shall take fire from the others. Listen. Tomorrow we'll hunt and get meat. Tonight I'll go along with two hunters— who'll come?"

Maurice and Roger put up their hands.

"Maurice—"

"Yes, Chief?"

"Where was their fire?"

"Back at the old place by the fire rock."

The chief nodded.

"The rest of you can go to sleep as soon as the sun sets. But us three, Maurice, Roger and me, we've got work to do. We'll leave just before sunset—"

Maurice put up his hand.

"But what happens if we meet—"

The chief waved his objection aside.

"We'll keep along by the sands. Then if he comes we'll do our, our dance again."

"Only the three of us?"

Again the murmur swelled and died away.

Piggy handed Ralph his glasses and waited to receive back his sight. The wood was damp; and this was the third time they had lighted it. Ralph stood back, speaking to himself.

"We don't want another night without fire."

He looked round guiltily at the three boys standing by. This was the first time he had admitted the double function of the fire. Certainly one was to send up a beckoning column of smoke; but the other was to be a hearth now and a comfort until they slept. Eric breathed on the wood till it glowed and sent out a little flame. A billow of white and yellow smoke reeked up. Piggy took back his glasses and looked at the smoke with pleasure.

"If only we could make a radio!"

"Or a plane—"

"—or a boat."

Ralph dredged in his fading knowledge of the world.

"We might get taken prisoner by the Reds."

Eric pushed back his hair.

"They'd be better than—"

He would not name people and Sam finished the sentence for him by nodding along the beach.

Ralph remembered the ungainly figure on a parachute.

"He said something about a dead man." He flushed painfully at this admission that he had been present at the dance. He made urging motions at the smoke and with his body. "Don't stop— go on up!"

"Smoke's getting thinner."

"We need more wood already, even when it's wet."

"My asthma—"

The response was mechanical.

"Sucks to your ass-mar."

"If I pull logs, I get my asthma bad. I wish I didn't, Ralph, but there it is."

The three boys went into the forest and fetched armfuls of rotten wood. Once more the smoke rose, yellow and thick.

"Let's get something to eat."

Together they went to the fruit trees, carrying their spears, saying little, cramming in haste. When they came out of the forest again the sun was setting and only embers glowed in the fire, and there was no smoke.

"I can't carry any more wood," said Eric. "I'm tired."

Ralph cleared his throat.

"We kept the fire going up there."

"Up there it was small. But this has got to be a big one."

Ralph carried a fragment to the fire and watched the smoke that drifted into the dusk.

"We've got to keep it going."

Eric flung himself down.

"I'm too tired. And what's the good?"

"Eric!" cried Ralph in a shocked voice. "Don't talk like that!"

Sam knelt by Eric.

"Well—what *is* the good?"

Ralph tried indignantly to remember. There was something good about a fire. Something overwhelmingly good.

"Ralph's told you often enough," said Piggy moodily. "How else are we going to be rescued?"

"Of course! If we don't make smoke—"

He squatted before them in the crowding dusk.

"Don't you understand? What's the good of wishing for radios and boats?"

He held out his hand and twisted the fingers into a fist.

"There's only one thing we can do to get out of this mess. Anyone can play at hunting, anyone can get us meat—"

He looked from face to face. Then, at the moment of greatest passion and conviction, that curtain flapped in his head and he forgot what he had been driving at. He knelt there, his fist clenched, gazing solemnly from one to the other. Then the curtain whisked back.

"Oh, yes. So we've got to make smoke; and more smoke—"

"But we can't keep it going! Look at that!"

The fire was dying on them.

"Two to mind the fire," said Ralph, half to himself, "that's twelve hours a day."

"We can't get any more wood, Ralph—"

"—not in the dark—"

"—not at night—"

"We can light it every morning," said Piggy. "Nobody ain't going to see smoke in the dark."

Sam nodded vigorously.

"It was different when the fire was—"

"—up there."

Ralph stood up, feeling curiously defenseless with the darkness pressing in.

"Let the fire go then, for tonight."

He led the way to the first shelter, which still stood, though battered. The bed leaves lay within, dry and noisy to the touch. In the next shelter a littlun was talking in his sleep. The four biguns crept into the shelter and burrowed under the leaves. The twins lay together and Ralph and Piggy at the other end. For a while there was the continual creak and rustle of leaves as they tried for comfort.

"Piggy."

"Yeah?"

"All right?"

"S'pose so."

At length, save for an occasional rustle, the shelter was silent. An oblong of blackness relieved with brilliant spangles hung before them and there was the hollow sound of surf on the reef. Ralph settled himself for his nightly game of supposing. . . .

Supposing they could be transported home by jet, then before morning they would land at that big airfield in Wiltshire. They would go by car; no, for things to be perfect they would go by train; all the way down to Devon and take that cottage again. Then at the foot of the garden the wild ponies would come and look over the wall. . . .

Ralph turned restlessly in the leaves. Dartmoor was wild and so were the ponies. But the attraction of wildness had gone.

His mind skated to a consideration of a tamed town where savagery could not set foot. What could be safer than the bus center with its lamps and wheels?

All at once, Ralph was dancing round a lamp standard. There was a bus crawling out of the bus station, a strange bus. . . .

"Ralph! Ralph!"

"What is it?"

"Don't make a noise like that—"

"Sorry."

From the darkness of the further end of the shelter came a dreadful moaning and they shattered the leaves in their fear. Sam and Eric, locked in an embrace, were fighting each other.

"Sam! Sam!"

"Hey—Eric!"

Presently all was quiet again.

Piggy spoke softly to Ralph.

"We got to get out of this."

"What d'you mean?"

"Get rescued."

For the first time that day, and despite the crowding blackness, Ralph sniggered.

"I mean it," whispered Piggy. "If we don't get home soon we'll be barmy."

"Round the bend."

"Bomb happy."

"Crackers."

Ralph pushed the damp tendrils of hair out of his eyes.

"You write a letter to your auntie."

Piggy considered this solemnly.

"I don't know where she is now. And I haven't got an envelope and a stamp. An' there isn't a mailbox. Or a postman."

The success of his tiny joke overcame Ralph. His sniggers became uncontrollable, his body jumped and twitched.

Piggy rebuked him with dignity.

"I haven't said anything all that funny."

Ralph continued to snigger though his chest hurt. His twitch-ings exhausted him till he lay, breathless and woebegone, waiting for the next spasm. During one of these pauses he was ambushed by sleep.

"Ralph! You been making a noise again. Do be quiet, Ralph—because."

Ralph heaved over among the leaves. He had reason to be thankful that his dream was broken, for the bus had been nearer and more distinct.

"Why—because?"

"Be quiet—and listen."

Ralph lay down carefully, to the accompaniment of a long sigh from the leaves. Eric moaned something and then lay still. The darkness, save for the useless oblong of stars, was blanket-thick.

"I can't hear anything."

"There's something moving outside."

Ralph's head prickled. The sound of his blood drowned all else and then subsided.

"I still can't hear anything."

"Listen. Listen for a long time."

Quite clearly and emphatically, and only a yard or so away from the back of the shelter, a stick cracked. The blood roared again in Ralph's ears, confused images chased each other through his mind. A composite of these things was prowling round the shelters. He could feel Piggy's head against his shoulder and the convulsive grip of a hand.

"Ralph! Ralph!"

"Shut up and listen."

Desperately, Ralph prayed that the beast would prefer littluns. A voice whispered horribly outside.

"Piggy—Piggy—"

"It's come!" gasped Piggy. "It's real!"

He clung to Ralph and reached to get his breath.

"Piggy, come outside. I want you, Piggy."

Ralph's mouth was against Piggy's ear.

"Don't say anything."

"Piggy—where are you, Piggy?"

Something brushed against the back of the shelter. Piggy kept still for a moment, then he had his asthma. He arched his back and crashed among the leaves with his legs. Ralph rolled away from him.

Then there was a vicious snarling in the mouth of the shelter and the plunge and thump of living things. Someone tripped over Ralph and Piggy's corner became a complication of snarls and crashes and flying limbs. Ralph hit out; then he and what seemed like a dozen others were rolling over and over, hitting, biting, scratching. He was torn and jolted, found fingers in his mouth and bit them. A fist withdrew and came back like a piston, so that the whole shelter exploded into light. Ralph twisted sideways on top of a writhing body and felt hot breath on his cheek. He began to pound the mouth below him, using his clenched fist as a hammer; he hit with more and more passionate hysteria as the face became slippery. A knee jerked up between his legs and he fell sideways, busying himself with his pain, and the fight rolled over him. Then the shelter collapsed with smothering finality; and the anonymous shapes fought their way out and through. Dark figures drew themselves out of the wreckage and flitted away, till the screams of the littluns and Piggy's gasps were once more audible.

Ralph called out in a quavering voice.

"All you littluns, go to sleep. We've had a fight with the others. Now go to sleep."

Samneric came close and peered at Ralph.

"Are you two all right?"

"I think so—"

"—I got busted."

"So did I. How's Piggy?"

They hauled Piggy clear of the wreckage and leaned him against a tree. The night was cool and purged of immediate terror. Piggy's breathing was a little easier.

"Did you get hurt, Piggy?"

"Not much."

"That was Jack and his hunters," said Ralph bitterly. "Why can't they leave us alone?"

"We gave them something to think about," said Sam. Honesty compelled him to go on. "At least you did. I got mixed up with myself in a corner."

"I gave one of 'em what for," said Ralph, "I smashed him up all right. He won't want to come and fight us again in a hurry."

"So did I," said Eric. "When I woke up one was kicking me in the face. I got an awful bloody face, I think, Ralph. But I did him in the end."

"What did you do?"

"I got my knee up," said Eric with simple pride, "and I hit him with it in the pills. You should have heard him holler! He won't come back in a hurry either. So we didn't do too badly."

Ralph moved suddenly in the dark; but then he heard Eric working his mouth.

"What's the matter?"

"Jus' a tooth loose."

Piggy drew up his legs.

"You all right, Piggy?"

"I thought they wanted the conch."

Ralph trotted down the pale beach and jumped on to the platform. The conch still glimmered by the chief's seat. He gazed for a moment or two, then went back to Piggy.

"They didn't take the conch."

"I know. They didn't come for the conch. They came for something else. Ralph—what am I going to do?"

Far off along the bowstave of beach, three figures trotted toward the Castle Rock. They kept away from the forest and down by the water. Occasionally they sang softly; occasionally they turned cartwheels down by the moving streak of phosphorescence. The chief led then, trotting steadily, exulting in his achievement. He was a chief now in truth; and he made stabbing motions with his spear. From his left hand dangled Piggy's broken glasses.

eleven

CASTLE
ROCK

IN THE SHORT CHILL OF DAWN THE FOUR BOYS gathered round the black smudge where the fire had been, while Ralph knelt and blew. Grey, feathery ashes scurried hither and thither at his breath but no spark shone among them. The twins watched anxiously and Piggy sat expressionless behind the luminous wall of his myopia. Ralph continued to blow till his ears were singing with the effort, but then the first breeze of dawn took the job off his hands and blinded him with ashes. He squatted back, swore, and rubbed water out of his eyes.

"No use."

Eric looked down at him through a mask of dried blood. Piggy peered in the general direction of Ralph.

"'Course it's no use, Ralph. Now we got no fire."

Ralph brought his face within a couple of feet of Piggy's.

"Can you see me?"

"A bit."

Ralph allowed the swollen flap of his cheek to close his eye again.

"They've got our fire."

Rage shrilled his voice.

"They stole it!"

"That's them," said Piggy. "They blinded me. See? That's Jack Merridew. You call an assembly, Ralph, we got to decide what to do."

"An assembly for only us?"

"It's all we got. Sam—let me hold on to you."

They went toward the platform.

"Blow the conch," said Piggy. "Blow as loud as you can."

The forests re-echoed; and birds lifted, crying out of the tree-tops, as on that first morning ages ago. Both ways the beach was deserted. Some littluns came from the shelters. Ralph sat down on the polished trunk and the three others stood before him. He nodded, and Samneric sat down on the right. Ralph pushed the conch into Piggy's hands. He held the shining thing carefully and blinked at Ralph.

"Go on, then."

"I just take the conch to say this. I can't see no more and I got to get my glasses back. Awful things has been done on this island. I voted for you for chief. He's the only one who ever got anything done. So now you speak, Ralph, and tell us what. Or else—"

Piggy broke off, sniveling. Ralph took back the conch as he sat down.

"Just an ordinary fire. You'd think we could do that, wouldn't you? Just a smoke signal so we can be rescued. Are we savages or what? Only now there's no signal going up. Ships may be passing. Do you remember how he went hunting and the fire went out and a ship passed by? And they all think he's best as chief. Then there was, there was...that's his fault, too. If it hadn't been for him it would never have happened. Now Piggy can't see, and they came, stealing"—Ralph's voice ran up—"at night, in darkness, and stole our fire. They stole it. We'd have given them fire if they'd asked. But they stole it and the signal's out and we can't ever be rescued. Don't you see what I mean? We'd have given them fire for themselves only they stole it. I—"

He paused lamely as the curtain flickered in his brain. Piggy held out his hands for the conch.

"What you goin' to do, Ralph? This is jus' talk without deciding. I want my glasses."

"I'm trying to think. Supposing we go, looking like we used to, washed and hair brushed—after all we aren't savages really and being rescued isn't a game—"

He opened the flap of his cheek and looked at the twins.

"We could smarten up a bit and then go—"

"We ought to take spears," said Sam. "Even Piggy."

"—because we may need them."

"You haven't got the conch!"

Piggy held up the shell.

"You can take spears if you want but I shan't. What's the good? I'll have to be led like a dog, anyhow. Yes, laugh. Go on, laugh. There's them on this island as would laugh at anything. And what happened? What's grownups goin' to think? Young Simon was murdered. And there was that other kid what had a mark on his face. Who's seen him since we first come here?"

"Piggy! Stop a minute!"

"I got the conch. I'm going to that Jack Merridew an' tell him, I am."

"You'll get hurt."

"What can he do more than he has? I'll tell him what's what. You let me carry the conch, Ralph. I'll show him the one thing he hasn't got."

Piggy paused for a moment and peered round at the dim figures. The shape of the old assembly, trodden in the grass, listened to him.

"I'm going to him with this conch in my hands. I'm going to hold it out. Look, I'm goin' to say, you're stronger than I am and you haven't got asthma. You can see, I'm goin' to say, and with both eyes. But I don't ask for my glasses back, not as a favor. I don't ask you to be a sport, I'll say, not because you're strong, but because what's right's right. Give me my glasses, I'm going to say—you got to!"

Piggy ended, flushed and trembling. He pushed the conch quickly into Ralph's hands as though in a hurry to be rid of it and wiped the tears from his eyes. The green light was gentle about them and the conch lay at Ralph's feet, fragile and white. A single drop of water that had escaped Piggy's fingers now flashed on the delicate curve like a star.

At last Ralph sat up straight and drew back his hair.

"All right. I mean—you can try if you like. We'll go with you."

"He'll be painted," said Sam, timidly. "You know how he'll be—"

"—he won't think much of us—"

"—if he gets waxy we've had it—"

Ralph scowled at Sam. Dimly he remembered something Simon had said to him once, by the rocks.

"Don't be silly," he said. And then he added quickly, "Let's go."

He held out the conch to Piggy who flushed, this time with pride.

"You must carry it."

"When we're ready I'll carry it—"

Piggy sought in his mind for words to convey his passionate willingness to carry the conch against all odds.

"I don't mind. I'll be glad, Ralph, only I'll have to be led."

Ralph put the conch back on the shining log.

"We better eat and then get ready."

They made their way to the devastated fruit trees. Piggy was helped to his food and found some by touch. While they ate, Ralph thought of the afternoon.

"We'll be like we were. We'll wash—"

Sam gulped down a mouthful and protested.

"But we bathe every day!"

Ralph looked at the filthy objects before him and sighed.

"We ought to comb our hair. Only it's too long."

"I've got both socks left in the shelter," said Eric, "so we could pull them over our heads like caps, sort of."

"We could find some stuff," said Piggy, "and tie your hair back."

"Like a girl!"

"No. 'Course not."

"Then we must go as we are," said Ralph, "and they won't be any better."

Eric made a detaining gesture.

"But they'll be painted! You know how it is."

The others nodded. They understood only too well the liberation into savagery that the concealing paint brought.

"Well, we won't be painted," said Ralph, "because we aren't savages."

Samneric looked at each other.

"All the same—"

Ralph shouted.

"No paint!"

He tried to remember.

"Smoke," he said, "we want smoke."

He turned on the twins fiercely.

"I said 'smoke'! We've got to have smoke."

There was silence, except for the multitudinous murmur of the bees. As last Piggy spoke, kindly.

" 'Course we have. 'Cos the smoke's a signal and we can't be rescued if we don't have smoke."

"I knew that!" shouted Ralph. He pulled his arm away from Piggy. "Are you suggesting—?"

"I'm jus' saying what you always say," said Piggy hastily. "I'd thought for a moment—"

"I hadn't," said Ralph loudly. "I knew it all the time. I hadn't forgotten."

Piggy nodded propitiatingly.

"You're chief, Ralph. You remember everything."

"I hadn't forgotten."

" 'Course not."

The twins were examining Ralph curiously, as though they were seeing him for the first time.

They set off along the beach in formation. Ralph went first, limping a little, his spear carried over one shoulder. He saw things partially, through the tremble of the heat haze over the flashing sands, and his own long hair and injuries. Behind him came the twins, worried now for a while but full of unquenchable vitality. They said little but trailed the butts of their wooden spears; for Piggy had found that, by looking down and shielding his tired sight from the sun, he could just see these moving along the sand. He walked between the trailing butts, therefore, the conch held carefully between his two hands. The boys made a compact little group that moved over the beach, four plate-like shadows dancing and mingling beneath them. There was no sign left of the storm, and the beach was swept clean like a blade that has been scoured.

The sky and the mountain were at an immense distance, shimmering in the heat; and the reef was lifted by mirage, floating in a kind of silver pool halfway up the sky.

They passed the place where the tribe had danced. The charred sticks still lay on the rocks where the rain had quenched them but the sand by the water was smooth again. They passed this in silence. No one doubted that the tribe would be found at the Castle Rock and when they came in sight of it they stopped with one accord. The densest tangle on the island, a mass of twisted stems, black and green and impenetrable, lay on their left and tall grass swayed before them. Now Ralph went forward.

Here was the crushed grass where they had all lain when he had gone to prospect. There was the neck of land, the ledge skirting the rock, up there were the red pinnacles.

Sam touched his arm.

"Smoke."

There was a tiny smudge of smoke wavering into the air on the other side of the rock.

"Some fire—I don't think."

Ralph turned.

"What are we hiding for?"

He stepped through the screen of grass on to the little open space that led to the narrow neck.

"You two follow behind. I'll go first, then Piggy a pace behind me. Keep your spears ready."

Piggy peered anxiously into the luminous veil that hung between him and the world.

"Is it safe? Ain't there a cliff? I can hear the sea."

"You keep right close to me."

Ralph moved forward on to the neck. He kicked a stone and it bounded into the water. Then the sea sucked down, revealing a red, weedy square forty feet beneath Ralph's left arm.

"Am I safe?" quavered Piggy. "I feel awful—"

High above them from the pinnacles came a sudden shout and then an imitation war-cry that was answered by a dozen voices from behind the rock.

"Give me the conch and stay still."

"Halt! Who goes there?"

Ralph bent back his head and glimpsed Roger's dark face at the top.

"You can see who I am!" he shouted. "Stop being silly!"

He put the conch to his lips and began to blow. Savages appeared, painted out of recognition, edging round the ledge toward the neck. They carried spears and disposed themselves to defend the entrance. Ralph went on blowing and ignored Piggy's terrors.

Roger was shouting.

"You mind out—see?"

At length Ralph took his lips away and paused to get his breath back. His first words were a gasp, but audible.

"—calling an assembly."

The savages guarding the neck muttered among themselves but made no motion. Ralph walked forwards a couple of steps. A voice whispered urgently behind him.

"Don't leave me, Ralph."

"You kneel down," said Ralph sideways, "and wait till I come back."

He stood halfway along the neck and gazed at the savages intently. Freed by the paint, they had tied their hair back and were more comfortable than he was. Ralph made a resolution to tie his own back afterwards. Indeed he felt like telling them to wait and doing it there and then; but that was impossible. The savages sniggered a bit and one gestured at Ralph with his spear. High above, Roger took his hands off the lever and leaned out to see what was going on. The boys on the neck stood in a pool of their own shadow, diminished to shaggy heads. Piggy crouched, his back shapeless as a sack.

"I'm calling an assembly."

Silence.

Roger took up a small stone and flung it between the twins, aiming to miss. They started and Sam only just kept his footing. Some source of power began to pulse in Roger's body.

Ralph spoke again, loudly.

"I'm calling an assembly."

He ran his eye over them.

"Where's Jack?"

The group of boys stirred and consulted. A painted face spoke with the voice of Robert.

"He's hunting. And he said we weren't to let you in."

"I've come to see about the fire," said Ralph, "and about Piggy's specs."

The group in front of him shifted and laughter shivered outwards from among them, light, excited laughter that went echoing among the tall rocks.

A voice spoke from behind Ralph.

"What do you want?"

The twins made a bolt past Ralph and got between him and the entry. He turned quickly. Jack, identifiable by personality and red hair, was advancing from the forest. A hunter crouched on either side. All three were masked in black and green. Behind them on the grass the headless and paunched body of a sow lay where they had dropped it.

Piggy wailed.

"Ralph! Don't leave me!"

With ludicrous care he embraced the rock, pressing himself to it above the sucking sea. The sniggering of the savages became a loud derisive jeer.

Jack shouted above the noise.

"You go away, Ralph. You keep to your end. This is my end and my tribe. You leave me alone."

The jeering died away.

"You pinched Piggy's specs," said Ralph, breathlessly. "You've got to give them back."

"Got to? Who says?"

Ralph's temper blazed out.

"I say! You voted for me for chief. Didn't you hear the conch? You played a dirty trick—we'd have given you fire if you'd asked for it—"

The blood was flowing in his cheeks and the bunged-up eye throbbed.

"You could have had fire whenever you wanted. But you didn't. You came sneaking up like a thief and stole Piggy's glasses!"

"Say that again!"

"Thief! Thief!"

Piggy screamed.

"Ralph! Mind me!"

Jack made a rush and stabbed at Ralph's chest with his spear. Ralph sensed the position of the weapon from the glimpse he caught of Jack's arm and put the thrust aside with his own butt. Then he brought the end round and caught Jack a stinger across the ear. They were chest to chest, breathing fiercely, pushing and glaring.

"Who's a thief?"

"You are!"

Jack wrenched free and swung at Ralph with his spear. By common consent they were using the spears as sabers now, no longer daring the lethal points. The blow struck Ralph's spear and slid down, to fall agonizingly on his fingers. Then they were apart once more, their positions reversed, Jack toward the Castle Rock and Ralph on the outside toward the island.

Both boys were breathing very heavily.

"Come on then—"

"Come on—"

Truculently they squared up to each other but kept just out of fighting distance.

"You come on and see what you get!"

"You come on—"

Piggy clutching the ground was trying to attract Ralph's attention. Ralph moved, bent down, kept a wary eye on Jack.

"Ralph—remember what we came for. The fire. My specs."

Ralph nodded. He relaxed his fighting muscles, stood easily and grounded the butt of his spear. Jack watched him inscrutably through his paint. Ralph glanced up at the pinnacles, then toward the group of savages.

"Listen. We've come to say this. First you've got to give back Piggy's specs. If he hasn't got them he can't see. You aren't playing the game—"

The tribe of painted savages giggled and Ralph's mind faltered. He pushed his hair up and gazed at the green and black mask before him, trying to remember what Jack looked like.

Piggy whispered.

"And the fire."

"Oh yes. Then about the fire. I say this again. I've been saying it ever since we dropped in."

He held out his spear and pointed at the savages.

"Your only hope is keeping a signal fire going as long as there's light to see. Then maybe a ship'll notice the smoke and come and rescue us and take us home. But without that smoke we've got to wait till some ship comes by accident. We might wait years; till we were old—"

The shivering, silvery, unreal laughter of the savages sprayed out and echoed away. A gust of rage shook Ralph. His voice cracked.

"Don't you understand, you painted fools? Sam, Eric, Piggy and me—we aren't enough. We tried to keep the fire going, but we couldn't. And then you, playing at hunting...."

He pointed past them to where the trickle of smoke dispersed in the pearly air.

"Look at that! Call that a signal fire? That's a cooking fire. Now you'll eat and there'll be no smoke. Don't you understand? There may be a ship out there—"

He paused, defeated by the silence and the painted anonymity of the group guarding the entry. Jack opened a pink mouth and addressed Samneric, who were between him and his tribe.

"You two. Get back."

No one answered him. The twins, puzzled, looked at each other; while Piggy, reassured by the cessation of violence, stood up carefully. Jack glanced back at Ralph and then at the twins.

"Grab them!"

No one moved. Jack shouted angrily.

"I said 'grab them'!"

The painted group moved round Samneric nervously and un-handily. Once more the silvery laughter scattered.

Samneric protested out of the heart of civilization.

"Oh, I say!"

"—honestly!"

Their spears were taken from them.

"Tie them up!"

Ralph cried out hopelessly against the black and green mask.

"Jack!"

"Go on. Tie them."

Now the painted group felt the otherness of Samneric, felt the power in their own hands. They felled the twins clumsily and excitedly. Jack was inspired. He knew that Ralph would attempt a rescue. He struck in a humming circle behind him and Ralph only just parried the blow. Beyond them the tribe and the twins were a loud and writing heap. Piggy crouched again. Then the twins lay, astonished, and the tribe stood round them. Jack turned to Ralph and spoke between his teeth.

"See? They do what I want."

There was silence again. The twins lay, inexpertly tied up, and the tribe watched Ralph to see what he would do. He numbered them through his fringe, glimpsed the ineffectual smoke.

His temper broke. He screamed at Jack.

"You're a beast and a swine and a bloody, bloody thief!"

He charged.

Jack, knowing this was the crisis, charged too. They met with a jolt and bounced apart. Jack swung with his fist at Ralph and caught him on the ear. Ralph hit Jack in the stomach and made him grunt. Then they were facing each other again, panting and furious, but unnerved by each other's ferocity. They became aware of the noise that was the background to this fight, the steady shrill cheering of the tribe behind them.

Piggy's voice penetrated to Ralph.

"Let me speak."

He was standing in the dust of the fight, and as the tribe saw his intention the shrill cheer changed to a steady booing.

Piggy held up the conch and the booing sagged a little, then came up again to strength.

"I got the conch!"

He shouted.

"I tell you, I got the conch!"

Surprisingly, there was silence now; the tribe were curious to hear what amusing thing he might have to say.

Silence and pause; but in the silence a curious air-noise, close by Ralph's head. He gave it half his attention—and there it was again; a faint "Zup!" Someone was throwing stones: Roger was dropping them, his one hand still on the lever. Below him, Ralph was a shock of hair and Piggy a bag of fat.

"I got this to say. You're acting like a crowd of kids."

The booing rose and died again as Piggy lifted the white, magic shell.

"Which is better—to be a pack of painted Indians like you are, or to be sensible like Ralph is?"

A great clamor rose among the savages. Piggy shouted again.

"Which is better—to have rules and agree, or to hunt and kill?"

Again the clamor and again—"Zup!"

Ralph shouted against the noise.

"Which is better, law and rescue, or hunting and breaking things up?"

Now Jack was yelling too and Ralph could no longer make himself heard. Jack had backed right against the tribe and they were a solid mass of menace that bristled with spears. The intention of a charge was forming among them; they were working up to it and the neck would be swept clear. Ralph stood facing them, a little to one side, his spear ready. By him stood Piggy still holding out the talisman, the fragile, shining beauty of the shell. The storm of sound beat at them, an incantation of hatred. High overhead, Roger, with a sense of delirious abandonment, leaned all his weight on the lever.

Ralph heard the great rock before he saw it. He was aware of a jolt in the earth that came to him through the soles of his feet, and the breaking sound of stones at the top of the cliff. Then the monstrous red thing bounded across the neck and he flung himself flat while the tribe shrieked.

The rock struck Piggy a glancing blow from chin to knee; the conch exploded into a thousand white fragments and ceased to exist. Piggy, saying nothing, with no time for even a grunt, traveled through the air sideways from the rock, turning over as he went. The rock bounded twice and was lost in the forest. Piggy fell forty feet and landed on his back across the square red rock in the sea. His head opened and stuff came out and turned red. Piggy's arms and legs twitched a bit, like a pig's after it has been killed. Then the sea breathed again in a long, slow sigh, the water boiled white and pink over the rock; and when it went, sucking back again, the body of Piggy was gone.

This time the silence was complete. Ralph's lips formed a word but no sound came.

Suddenly Jack bounded out from the tribe and began screaming wildly.

"See? See? That's what you'll get! I meant that! There isn't a tribe for you any more! The conch is gone—"

He ran forward, stooping.

"I'm chief!"

Viciously, with full intention, he hurled his spear at Ralph. The point tore the skin and flesh over Ralph's ribs, then sheared off and fell in the water. Ralph stumbled, feeling not pain but panic, and the tribe, screaming now like the chief, began to advance. Another spear, a bent one that would not fly straight, went past his face and one fell from on high where Roger was. The twins lay hidden behind the tribe and the anonymous devils' faces swarmed across the neck. Ralph turned and ran. A great noise as of sea gulls rose behind him. He obeyed an instinct that he did not know he possessed and swerved over the open space so that the spears went wide. He saw the headless body of the sow and jumped in time. Then he was crashing through foliage and small boughs and was hidden by the forest.

The chief stopped by the pig, turned and held up his hands.

"Back! Back to the fort!"

Presently the tribe returned noisily to the neck where Roger joined them.

The chief spoke to him angrily.

"Why aren't you on watch?"

Roger looked at him gravely.

"I just came down—"

The hangman's horror clung round him. The chief said no more to him but looked down at Samneric.

"You got to join the tribe."

"You lemme go—"

"—and me."

The chief snatched one of the few spears that were left and poked Sam in the ribs.

"What d'you mean by it, eh?" said the chief fiercely. "What d'you mean by coming with spears? What d'you mean by not joining my tribe?"

The prodding became rhythmic. Sam yelled.

"That's not the way."

Roger edged past the chief, only just avoiding pushing him with his shoulder. The yelling ceased, and Samneric lay looking up in quiet terror. Roger advanced upon them as one wielding a nameless authority.

CRY OF THE HUNTERS

RALPH LAY IN A COVERT, WONDERING ABOUT HIS wounds. The bruised flesh was inches in diameter over his right ribs, with a swollen and bloody scar where the spear had hit him. His hair was full of dirt and tapped like the tendrils of a creeper. All over he was scratched and bruised from his flight through the forest. By the time his breathing was normal again, he had worked out that bathing these injuries would have to wait. How could you listen for naked feet if you were splashing in water? How could you be safe by the little stream or on the open beach?

Ralph listened. He was not really far from the Castle Rock, and during the first panic he had thought he heard sounds of pursuit. But the hunters had only sneaked into the fringes of the greenery, retrieving spears perhaps, and then had rushed back to the sunny rock as if terrified of the darkness under the leaves. He had even glimpsed one of them, striped brown, black, and red, and had judged that it was Bill. But really, thought Ralph, this was not Bill. This was a savage whose image refused to blend with that ancient picture of a boy in shorts and shirt.

The afternoon died away; the circular spots of sunlight moved steadily over green fronds and brown fiber but no sound came from behind the rock. At last Ralph wormed out of the ferns and sneaked forward to the edge of that impenetrable thicket that fronted the neck of land. He peered with elaborate caution between branches at the edge and could see Robert sitting on guard at the top of the cliff. He held a spear in his left hand and was tossing up a pebble and catching it again with the right. Behind him a column of smoke rose thickly, so that Ralph's nostrils flared and his mouth dribbled. He wiped his nose and mouth with the back of his hand and for the first time since the morning felt hungry. The tribe must be sitting round the gutted pig, watching the fat ooze and burn among the ashes. They would be intent.

Another figure, an unrecognizable one, appeared by Robert and gave him something, then turned and went back behind the rock. Robert laid his spear on the rock beside him and began to gnaw between his raised hands. So the feast was beginning and the watchman had been given his portion.

Ralph saw that for the time being he was safe. He limped away through the fruit trees, drawn by the thought of the poor food yet bitter when he remembered the feast. Feast today, and then tomorrow....

He argued unconvincingly that they would let him alone, perhaps even make an outlaw of him. But then the fatal unreasoning knowledge came to him again. The breaking of the conch and the deaths of Piggy and Simon lay over the island like a vapor. These painted savages would go further and further. Then there was that indefinable connection between himself and Jack; who therefore would never let him alone; never.

He paused, sun-flecked, holding up a bough, prepared to duck under it. A spasm of terror set him shaking and he cried aloud.

"No. They're not as bad as that. It was an accident."

He ducked under the bough, ran clumsily, then stopped and listened.

He came to the smashed acres of fruit and ate greedily. He saw two littluns and, not having any idea of his own appearance, wondered why they screamed and ran.

When he had eaten he went toward the beach. The sunlight was slanting now into the palms by the wrecked shelter. There was the platform and the pool. The best thing to do was to ignore this leaden feeling about the heart and rely on their common sense, their daylight sanity. Now that the tribe had eaten, the thing to do was to try again. And anyway, he couldn't stay here all night in an empty shelter by the deserted platform. His flesh crept and he shivered in the evening sun. No fire; no smoke; no rescue. He turned and limped away through the forest toward Jack's end of the island.

The slanting sticks of sunlight were lost among the branches. At length he came to a clearing in the forest where rock prevented vegetation from growing. Now it was a pool of shadows and Ralph nearly flung himself behind a tree when he saw something standing in the center; but then he saw that the white face was bone and that the pig's skull grinned at him from the top of a stick. He walked slowly into the middle of the clearing and looked steadily at the skull that gleamed as white as ever the conch had done and seemed to jeer at him cynically. An inquisitive ant was busy in one of the eye sockets but otherwise the thing was lifeless.

Or was it?

Little prickles of sensation ran up and down his back. He stood, the skull about on a level with his face, and held up his hair with two hands. The teeth grinned, the empty sockets seemed to hold his gaze masterfully and without effort.

What was it?

The skull regarded Ralph like one who knows all the answers and won't tell. A sick fear and rage swept him. Fiercely he hit out at the filthy thing in front of him that bobbed like a toy and came back, still grinning into his face, so that he lashed and cried out in loathing. Then he was licking his bruised knuckles and looking at the bare stick, while the skull lay in two pieces, its grin now six feet across. He wrenched the quivering stick from the crack and held it as a spear between him and the white pieces. Then he backed away, keeping his face to the skull that lay grinning at the sky.

When the green glow had gone from the horizon and night was fully accomplished, Ralph came again to the thicket in front of the Castle Rock. Peeping through, he could see that the height was still occupied, and whoever it was up there had a spear at the ready.

He knelt among the shadows and felt his isolation bitterly. They were savages it was true; but they were human, and the ambushing fears of the deep night were coming on.

Ralph moaned faintly. Tired though he was, he could not relax and fall into a well of sleep for fear of the tribe. Might it not be possible to walk boldly into the fort, say—"I've got pax," laugh lightly and sleep among the others? Pretend they were still boys, schoolboys who had said, "Sir, yes, Sir"—and worn caps? Daylight might have answered yes; but darkness and the horrors of death said no. Lying there in the darkness, he knew he was an outcast.

" 'Cos I had some sense."

He rubbed his cheek along his forearm, smelling the acrid scent of salt and sweat and the staleness of dirt. Over to the left, the waves of ocean were breathing, sucking down, then boiling back over the rock.

There were sounds coming from behind the Castle Rock. Listening carefully, detaching his mind from the swing of the sea, Ralph could make out a familiar rhythm.

"Kill the beast! Cut his throat! Spill his blood!"

The tribe was dancing. Somewhere on the other side of this rocky wall there would be a dark circle, a glowing fire, and meat. They would be savoring food and the comfort of safety.

A noise nearer at hand made him quiver. Savages were clambering up the Castle Rock, right up to the top, and he could hear voices. He sneaked forward a few yards and saw the shape at the top of the rock change and enlarge. There were only two boys on the island who moved or talked like that.

Ralph put his head down on his forearms and accepted this new fact like a wound. Samneric were part of the tribe now. They were guarding the Castle Rock against him. There was no chance of rescuing them and building up an outlaw tribe at the other end of the island. Samneric were savages like the rest; Piggy was dead, and the conch smashed to powder.

At length the guard climbed down. The two that remained seemed nothing more than a dark extension of the rock. A star appeared behind them and was momentarily eclipsed by some movement.

Ralph edged forward, feeling his way over the uneven surface as though he were blind. There were miles of vague water at his right and the restless ocean lay under his left hand, as awful as the shaft of a pit. Every minute the water breathed round the death rock and flowered into a field of whiteness. Ralph crawled until he found the ledge of the entry in his grasp. The lookouts were immediately above him and he could see the end of a spear projecting over the rock.

He called very gently.

"Samneric—"

There was no reply. To carry he must speak louder; and this would rouse those striped and inimical creatures from their feasting by the fire. He set his teeth and started to climb, finding the holds by touch. The stick that had supported a skull hampered him but he would not be parted from his only weapon. He was nearly level with the twins before he spoke again.

"Samneric—"

He heard a cry and a flurry from the rock. The twins had grabbed each other and were gibbering.

"It's me. Ralph."

Terrified that they would run and give the alarm, he hauled himself up until his head and shoulders stuck over the top. Far below his armpit he saw the luminous flowering round the rock.

"It's only me. Ralph."

At length they bent forward and peered in his face.

"We thought it was—"

"—we didn't know what it was—"

"—we thought—"

Memory of their new and shameful loyalty came to them. Eric was silent but Sam tried to do his duty.

"You got to go, Ralph. You go away now—"

He wagged his spear and essayed fierceness.

"You shove off. See?"

Eric nodded agreement and jabbed his spear in the air. Ralph leaned on his arms and did not go.

"I came to see you two."

His voice was thick. His throat was hurting him now though it had received no wound.

"I came to see you two—"

Words could not express the dull pain of these things. He fell silent, while the vivid stars were split and danced all ways.

Sam shifted uneasily.

"Honest, Ralph, you'd better go."

Ralph looked up again.

"You two aren't painted. How can you—? If it were light—"

If it were light shame would burn them at admitting these things. But the night was dark. Eric took up; and then the twins started their antiphonal speech.

"You got to go because it's not safe—"

"—they made us. They hurt us—"

"Who? Jack?"

"Oh no—"

They bent to him and lowered their voices.

"Push off, Ralph—"

"—it's a tribe—"

"—they made us—"

"—we couldn't help it—"

When Ralph spoke again his voice was low, and seemed breathless.

"What have I done? I liked him—and I wanted us to be rescued—"

Again the stars spilled about the sky. Eric shook his head, earnestly.

"Listen, Ralph. Never mind what's sense. That's gone—"

"Never mind about the chief—"

"—you got to go for your own good."

"The chief and Roger—"

"—yes, Roger—"

"They hate you, Ralph. They're going to do you."

"They're going to hunt you tomorrow."

"But why?"

"I dunno. And Ralph, Jack, the chief, says it'll be dangerous—"

"—and we've got to be careful and throw our spears like at a pig."

"We're going to spread out in a line across the island—"

"—we're going forward from this end—"

"—until we find you."

"We've got to give signals like this."

Eric raised his head and achieved a faint ululation by beating on his open mouth. Then he glanced behind him nervously.

"Like that—"

"—only louder, of course."

"But I've done nothing," whispered Ralph, urgently. "I only wanted to keep up a fire!"

He paused for a moment, thinking miserably of the morrow. A matter of overwhelming importance occurred to him.

"What are you—?"

He could not bring himself to be specific at first; but then fear and loneliness goaded him.

"When they find me, what are they going to do?"

The twins were silent. Beneath him, the death rock flowered again.

"What are they—oh God! I'm hungry—"

The towering rock seemed to sway under him.

"Well—what—?"

The twins answered his question indirectly.

"You got to go now, Ralph."

"For your own good."

"Keep away. As far as you can."

"Won't you come with me? Three of us—we'd stand a chance."

After a moment's silence, Sam spoke in a strangled voice.

"You don't know Roger. He's a terror."

"And the chief—they're both—"

"—terrors—"

"—only Roger—"

Both boys froze. Someone was climbing toward them from the tribe.

"He's coming to see if we're keeping watch. Quick, Ralph!"

As he prepared to let himself down the cliff, Ralph snatched at the last possible advantage to be wrung out of this meeting.

"I'll lie up close; in that thicket down there," he whispered, "so keep them away from it. They'll never think to look so close—"

The footsteps were still some distance away.

"Sam—I'm going to be all right, aren't I?"

The twins were silent again.

"Here!" said Sam suddenly. "Take this—"

Ralph felt a chunk of meat pushed against him and grabbed it.

"But what are you going to do when you catch me?"

Silence above. He sounded silly to himself. He lowered himself down the rock.

"What are you going to do—?"

From the top of the towering rock came the incomprehensible reply.

"Roger sharpened a stick at both ends."

Roger sharpened a stick at both ends. Ralph tried to attach a meaning to this but could not. He used all the bad words he could think of in a fit of temper that passed into yawning. How long could you go without sleep? He yearned for a bed and sheets—but the only whiteness here was the slow spilt milk, luminous round the rock forty feet below, where Piggy had fallen. Piggy was everywhere, was on this neck, was become terrible in darkness and death. If Piggy were to come back now out of the water, with his empty head—Ralph whimpered and yawned like a littlun. The stick in his hand became a crutch on which he reeled.

Then he tensed again. There were voices raised on the top of the Castle Rock. Samneric were arguing with someone. But the ferns and the grass were near. That was the place to be in, hidden, and next to the thicket that would serve for tomorrow's hideout. Here—and his hands touched grass—was a place to be in for the night, not far from the tribe, so that if the horrors of the supernatural emerged one could at least mix with humans for the time being, even if it meant ...

What did it mean? A stick sharpened at both ends. What was there in that? They had thrown spears and missed; all but one. Perhaps they would miss next time, too.

He squatted down in the tall grass, remembered the meat that Sam had given him, and began to tear at it ravenously. While he was eating, he heard fresh noises—cries of pain from Samneric, cries of panic, angry voices. What did it mean? Someone besides himself was in trouble, for at least one of the twins was catching it. Then the voices passed away down the rock and he ceased to think of them. He felt with his hands and found cool, delicate fronds backed against the thicket. Here then was the night's lair. At first light he would creep into the thicket, squeeze between the twisted stems, ensconce himself so deep that only a crawler like himself could come through, and that crawler would be jabbed. There he would sit, and the search would pass him by, and the cordon waver on, ululating along the island, and he would be free.

He pulled himself between the ferns, tunneling in. He laid the stick beside him, and huddled himself down in the blackness. One must remember to wake at first light, in order to diddle the savages—and he did not know how quickly sleep came and hurled him down a dark interior slope.

He was awake before his eyes were open, listening to a noise that was near. He opened an eye, found the mold an inch or so from his face and his fingers gripped into it, light filtering between the fronds of fern. He had just time to realize that the age-long nightmares of falling and death were past and that the morning was come, when he heard the sound again. It was an ululation over by the seashore—and now the next savage answered and the next. The cry swept by him across the narrow end of the island from sea to lagoon, like the cry of a flying bird. He took no time to consider but grabbed his sharp stick and wriggled back among the ferns. Within seconds he was worming his way into the thicket; but not before he had glimpsed the legs of a savage coming toward him. The ferns were thumped and beaten and he heard legs moving in the long grass. The savage, whoever he was, ululated twice; and the cry was repeated in both directions, then died away. Ralph crouched still, tangled in the ferns, and for a time he heard nothing.

At last he examined the thicket itself. Certainly no one could attack him here—and moreover he had a stroke of luck. The great rock that had killed Piggy had bounded into this thicket and bounced there, right in the center, making a smashed space a few feet in extent each way. When Ralph had wriggled into this he felt secure, and clever. He sat down carefully among the smashed stems and waited for the hunt to pass. Looking up between the leaves he caught a glimpse of something red. That must be the top of the Castle Rock, distant and unmenacing. He composed himself triumphantly, to hear the sounds of the hunt dying away.

Yet no one made a sound; and as the minutes passed, in the green shade, his feeling of triumph faded.

At last he heard a voice—Jack's voice, but hushed.

"Are you certain?"

The savage addressed said nothing. Perhaps he made a gesture.

Roger spoke.

"If you're fooling us—"

Immediately after this, there came a gasp, and a squeal of pain. Ralph crouched instinctively. One of the twins was there, outside the thicket, with Jack and Roger.

"You're sure he meant in there?"

The twin moaned faintly and then squealed again.

"He meant he'd hide in there?"

"Yes—yes—oh—!"

Silver laughter scattered among the trees.

So they knew.

Ralph picked up his stick and prepared for battle. But what could they do? It would take them a week to break a path through the thicket; and anyone who wormed his way in would be helpless. He felt the point of his spear with his thumb and grinned without amusement. Whoever tried that would be stuck, squealing like a pig.

They were going away, back to the tower rock. He could hear feet moving and then someone sniggered. There came again that high, bird-like cry that swept along the line. So some were still watching for him; but some—?

There was a long, breathless silence. Ralph found that he had bark in his mouth from the gnawed spear. He stood and peered upwards to the Castle Rock.

As he did so, he heard Jack's voice from the top.

"Heave! Heave! Heave!"

The red rock that he could see at the top of the cliff vanished like a curtain, and he could see figures and blue sky. A moment later the earth jolted, there was a rushing sound in the air, and the top of the thicket was cuffed as with a gigantic hand. The rock bounded on, thumping and smashing toward the beach, while a shower of broken twigs and leaves fell on him. Beyond the thicket, the tribe was cheering.

Silence again.

Ralph put his fingers in his mouth and bit them. There was only one other rock up there that they might conceivably move; but that was half as big as a cottage, big as a car, a tank. He visualized its probable progress with agonizing clearness—that one would start slowly, drop from ledge to ledge, trundle across the neck like an outsize steamroller.

"Heave! Heave! Heave!"

Ralph put down his spear, then picked it up again. He pushed his hair back irritably, took two hasty steps across the little space and then came back. He stood looking at the broken ends of branches.

Still silence.

He caught sight of the rise and fall of his diaphragm and was surprised to see how quickly he was breathing. Just left of center his heart-beats were visible. He put the spear down again.

"Heave! Heave! Heave!"

A shrill, prolonged cheer.

Something boomed up on the red rock, then the earth jumped and began to shake steadily, while the noise as steadily increased. Ralph was shot into the air, thrown down, dashed against branches. At his right hand, and only a few feet away, the whole thicket bent and the roots screamed as they came out of the earth together. He saw something red that turned over slowly as a mill wheel. Then the red thing was past and the elephantine progress diminished toward the sea.

Ralph knelt on the plowed-up soil, and waited for the earth to come back. Presently the white, broken stumps, the split sticks and the tangle of the thicket refocused. There was a kind of heavy feeling in his body where he had watched his own pulse.

Silence again.

Yet not entirely so. They were whispering out there; and suddenly the branches were shaken furiously at two places on his right. The pointed end of a stick appeared. In panic, Ralph thrust his own stick through the crack and struck with all his might.

"Aaa-ah!"

His spear twisted a little in his hands and then he withdrew it again.

"Ooh-ooh—"

Someone was moaning outside and a babble of voices rose. A fierce argument was going on and the wounded savage kept groaning. Then when there was silence, a single voice spoke and Ralph decided that it was not Jack's.

"See? I told you—he's dangerous."

The wounded savage moaned again.

What else? What next?

Ralph fastened his hands round the chewed spear and his hair fell. Someone was muttering, only a few yards away toward the Castle Rock. He heard a savage say "No!" in a shocked voice; and then there was suppressed laughter. He squatted back on his heels and showed his teeth at the wall of branches. He raised his spear, snarled a little, and waited.

Once more the invisible group sniggered. He heard a curious trickling sound and then a louder crepitation as if someone were unwrapping great sheets of cellophane. A stick snapped and he stifled a cough. Smoke was seeping through the branches in white and yellow wisps, the patch of blue sky overhead turned to the color of a storm cloud, and then the smoke billowed round him.

Someone laughed excitedly, and a voice shouted.

"Smoke!"

He wormed his way through the thicket toward the forest, keeping as far as possible beneath the smoke. Presently he saw open space, and the green leaves of the edge of the thicket. A smallish savage was standing between him and the rest of the forest, a savage striped red and white, and carrying a spear. He was coughing and smearing the paint about his eyes with the back of his hand as he tried to see through the increasing smoke. Ralph launched himself like a cat; stabbed, snarling, with the spear, and the savage doubled up. There was a shout from beyond the thicket and then Ralph was running with the swiftness of fear through the undergrowth. He came to a pig-run, followed it for perhaps a hundred yards, and then swerved off. Behind him the ululation swept across the island once more and a single voice shouted three times. He guessed that was the signal to advance and sped away again, till his chest was like fire. Then he flung himself down under a bush and waited for a moment till his breathing steadied. He passed his tongue tentatively over his teeth and lips and heard far off the ululation of the pursuers.

There were many things he could do. He could climb a tree; but that was putting all his eggs in one basket. If he were detected, they had nothing more difficult to do than wait.

If only one had time to think!

Another double cry at the same distance gave him a clue to their plan. Any savage balked in the forest would utter the double shout and hold up the line till he was free again. That way they might hope to keep the cordon unbroken right across the island. Ralph thought of the boar that had broken through them with such ease. If necessary, when the chase came too close, he could charge the cordon while it was still thin, burst through, and run back. But run back where? The cordon would turn and sweep again. Sooner or later he would have to sleep or eat—and then he would awaken with hands clawing at him; and the hunt would become a running down.

What was to be done, then? The tree? Burst the line like a boar? Either way the choice was terrible.

A single cry quickened his heart-beat and, leaping up, he dashed away toward the ocean side and the thick jungle till he was hung up among creepers; he stayed there for a moment with his calves quivering. If only one could have quiet, a long pause, a time to think!

And there again, shrill and inevitable, was the ululation sweeping across the island. At that sound he shied like a horse among the creepers and ran once more till he was panting. He flung himself down by some ferns. The tree, or the charge? He mastered his breathing for a moment, wiped his mouth, and told himself to be calm. Samneric were somewhere in that line, and hating it. Or were they? And supposing, instead of them, he met the chief, or Roger who carried death in his hands?

Ralph pushed back his tangled hair and wiped the sweat out of his best eye. He spoke aloud.

"Think."

What was the sensible thing to do?

There was no Piggy to talk sense. There was no solemn assembly for debate nor dignity of the conch.

"Think."

Most, he was beginning to dread the curtain that might waver in his brain, blacking out the sense of danger, making a simpleton of him.

A third idea would be to hide so well that the advancing line would pass without discovering him.

He jerked his head off the ground and listened. There was another noise to attend to now, a deep grumbling noise, as though the forest itself were angry with him, a somber noise across which the ululations were scribbled excruciatingly as on slate. He knew he had heard it before somewhere, but had no time to remember.

Break the line.

A tree.

Hide, and let them pass.

A nearer cry stood him on his feet and immediately he was away again, running fast among thorns and brambles. Suddenly he blundered into the open, found himself again in that open space—and there was the fathom-wide grin of the skull, no longer ridiculing a deep blue patch of sky but jeering up into a blanket of smoke. Then Ralph was running beneath trees, with the grumble of the forest explained. They had smoked him out and set the island on fire.

Hide was better than a tree because you had a chance of breaking the line if you were discovered.

Hide, then.

He wondered if a pig would agree, and grimaced at nothing. Find the deepest thicket, the darkest hole on the island, and creep in. Now, as he ran, he peered about him. Bars and splashes of sunlight flitted over him and sweat made glistening streaks on his dirty body. The cries were far now, and faint.

At last he found what seemed to him the right place, though the decision was desperate. Here, bushes and a wild tangle of creeper made a mat that kept out all the light of the sun. Beneath it was a space, perhaps a foot high, though it was pierced everywhere by parallel and rising stems. If you wormed into the middle of that you would be five yards from the edge, and hidden, unless the savage chose to lie down and look for you; and even then, you would be in darkness—and if the worst happened and he saw you, then you had a chance to burst out at him, fling the whole line out of step and double back.

Cautiously, his stick trailing behind him, Ralph wormed between the rising stems. When he reached the middle of the mat he lay and listened.

The fire was a big one and the drum-roll that he had thought was left so far behind was nearer. Couldn't a fire outrun a galloping horse? He could see the sun-splashed ground over an area of perhaps fifty yards from where he lay, and as he watched, the sunlight in every patch blinked at him. This was so like the curtain that flapped in his brain that for a moment he thought the blinking was inside him. But then the patches blinked more rapidly, dulled and went out, so that he saw that a great heaviness of smoke lay between the island and the sun.

If anyone peered under the bushes and chanced to glimpse human flesh it might be Samneric who would pretend not to see and say nothing. He laid his cheek against the chocolate-colored earth, licked his dry lips and closed his eyes. Under the thicket, the earth was vibrating very slightly; or perhaps there was a sound beneath the obvious thunder of the fire and scribbled ululations that was too low to hear.

Someone cried out. Ralph jerked his cheek off the earth and looked into the dulled light. They must be near now, he thought, and his chest began to thump. Hide, break the line, climb a tree—which was the best after all? The trouble was you only had one chance.

Now the fire was nearer; those volleying shots were great limbs, trunks even, bursting. The fools! The fools! The fire must be almost at the fruit trees—what would they eat tomorrow?

Ralph stirred restlessly in his narrow bed. One chanced nothing! What could they do? Beat him? So what? Kill him? A stick sharpened at both ends.

The cries, suddenly nearer, jerked him up. He could see a striped savage moving hastily out of a green tangle, and coming toward the mat where he hid, a savage who carried a spear. Ralph gripped his fingers into the earth. Be ready now, in case.

Ralph fumbled to hold his spear so that it was point foremost; and now he saw that the stick was sharpened at both ends.

The savage stopped fifteen yards away and uttered his cry.

Perhaps he can hear my heart over the noises of the fire. Don't scream. Get ready.

The savage moved forward so that you could only see him from the waist down. That was the butt of his spear. Now you could see him from the knee down. Don't scream.

A herd of pigs came squealing out of the greenery behind the savage and rushed away into the forest. Birds were screaming, mice shrieking, and a little hopping thing came under the mat and cowered.

Five yards away the savage stopped, standing right by the thicket, and cried out. Ralph drew his feet up and crouched. The stake was in his hands, the stake sharpened at both ends, the stake that vibrated so wildly, that grew long, short, light, heavy, light again.

The ululation spread from shore to shore. The savage knelt down by the edge of the thicket, and there were lights flickering in the forest behind him. You could see a knee disturb the mold. Now the other. Two hands. A spear.

A face.

The savage peered into the obscurity beneath the thicket. You could tell that he saw light on this side and on that, but not in the middle—there. In the middle was a blob of dark and the savage wrinkled up his face, trying to decipher the darkness.

The seconds lengthened. Ralph was looking straight into the savage's eyes.

Don't scream.

You'll get back.

Now he's seen you. He's making sure. A stick sharpened.

Ralph screamed, a scream of fright and anger and desperation. His legs straightened, the screams became continuous and foaming. He shot forward, burst the thicket, was in the open, screaming, snarling, bloody. He swung the stake and the savage tumbled over; but there were others coming toward him, crying out. He swerved as a spear flew past and then was silent, running. All at once the lights flickering ahead of him merged together, the roar of the forest rose to thunder and a tall bush directly in his path burst into a great fan-shaped flame. He swung to the right, running desperately fast, with the heat beating on his left side and the fire racing forward like a tide. The ululation rose behind him and spread along, a series of short sharp cries, the sighting call.

A brown figure showed up at his right and fell away. They were all running, all crying out madly. He could hear them crashing in the undergrowth and on the left was the hot, bright thunder of the fire. He forgot his wounds, his hunger and thirst, and became fear; hopeless fear on flying feet, rushing through the forest toward the open beach. Spots jumped before his eyes and turned into red circles that expanded quickly till they passed out of sight. Below him someone's legs were getting tired and the desperate ululation advanced like a jagged fringe of menace and was almost overhead.

He stumbled over a root and the cry that pursued him rose even higher. He saw a shelter burst into flames and the fire flapped at his right shoulder and there was the glitter of water. Then he was down, rolling over and over in the warm sand, crouching with arm to ward off, trying to cry for mercy.

He staggered to his feet, tensed for more terrors, and looked up at a huge peaked cap. It was a white-topped cap, and above the green shade of the peak was a crown, an anchor, gold foliage. He saw white drill, epaulettes, a revolver, a row of gilt buttons down the front of a uniform.

A naval officer stood on the sand, looking down at Ralph in wary astonishment. On the beach behind him was a cutter, her bows hauled up and held by two ratings. In the stern-sheets another rating held a sub-machine gun.

The ululation faltered and died away.

The officer looked at Ralph doubtfully for a moment, then took his hand away from the butt of the revolver.

"Hullo."

Squirming a little, conscious of his filthy appearance, Ralph answered shyly.

"Hullo."

The officer nodded, as if a question had been answered.

"Are there any adults—any grownups with you?"

Dumbly, Ralph shook his head. He turned a half-pace on the sand. A semicircle of little boys, their bodies streaked with colored clay, sharp sticks in their hands, were standing on the beach making no noise at all.

"Fun and games," said the officer.

The fire reached the coconut palms by the beach and swallowed them noisily. A flame, seemingly detached, swung like an acrobat and licked up the palm heads on the platform. The sky was black.

The officer grinned cheerfully at Ralph.

"We saw your smoke. What have you been doing? Having a war or something?"

Ralph nodded.

The officer inspected the little scarecrow in front of him. The kid needed a bath, a haircut, a nose-wipe and a good deal of ointment.

"Nobody killed, I hope? Any dead bodies?"

"Only two. And they've gone."

The officer leaned down and looked closely at Ralph.

"Two? Killed?"

Ralph nodded again. Behind him, the whole island was shuddering with flame. The officer knew, as a rule, when people were telling the truth. He whistled softly.

Other boys were appearing now, tiny tots some of them, brown, with the distended bellies of small savages. One of them came close to the officer and looked up.

"I'm, I'm—"

But there was no more to come. Percival Wemys Madison sought in his head for an incantation that had faded clean away.

The officer turned back to Ralph.

"We'll take you off. How many of you are there?"

Ralph shook his head. The officer looked past him to the group of painted boys.

"Who's boss here?"

"I am," said Ralph loudly.

A little boy who wore the remains of an extraordinary black cap on his red hair and who carried the remains of a pair of spectacles at his waist, started forward, then changed his mind and stood still.

"We saw your smoke. And you don't know how many of you there are?"

"No, sir."

"I should have thought," said the officer as he visualized the search before him, "I should have thought that a pack of British boys—you're all British, aren't you?—would have been able to put up a better show than that—I mean—"

"It was like that at first," said Ralph, "before things—"

He stopped.

"We were together then—"

The officer nodded helpfully.

"I know. Jolly good show. Like the Coral Island."

Ralph looked at him dumbly. For a moment he had a fleeting picture of the strange glamour that had once invested the beaches. But the island was scorched up like dead wood—Simon was dead—and Jack had.... The tears began to flow and sobs shook him. He gave himself up to them now for the first time on the island; great, shuddering spasms of grief that seemed to wrench his whole body. His voice rose under the black smoke before the burning wreckage of the island; and infected by that emotion, the other little boys began to shake and sob too. And in the middle of them, with filthy body, matted hair, and unwiped nose, Ralph wept for the end of innocence, the darkness of man's heart, and the fall through the air of the true, wise friend called Piggy.

The officer, surrounded by these noises, was moved and a little embarrassed. He turned away to give them time to pull themselves together; and waited, allowing his eyes to rest on the trim cruiser in the distance.

NOTES ON
*Lord of the Flies**

I<small>N ANSWER TO A PUBLICITY QUESTIONNAIRE FROM</small>
the American publishers of L<small>ORD OF THE FLIES</small>, William Golding (born Cornwall, 1911) declared that he was brought up to be a scientist, and revolted; after two years of Oxford he changed his educational emphasis from science to English literature, and became devoted to Anglo-Saxon. After publishing a volume of poetry he "wasted the next four years," and when World War II broke out he joined the Royal Navy. For the next five years he was involved in naval matters except for a few months in New York and six months with Lord Cherwell in a "research establishment." He finished his naval career as a lieutenant in command of a rocket ship; he had seen action against battleships, submarines and aircraft, and had participated in the Walcheren and D-Day operations. After the war he began teaching and writing. Today, his novels include L<small>ORD OF THE FLIES</small> (Coward-McCann), <small>THE INHERITORS</small> (which may loosely be described as a novel of prehistory but is, like all of Golding's work, much more), and <small>PINCHER MARTIN</small> (published in hardcover by Harcourt Brace as

---

*The above *Notes* pretend to be no more than a series of reflections on aspects of L<small>ORD</small> <small>OF THE FLIES</small>. An exhaustive study of its symbolism has not yet been attempted.

THE TWO DEATHS OF CHRISTOPHER MARTIN). He lists his Hobbies as thinking, classical Greek, sailing and archaeology, and his Literary Influences as Euripides and the anonymous Anglo-Saxon author of THE BATTLE OF MALDON.

The theme of LORD OF THE FLIES is described by Golding as follows (in the same publicity questionnaire): "The theme is an attempt to trace the defects of society back to the defects of human nature. The moral is that the shape of a society must depend on the ethical nature of the individual and not on any political system however apparently logical or respectable. The whole book is symbolic in nature except the rescue in the end where adult life appears, dignified and capable, but in reality enmeshed in the same evil as the symbolic life of the children on the island. The officer, having interrupted a man-hunt, prepares to take the children off the island in a cruiser which will presently be hunting its enemy in the same implacable way. And who will rescue the adult and his cruiser?"

This is, of course, merely a casual summing-up on Mr. Golding's part of his extremely complex and beautifully woven symbolic web which becomes apparent as we follow through the book, but it does indicate that LORD OF THE FLIES is not, to say the least, a simple adventure story of boys on a desert island. In fact, the implications of the story go far beyond the degeneration of a few children. What is unique about the work of Golding is the way he has combined and synthesized all of the characteristically twentieth-century methods of analysis of the human being and human society and used this unified knowledge to comment on a "test situation." In this book, as in few others at the present time, are findings of psychoanalysts of all schools, anthropologists, social psychologists and philosophical historians mobilized into an attack upon the central problem of modern thought: the nature of the human personality and the reflection of personality on society.

Another feature of Golding's work is the superb use of symbolism, a symbolism that "works." The central symbol itself, the "lord of the flies," is, like any true symbol, much more than the sum of its parts; but some elements of it may be isolated. The "lord of the flies" is a translation of the Hebrew *Ba'alzevuv* (*Beelzebub* in Greek). It has been suggested that it was a mistranslation of a mistransliterated word which gave us this pungent and suggestive name for the Devil, a devil whose name suggests that he is devoted to decay, destruction, demoralization, hysteria and panic and who therefore fits in very well with Golding's theme.

The Devil is not present in any traditional religious sense; Golding's Beelzebub is the modern equivalent, the anarchic, amoral, driving force that Freudians call the Id, whose only function seems to be to insure the survival of the host in which it is embedded or embodied, which function it performs with tremendous and single-minded tenacity. Although it is possible to find other names for this force, the modern picture of the personality, whether drawn by theologians or psychoanalysts, inevitably includes this force or psychic structure as the fundamental principle of the Natural Man. The tenets of civilization, the moral and social codes, the Ego, the intelligence itself, form only a veneer over this white-hot power, this uncontrollable force, "the fury and the mire of human veins." Dostoievsky found salvation in this freedom, although he found damnation in it also. Yeats found in it the only source of creative genius ("Whatever flames upon the night,/Man's own resinous heart has fed."). Conrad was appalled by this "heart of darkness," and existentialists find in the denial of this freedom the source of perversion of all human values. Indeed one could, if one were so minded, go through the entire canon of modern literature, philosophy and psychology and find this great basic drive defined as underlying the most fundamental conclusions of modern thought.

The emergence of this concealed, basic wildness is the theme of the book; the struggle between Ralph, the representative of civilization with his parliaments and his brain trust (Piggy, the intellectual whose shattering spectacles mark the progressive decay of rational influence as the story progresses), and Jack, in whom the spark of wildness burns hotter and closer to the surface than in Ralph and who is the leader of the forces of anarchy on the island, is also, of course, the struggle in modern society between those same forces translated onto a worldwide scale.

The turning point in the struggle between Ralph and Jack is the killing of the sow (pp. 151–154). The sow is a mother: "sunk in deep maternal bliss lay the largest of the lot . . . the great bladder of her belly was fringed with a row of piglets that slept or burrowed and squeaked." The killing of the sow is accomplished in terms of sexual intercourse.

They were just behind her when she staggered into an open space where bright flowers grew and butterflies danced round each other and the air was hot and still.

Here, struck down by the heat, the sow fell and the hunters hurled themselves at her. This dreadful eruption from an unknown world made her frantic; she squealed and bucked and the air was full of sweat and noise and blood and terror. Roger ran round the heap, prodding with his spear whenever pigflesh appeared. Jack was on top of the sow, stabbing downward with his knife. Roger [a natural sadist, who becomes the "official" torturer and executioner for the tribe] found a lodgment for his point and began to push till he was leaning with his whole weight. The spear moved forward inch by inch, and the terrified squealing became a high-pitched scream. Then Jack found the throat and the hot blood spouted over his hands. The sow collapsed under them and they were heavy and fulfilled upon her. The butterflies still danced, preoccupied in the center of the clearing.

The pig's head is cut off; a stick is sharpened at both ends and "jammed in a crack" in the earth. (The death planned for Ralph at the end of the book involves a stick sharpened at both ends.) The pig's head is impaled on the stick; "... the head hung there, a little blood dribbling down the stick. Instinctively the boys drew back too; and the forest was very still. They listened, and the loudest noise was the buzzing of flies over the spilled guts." Jack offers this grotesque trophy to "the Beast," the terrible animal that the littler children had been dreaming of, and which seems to be lurking on the island wherever they were not looking. The entire incident forms a horrid parody of an Oedipal wedding night; these emotions, the sensations aroused by murder and death, and the overpowering and unaccustomed emotions of sexual love experienced by the half-grown boys, plus their own irrational fears and blind terrors, release the forces of death and the devil on the island.

After this occurs the most deeply symbolic incident in the book, the "interview" of Simon, an embryo mystic, with the head. The head seems to be saying, to Simon's heightened perceptions, that "everything was a bad business.... The half-shut eyes were dim with the infinite cynicism of adult life." Simon fights with all his feeble power against the message of the head, against the "ancient, inescapable recognition," the recognition of human capacities for evil and the superficial nature of human moral systems. It is the knowledge of the end of innocence, for which Ralph is to weep at the close of the book. " 'Fancy thinking the Beast was something you could hunt and kill!' said the head. For a moment or two the forest and all the other dimly appreciated places echoes with the parody of laughter. 'You knew, didn't you? I'm part of you? Close, close, close! I'm the reason why it's no go? Why things are what they are?' "

At the end of this fantastic scene Simon imagines he is looking into a vast mouth. "There was blackness within, a blackness that spread. . . . Simon was inside the mouth. He fell down and lost consciousness." This mouth,* the symbol of ravenous, unreasoning and eternally insatiable nature, appears again in PINCHER MARTIN, in which the development of the theme of a Nature inimical to the conscious personality of man is developed in a stunning fashion. In LORD OF THE FLIES, however, only the outline of a philosophy is sketched, and the boys of the island are figures in a parable or fable which like all great parables or fables reveals to the reader an intimate, disquieting connection between the innocent, time-passing, story-telling aspect of its surface and the great, "dimly appreciated" depths of its interior.

—E. L. EPSTEIN

*cf. Conrad's "Heart of Darkness": "I saw [the dying Kurtz] open his mouth wide— it gave him a weirdly voracious aspect, as though he wanted to swallow all the air, all the earth, all the men before him." Indeed Golding seems very close to Conrad, both in basic principles and in artistic method.

LORD OF THE FLIES
Selected Highlights of Critical Analysis

EW WORKS OF 20TH-CENTURY LITERATURE HAVE enjoyed such a wide diversity of both popular and critical attention as William Golding's first novel, *Lord of the Flies*. The following excerpts have been selected from five decades of analysis, and are presented here to give the reader an overview of the complex, and often conflicting, reactions the book has provoked. Since its publication in 1954, *Lord of the Flies* has been compared to the timeless dramas of Shakespeare and Euripides, the psychological theories of Freud and Jung, the philosophies of Rousseau and Sartre, the political satires of Orwell and Swift, and the metaphoric journeys of Conrad. It has become a cult classic among several generations of readers, hailed as one of the definitive narratives of youth itself. It is at once a companion piece and a dark mirror to Salinger's *The Catcher in the Rye*. In fact, it is the book's enormous popularity among college students of the 1950s and early 1960s that inspired literary critics to take a closer look at *Lord of the Flies*, which was largely ignored in its first publication. Now, five decades later, the number and variety of essays, articles, and books written about Golding and his first novel seem inexhaustible. *Lord of the Flies* continues to fascinate.

And it is clear that no single assessment of the work can account for its enduring literary impact and appeal.

Here then is a sampling of critical writing on William Golding's *Lord of the Flies*. The selections have been arranged thematically rather than chronologically to provide readers with alternating viewpoints and insights. The excerpts represent only a small portion of the critics' longer works, but hopefully convey the richness and diversity of analysis the book has received. They are springboards for deeper discussions, or simply food for thought. On the subject of critics, Golding himself remarked in a 1964 interview with James Keating: "[S]ome of them say things which I agree with and some say things which I don't agree with.... The critic has as much right as any man to get what he can out of a book ..." We can only assume the same rights apply to the reader.

"When we first begin to write and talk about Mr. Golding's novel, it is the aspect of fable which occupies our attention. And this is very natural because the book is a very satisfying one to talk about. Mr. Golding, our account might run, is examining what human nature is really like if we could consider it apart from the mass of social detail which gives a recognizable feature to our daily lives.... And it was in Ballantyne's *Coral Island*, a book published in the middle of the last century, that Mr. Golding found the suggestion for his 'external scene.' This is not a question of turning Ballantyne inside out, so that where his boys are endlessly brave, resourceful and Christian, Mr. Golding's are frightened, anarchic and savage; rather Mr. Golding's adventure story is to point up in a forceful and economic way the terrifying gap between the appearance and the reality.... If we take Ralph's remark about 'the darkness of man's heart' as coming very close to the subject of the book, it is worth just remembering that this book, published in 1954, was written in a world very different from Ballantyne's, one which had seen within twenty years the systematic destruction of the Jewish race, a world war revealing unnumbered atrocities of what man had done to man, and in 1945 the mushroom cloud of the atomic bomb which has come to dominate all our political and moral thinking.... Ultimately, Mr. Golding's book is valuable to us, not because it *tells us about* the darkness of man's heart, but because it shows it, because it is a work of art which enables us to enter into the world it creates and live at the level of a deeply perceptive and intelligent man. His vision becomes ours, and such a translation should make us realize the truth of Shelley's remark that 'the great instrument for the moral good is the imagination.' "

> —from the Introduction to the
> "School Edition" of *Lord of the Flies*
> by Ian Gregor and Mark Kinkead-Weekes, 1962

"William Golding's novel is not antihuman; it is anti-Rousseau. It does not portray human nature as such; it presents human nature as infected with the romantic chimera of inevitable human progress, a progress which will be achieved because of the innate nobility and innocence of the human species.... *Lord of the Flies* begins with all the paraphernalia of the romantic, and sentimental, preconceptions that owe so much to Rousseau's social philosophy. In the first chapter we are presented with a group of children, the contemporary world's symbol of innocence. They are placed on a tropical island, an earthly paradise, Rousseau's habitat for the 'noble savage.' But these boys are not Adam-figures; they are not innocent. Each of them, in varying degrees, reflects the influence of the serpent—which, by the way, is introduced in the first chapter when Ralph unfastens 'the snake-clasp of his belt.' Here begins the terrible irony that runs through the whole novel. Romantic man thinks he can rid himself of evil merely by taking off his clothes, the symbol of civilization and its effects. . . . If, as the Western world seems to believe, the democratic process of government is the best devised by man throughout his history, why doesn't it work always and everywhere? It is at this level that Golding suggests symbolically the inadequacy, not the depravity, of the solely human; it is at this level that he directs his devastatingly ironic commentary on the Rousseauvian myth . . . of the natural goodness of the human species.

In effect, Golding's modern fable puts Rousseau's social contract to the test: *Lord of the Flies* takes man back to the primitive condition of things, which the French social reformer had advocated as the one sure way of restoring man to his proper dignity. Then it shows that, far from being naturally good, man has some type of defect for which civilization is not responsible. Rousseau's social philosophy fails the test, and the essentially confused notion of nature which Rousseau bequeathed to the contemporary world is exposed for the fraud that it is."

—from "Is Golding Calvinistic?"
by Thomas Marcellus Coskren, O.P., 1963

"*Lord of the Flies*, a grim parable that holds out precious little hope for humanity . . . is the most influential novel among U.S. undergraduates since Salinger's *Catcher in the Rye*. . . . The British schoolboys in *Lord of the Flies* are a few years younger than Salinger's Holden Caulfield—they are six to twelve—but are not self-pitying innocents in a world made miserable by adults. They create their own world, their own misery.... What accounts for the appeal? Part of it is, of course, pure identification. A Harvard undergraduate says the book 'rounds up all the people I knew in camp when I was a counselor.' On another level, Golding believes students 'seem to have it in for the whole world of organization. They're very cynical. And here was someone who was not making excuses for society. It was new to find someone who believes in original sin.' "

—from "Lord of the Campus,"
Time: The Weekly Newsmagazine, 1962

"The Nature-Nurture controversy which has engaged the attention of psychologists, philosophers, and anthropologists for long finds expression in literature too. Whereas Salinger's *The Catcher in the Rye* published three years before *Lord of the Flies* stresses social depravity, Golding's novel shows natural depravity to be the true source of evil. Evil is traced by Salinger to defective education and institutions; Golding traces the defects of society back to the defects of human nature. Like *Lord of the Flies, The Catcher in the Rye* is a reaction of an adolescent to the world around. Ralph's struggle against Jack and his savages recalls Holden's attempts as the 'Catcher' to prevent the children from falling off the cliff of childhood into adulthood. While Salinger subscribes to the cult of childhood innocence, Golding shows the children to be no better than adults. *The Catcher in the Rye* depicts the fall from adolescence into adulthood; *Lord of the Flies* shows that children are already fallen. Their innocence is just ignorance."

—from *William Golding: A Study*
by V. V. Subbarao, 1987

"The abrupt return to childhood, to insignificance, underscores the argument of the narrative: that Evil is inherent in the human mind itself, whatever innocence may cloak it, ready to put forth its strength as soon as the occasion is propitious. This is Golding's theme, and it takes on a frightful force by being presented in juvenile terms, in a setting that is twice deliberately likened to the sunny Coral Island of R. M. Ballantyne. The boys' society represents, in embryo, the society of the adult world, their impulses and convictions are those of adults incisively abridged, and the whole narrative is a powerfully ironic commentary on the nature of Man, an accusation levelled at us all.... Like any orthodox moralist Golding insists that Man is a fallen creature, but he refuses to hypostatize Evil or to locate it in a dimension of its own. On the contrary Beelzebub, Lord of the Flies, is Roger and Jack and you and I, ready to declare himself as soon as we permit him to."

—from "The Fables of William Golding"
by John Peter, 1957

"At all events, one readily sees that Golding's formal approach to the novel shows the marks of his early interest in ancient literature, both Greek and Anglo-Saxon, even in a list of such general characteristics of his fiction as the following: 1) his desire to be seen as a 'maker of myths'; 2) his general reliance on simple situations and plots that either partake of or suggest mythical archetypes; 3) his concern in making his novels the concrete expressions of spiritual or moral assumptions; 4) his suggestion of an inevitability in human actions akin to the ancient concept of Fate; 5) his primary use of the process of gradual self-discovery as plot device; 6) his use of irony as a major narrative technique. . . . [E]ven his use of contemporary sources may be seen as a way of giving a sense of archetypal continuity between the complex, interwoven structure of ancient myth and the 'myths' of the present."

—from *Of Earth and Darkness: The Novels of William Golding* by Arnold Johnston, 1980

"Golding himself has called his books both *myths* and *fables*, and both terms do point to a quality in the novels that it is necessary to recognize—that they are unusually tight, conceptualized, analogical expressions of moral ideas. Still, neither term is quite satisfactory . . . [I]t seems clear that *Lord of the Flies* should be read as a moral novel embodying a conception of human depravity which is compatible with, but not limited to, the Christian doctrine of Original Sin. To call the novel religious is to suggest that its values are more developed, and more affirmative, than in fact they are; Golding makes no reference to Grace, or to Divinity, but only to the darkness of men's hearts, and to the God of Dung and Filth who rules there. . . . The novel tells us a good deal about evil; but about salvation it is silent."

—from "William Golding's *Lord of the Flies*" by Samuel Hynes, 1968

"Without subscribing to any single religion, [Golding] is none-theless an old-fashioned Christian moralist whose novels characteristically depict the conflict between good and evil within the human soul. In an age of unbelief founded on technocratic rationalism Golding asserts the limits of human knowledge and power. His is an eschatological fiction whose characters are saved or damned according to their ability to recognize and to overcome the darkness within. It follows then that Golding's moral actors struggle not so much to conquer the outer world as to master the inner self.... Golding has often acknowledged the formative influence of the ancients. Together with the biblical version of man's fate expressed in the doctrine of original sin, Greek drama fleshes out the myth of the fall.... Both *Lord of the Flies* and *The Bacchae* are anthropological passion plays in which individuals—children in Golding, adults in Euripides—revert to savagery and murder during a frenzied ritual.... Morally diseased, mired in original sin, fallen man can rise only by the apparently impossible means of transcending his very nature. In man's apparent inability to re-create himself lies the tragedy of *Lord of the Flies.*"

—from *William Golding*
by Lawrence S. Friedman, 1993

"The bleakness of the novel's vision has been eloquently encapsulated by Golding himself in a sentence which recalls the despair of [Shakespeare's King] Lear in its bludgeoning repetitions: 'The theme of *Lord of the Flies* is grief, sheer grief, grief, grief, grief.' The grief which Golding expresses and powerfully elicits in the novel is grief at man's very nature and the nature of his world, grief that the boys, and we too, are 'suffering from the terrible disease of being human.' Shakespeare's tragedy and Golding's novel both present us with a fearless and savage close-up of human nature, a stripping-down of man to what essentially he is. The effect is appalling and humiliating: we are, in Golding's words, a species that 'produces evil as a bee produces honey.' . . . The South-Sea island setting suggests everyone's fantasy of lotus-eating escape or refuge from troubles and cares. But for Golding this is the sheerest fantasy: there is no escape from the agony of being human, no possibility of erecting utopian political systems where all will go well. Man's inescapable depravity makes sure 'it's no go' on Golding's island just as it does on the various islands visited by Gulliver in Swift's excoriating examination of the realities of the human condition. . . . The overall picture of man's nature which emerges from *Lord of the Flies* is indeed similar to the one we find in *Heart of Darkness*. A return to the state of nature, an escape into primitivism such as that attempted by Conrad's Kurtz, leads only to the unleashing of brutality, greed for power, and sadism in the most naked and brutal forms, to the horror of orgiastic and murderous midnight dances and human heads stuck on poles. But the forces of civilization, clad in shiny white to proclaim their moral excellence, are mere whited sepulchres, every bit as guilty as Kurtz and lacking even the honesty of open savagery. Both books offer this grim view of the human condition: there is no rescue, no way out, and the ending of *Lord of the Flies* is anything but happy."

—from *The Novels of William Golding*
by S. J. Boyd, 1988

"In 1954, as every schoolboy now knows, *Lord of the Flies* was published, a modern 'classic' was born. This first book was not immediately praised and given such status, for it appeared in an angry decade committed to political and social change, to nothing less than overthrow of 'the Establishment,' inspired by revival of the many hopes for the future that had been set aside during the traumatic war years. . . . Inevitably, the earliest reviewers and critics favored the work of the new social realists who appeared after the war, because their efforts continued the great tradition of the literature of hope; while Golding, searching in anthropology and in the mythic structures of classical Greek tragedy for some more essential truth that would explain why human hopes had been so often defeated, began with three contributions to the literature of disillusionment. About the only contemporary, or near-contemporary, Golding could acknowledge as a spiritual cousin (and fellow fabulist) was the late George Orwell. *Animal Farm* (1945), that nearly perfect Swiftian satire, had summed up the failure of the Russian Revolution—perhaps the failure of all utopian aspiration—as a result of human inequality. On both Orwell's farm and Golding's island this natural imbalance triggers the dialectics of behavior which must end with the triumph of the strong and wily beasts. *Nineteen Eighty-Four* (1949), just like *Lord of the Flies*, projects us into a near-future to portray an apocalypse—the collapse of humanistic hopes, the defeat of man, the pyramid waiting at the end of his violent history. . . . But time may bring them together, perhaps already it is doing so: the topical and seemingly vital literature of the angry 'realists' of the 1950s now fades from view, while the great negative 'fables' left by Orwell and Golding stand as dark monuments to the romantic humanism of the past."

—from *Critical Essays on William Golding*
by James R. Baker, 1988

"In analyzing William Golding's *Lord of the Flies*, the critic should assume that Golding knows psychological literature, and must then attempt to show how an author's knowledge of theory can vitalize his prose and characterization. The plot itself is uncomplicated; so simple, indeed, that one wonders how it so effortlessly absorbs the burden of meaning.... The narrative follows the children's gradual return to the amorality of childhood, a non-innocence which makes them small savages. Or we might make the analogy to the childhood of races and compare the child to the primitive. Denied the sustaining and repressing authority of parents, church, and state, the boys form a new culture, the development of which reflects that of the genuine primitive society, evolving its gods and demons, its rituals and taboos, its whole social structure. On the level of pure narrative, the action proceeds from the gradual struggle between Ralph and Jack, the two oldest boys, for precedence. Consistent clusters of imagery imply that one boy is godlike, the other satanic—thus making a symbolic level of meaning by transforming narrative events into an allegorical struggle between the forces of Good and those of Evil.... But, as Freud reminds us, 'metaphysics' becomes 'metapsychology'; gods and devils are 'nothing other than processes projected into the outer world.' If Ralph is a projection of man's good impulses from which we derive authority figures—whether god, king, or father—who establish the necessity for our valid ethical and social action, then Jack becomes an externalization of the evil instinctual forces of the unconscious; the allegorical has become the psychological.

The temptation is to regard the island on which the children are marooned as a kind of Eden, uncorrupted and Eveless. But the actions of the children negate any romantic assumptions about childhood innocence. Even though Golding himself momentarily becomes a victim of his Western culture and states at the end that Ralph wept for the 'end of innocence,' events have simply supported Freud's conclusion that no child is innocent.... Paradoxically, the children not only regress to a primitive and infantile morality, but they also degenerate into adults. They prove that, indeed, 'children are but men of a smaller growth.'"

—from "Men of a Smaller Growth:
A Psychological Analysis of William
Golding's *Lord of the Flies*"
by Claire Rosenfield, 1961

"Several 'levels' of meaning operate in *Lord of the Flies,* apart from the surface narrative. First, from a particular psychological viewpoint, the tripartite organization of the human psyche—ego, id, superego—is dramatized symbolically in the characters of Ralph, Jack, and Piggy, respectively.... A second level of symbolism emerges from the archetypal patterns in the novel. The quest motif is represented by Ralph's stumbling attempts at self-knowledge. His is literally an initiation by fire. Ironically the knowledge he acquires does not allow him to become an integrated member of adult society, but rather it causes him to recoil from the nightmare world he discovers.... On still another level, *Lord of the Flies* accommodates a political allegory in which Ralph represents democracy and Jack totalitarianism.... [T]he island society of *Lord of the Flies* demonstrates the inefficacy of political organizations that attempt to check human beings' worst destructive instincts. It is only by first recognizing these dark powers that democracy can hope to control them.

The fourth level of meaning is the moral allegory, which focuses on the conflicts between good and evil, and ecourages philosophical or theological interpretations. Golding is defining the nature of evil. Whether it is embodied in a destructive, unconscious force, a mistaken sacrifice that unsuccessfully atones for the boys' collective guilt, or a dictatorial power opposing the democratic order (corresponding to the psychological, archetypal, and politico-sociological levels, respectively), the problems of moral choice, the inevitability of original sin and human fallibility, the blindness of self-deception create a fourth level of meaning ...If *Lord of the Flies* 'teaches' through its moral allegory, it is the lesson of self-awareness..."

—from *The Modern Allegories of William Golding* by L. L. Dickson, 1990

"It is little wonder that some readers have judged [Golding] offensive, revolting, depravedly sensational, utterly wicked. He has been impelled to say that many human beings, left unrestrainedly to their own devices, will find the most natural expression of their desires to lie in human head-hunting. Those who affirm that man is made in God's image will be given some pause, but upon reflection they will probably interpret the novel as a portrayal of the inevitable and ultimate condition of a world without grace. Those who affirm that man is basically and inherently good— and becoming better—may simply find the novel a monstrous perpetuation of falsehood.

Golding's main offense, I suppose, is that he profanes what many men hold most precious: belief that the human being is essentially good and the child essentially innocent. Yet his offense, as well as his genius, lies not in any originality of view or statement but in his startling ability to make his story real, so real that many readers can only draw back in terror.... The ultimate purpose of the novel is not to leave its readers in a state of paralytic horror. The intention is certainly to impress upon them man's, any man's, miraculous ingenuity in perpetrating evil; but it is also to impress upon them the gift of a saving recognition which, to Golding, is apparently the *only* saving recognition...."

—from "An Old Story Well Told"
by William R. Mueller, 1963